THE
RED
EAGLES

THE
RED
EAGLES

David
Downing

MACMILLAN PUBLISHING COMPANY · NEW YORK

Macmillan Publishing Company
866 Third Avenue, New York, N.Y. 10022
Collier Macmillan Canada, Inc.

Library of Congress Cataloging-in-Publication Data
Downing, David.
    The red eagles.
    I. Title.
PR6054.0868R4   1987   823'.914   86-21862
ISBN 0-02-533380-1

Extracts from Attila Jozsef's poem "Consciousness" are taken from
the Michael Beevor translation in *Poems: Attila Jozsef* (London: The Danubia Book
Co., 1966). Permission to quote is courtesy of the editor, Thomas Kabdebo.

10 9 8 7 6 5 4 3 2 1

Designed by Jack Meserole

Printed in the United States of America

He has fully become a man
who has in his heart no mother, father
who knows that he gets life
only as an extra to death
and, like something found, he will give it back
at any time, that's why he keeps it safe,
who is not a god and not a priest
either to himself or anyone.

  —from "Consciousness" by Attila Jozsef

THE
RED
EAGLES

prologue

New York City, 1944

HER CONTACT stood with his back to the delicatessen window, in one hand the book with the green binding, in the other the spare pair of gloves. Though it was night, Amy could tell he had a rather nice face; there was a hint of innocence about it. As if by rote, she glanced up and down the street one more time, saw nothing, and then took the orange out of her bag and started walking toward him.

Amy was strangely nervous—she could tell from the way the sound of her heels on the sidewalk seemed to echo. He noticed her and the orange, looked surprised for an instant, then wary.

"Can you tell me the way to Grand Central Station?" she asked.

His face relaxed. "I'm going that way myself," he said, as if it were an old joke.

"Harry's sick and couldn't make it," she said, and it was at that moment that she saw, reflected in a window, a man staring at them. Her reaction was so quick she even startled herself. She took her companion's arm and forced them both into motion with a suddenness that almost knocked him over.

"What . . ."

"We're being watched. Don't turn around," she whispered.

They walked west toward Lexington Avenue, the clicking of her heels sounding louder than ever.

"What do we do?" he asked.

"Where are you staying?"

"The Pierre."

"Stop and tie your shoelaces."

As he did she looked back. The man was there, staring at a fire hydrant. "Damn," she murmured to herself. She'd been so careful and still it hadn't been careful enough.

They resumed walking, turning onto Lexington past a newsstand announcing the Allied attack on Monte Cassino.

"They must know something," he said, but there was no panic in his voice, and for that she was grateful.

"If they knew anything, you wouldn't still be on the street," she said, as much to convince herself as him. "It's just routine surveillance. I've got an idea. It's risky, but there's nothing else we can do. You're a single man in New York. If they believe I'm a hooker . . ."

"But . . ."

"Can you think of anything better?"

He said nothing. She hailed a cab and watched through the rear window as their tail signaled a car that had been cruising along behind him.

Reaching the hotel, they crossed the lobby to the elevators. Amy was conscious of the stares she received from the men as she tried to strut by with a slightly exaggerated sway of her hips. She hoped she wasn't overdoing it for her intended audience.

He had a suite on the fifth floor. It was large and luxurious; the United States Government obviously was not economizing when it came to important scientists. "We'd better get undressed," she said, kicking off her shoes and taking off her coat.

He looked at her as if she'd gone mad.

2

"They'll check," she said patiently. If they're any good, they will, she added to herself.

She peeled off her precious nylons, unbuttoned her skirt and blouse. "I'll get in bed," she said, carrying her clothes through to the bedroom.

"Shall I?" he asked almost apologetically.

"They won't check *that* thoroughly."

A few moments later he came in and sat on the end of the bed, looking extremely ill at ease in his underpants. She smiled at him reassuringly, though she felt anything but assured. Excited perhaps. He did have a nice face, and his body, though thin, was well-proportioned. It was a long time since she'd made love with a complete stranger . . . but this wasn't the time for thinking about it.

They sat silently, waiting for more than ten minutes. "No one's coming," he said at last, but before he could utter his next thought there was a firm rap on the outer door.

"Put the dressing gown on," she said. "Take your time answering. Be annoyed." She removed her brassiere, and he got a glimpse of small, perfectly formed breasts with large dark nipples.

She heard him open the door amid his angry protests.

"I'm sorry, Mr. Fuchs," a voice replied, "but we have to check the water in all the rooms. It won't take but a second."

She slipped out of bed and stood with her back to the window, completely naked. The door opened abruptly and the man walked in, stared at her for what seemed an eternity and then backed out muttering apologies. She could hear him still apologizing in the living room as the scientist resumed his protests. Then the outer door slammed, leaving silence.

She began to dress. He came back into the bedroom and did the same, neither of them speaking. Amy felt an almost incontrollable urge to laugh, but the young scientist's face was pale, his mouth pursed in a grim line.

"Was it the same man?" he asked.

"Yes."

"He didn't even *check* the water." He looked at her. "You weren't in bed when he walked in on you."

"I didn't want him to look at my face," she said coolly.

He looked at her with admiration. "Well, we fooled them!"

"It's not over yet. Let me think by myself a minute."

He left her sitting on the bed, straightening her nylons. What was going to happen when she left? Would they check her out? They might be satisfied.

He returned a few minutes later with a small manila envelope. "That's what Harry asked for," he said.

She folded it in two and put it in her handbag. "Is there any reason why you shouldn't have had it in your possession, innocently I mean?"

"No. We're always scribbling things like that."

"Good. If I'm arrested, tell them I stole it. Say you threw me out when you caught me looking through your wallet but you didn't realize I'd taken anything."

"Would they believe it?"

She shrugged. "It's better than nothing. They need you presumably, so they'll want to give you the benefit of the doubt. And tomorrow you'd better bring a real hooker up here."

"But I . . ."

"You must. They can't remember this night in particular. Believe me, it's more fun than the electric chair."

"You're right."

She grimaced. "Look, if they're waiting to question me, they'll be in the lobby. I don't think they'll approach me if you're there, so why don't you call a cab for me and then see me to it. I'll take it from there."

"I thought I threw you out."

"You threw me out like a gentleman."

He called down to reception, watched her applying her lipstick as he waited, a dark crimson shade that suited her shining black hair.

"What name should I know you by?" he asked.

"Rosa. But Harry should be back next time."

They went down in the elevator and walked across the lobby as fast as they could without arousing suspicion. She saw the man out of the corner of her eye, pulling himself out of an armchair.

The taxi was waiting. "Times Square," she told the driver as he pulled out onto Fifth Avenue. Looking back, she saw Fuchs walking back into the hotel and the man getting into a car that had pulled up for him.

Damn, damn, damn. For the first time she felt really frightened, and almost wished she'd brought the scientist with her—as long as she'd had him to worry about she hadn't had time to worry about herself. She reached inside her bag, felt the butt of the small revolver, but it offered no comfort. There was no way she could lose the pursuit in a cab, and the moment it stopped he'd have her.

"Make that Forty-second and Madison," she told the driver.

He swore and swung the cab under the nose of a bus and down another canyon. "Tell me when you change your mind again."

Amy ignored him and noticed that her fists were clenched tightly in her lap. She took out a cigarette and fumbled with the lighter. The cab screeched to a halt. "You're there, lady."

She paid the driver and got out, not daring to look back. After stamping out the cigarette she began walking east on Forty-second Street, unbuttoning her coat and avoiding the eyes of the women who occupied the doorways. Eventually finding one empty, she leaned against the doorjamb wondering what she was supposed to do next. The man's car stopped right in front of her. Amy forced a smile to her face. He was sitting in the back, pulling down the window to stare straight at her, a lecherous grin on his face.

Drive on, she pleaded silently.

He got out of the car and walked over to her, showed her his police shield. "Come with me, miss," he said, looking her up and down.

"What for? Why are you picking on me?"

He took her arm and threw her into the backseat of the car, then got in beside her, holding his thigh tight against hers. He stank of sweat and stale beer. "Drive, Junior," he told the man in front.

"What's your name, honey?" he asked.

"Eileen. Where . . ."

"Eileen what?"

"Eileen McCarthy."

"How long have you been a whore?"

"Not long. Look . . ."

"You're gorgeous naked."

Now she knew. More fun than the electric chair, she'd told Fuchs.

"Wasted on that egghead, I thought," he said, placing his hand on her thigh.

"He was rather sweet," she said, frantically trying to think of something that would stop him.

He guffawed. "Yeah? So am I, so am I. Look, honey," he said, suddenly tightening his grip on her thigh, "we can take you in and you'll get twenty-four hours in the slammer and a fifty-dollar fine, or you can give me twenty-five dollars' worth of your time and be back on the street in half an hour. Your choice."

They were entering Central Park. There was no way out of it, no way at all. If she was taken in, they'd find the gun and the envelope and her real name. "Okay, I'm yours," she said.

He smiled that smile. "You know where, Junior," he told his partner.

A few minutes later they turned off the road and coasted down a slope and into the trees. "Junior'll make sure we have some privacy," he said, and the young driver, with one disinterested glance at her, got out of the car and walked away.

"Look," she said, but he was already opening up her blouse, squeezing a breast as if he was testing the ripeness of

6

a peach. She felt her hand brush the metal clasp of her bag, and for a second almost succumbed to the urge to pull out the gun. But somehow it helped just knowing it was there, knowing that she could blow his head off if she wanted to.

He wasn't gentle but at least it was quick. She pulled up her skirt and buttoned up her blouse, not daring to look him in the face.

"I'm pretty sweet too, eh?" he said.

"Can I go now?" she asked quietly.

"We'll take you back."

"I'd rather walk."

"Your choice. I'll see you again, Eileen."

She got out of the car, clasping her handbag, and walked away, passing Junior. At least it had been only one of them.

After walking for several minutes she suddenly felt weak and sat down on the grass, her back against a tree. She wanted to cry but she couldn't. She wanted to be angry with the cop, but he really *had* thought she was a hooker. She'd been so goddamn clever. "I didn't want him to see my face"—she could hear herself say it, so cool and collected and pleased with herself. Well, he'd seen it now.

With an effort she pulled herself to her feet and walked out of the Park at Columbus Circle. Then she took a cab to Penn Station and caught a train back home to Washington with minutes to spare.

In the washroom at the end of the car she stripped and washed herself. She stood still, her arms astride the basin, looking at her face in the mirror.

Ten years, she thought, ten years of deception. Deceiving others, and maybe herself as well. She was thirty-three years old. No husband, no children, no country. No future.

Remembering the manila envelope, she took it from her bag and opened it. Inside there was a single sheet of paper, and on it a complicated diagram surrounded by notes written in her and Fuchs's native tongue. At the head of the sheet were two heavily underlined words—*"Die Atombombe."*

CONCEPTION

one

JOSEF STALIN stared gloomily out of the limousine window at the rain-swept Moscow streets. It was only eleven o'clock, but the city seemed already to have put itself to bed, and the swish of the limousine's tires seemed to echo in the emptiness. His eyes returned again to the piece of paper that rested on his knees, this diagram drawn by a German scientist in far-off America. Just one sheet of paper. *There has to be some way of speeding up the process.*

But deep down he feared that there wasn't, that this time the odds were stacked against him. Ten years earlier he'd told the Party of the German danger, had spelled out what needed to be done to prevent the Soviet State from being crushed. It had been close, closer than even the Germans knew, but he'd done it. This, though, was something altogether different. Some things could not be simply commanded, no matter how great a sacrifice was made.

Eighteen months, the GRU told him. The American bomb would be ready in eighteen months, ready for the "peace." The Soviet Union would have less than three years to match the American achievement while war weariness and the sentimental attachment to the "Grand Alliance" remorselessly ebbed away. A collision course was set. He'd had no illusions about the Germans, he had none about the Americans. A bare twelve months ago the taking of half of Europe had promised an impregnable buffer, and now it seemed almost irrelevant.

He felt a surge of self-pity. Were all his achievements to be reduced to nothing by this single sheet of paper? It was not long since he'd told Beria that he almost felt sorry for Churchill and the English, whose world was being dragged out from under them, who would soon be no more than the curators of an island museum. But was Churchill, with his pathetic faith in American generosity, the only deluded one? He himself had talked to the American generals at Tehran, and it had been like talking to the Germans at the time of the Pact. The stench of raw arrogance. The moment the Germans and Japanese were beaten the Americans would be everywhere, easing out the British and French, buying up the biggest empire the world had ever seen, brandishing their new bomb. Russia would be alone again. And defenseless. He slammed his fist on the seat, making the chauffeur jump. *There* must *be some way of speeding up the process.*

The limousine swept through the Spassky Gate and into the Kremlin, which was ablaze with lights now that the air-raid precautions had been lifted. He was, as usual, an hour late for the council meeting and felt able to expend some of his frustration on a brisk walk to the chamber overlooking the Alexandrov Gardens. *Perhaps*, he thought to himself as he climbed the stairs, but any lingering hopes were erased by the twin rows of gloomy faces lining the table. He wasted no time on preliminaries.

"Well, Andrei Andreyevich?" he barked as he eased himself into his chair.

Comrade Zhdanov, the head of the newly formed Atomic Division, shuffled his papers.

"Well?" Stalin repeated. "Tell me about *our* atom bomb."

"Yes, Comrade Secretary," Zhdanov began. "I have conducted the investigations required, but I regret to have to inform the council that there is no significant change in the forecasts. We simply do not have the materials. It may be possible to complete the ten-year development program in eight years, but the consequences of such a concentration of resources will put immeasurable strains on the rest of the economy.

"And," he added morosely, "it would also have a severe effect on the development of the aircraft required for delivery."

It was as he had feared.

"The other option?" he asked.

Zhdanov shuffled his papers again. "The possibility of stealing the material required has been thoroughly investigated. The trains the Americans use to carry their refined uranium from the plant in Oak Ridge, Tennessee, to Los Alamos are not heavily guarded. The actual theft could probably be accomplished by one of our partisan bands without too much trouble. Getting it and them back home might be difficult, and the political consequences of exposure would undoubtedly be grave. But these problems can be overcome.

"Unfortunately," he continued, "there is another which cannot be. Each train carries only enough atomic material for the making of, at most, two bombs. For us to have anything less than thirty would be worse than useless. The Americans would not take us seriously. We could hardly hope to hold up fifteen trains."

Zhdanov turned to look at Stalin for the first time, but the General Secretary's face held a strange expression, almost a quizzical smile. He was in fact remembering a train holdup he'd organized forty years before, in the days of the Georgian armed bands. One hundred thousand rubles had been the prize, but the denominations of the bills had been so large that anyone who'd tried to cash one had been instantly arrested. *Those were simpler days.*

"Thank you, Andrei Andreyevich," he said perfunctorily. "Has anyone anything *positive* to suggest?"

He was answered with a stony silence.

"So we cannot make it, and we cannot steal it," Stalin said softly. "But make no mistake, we must have it. The alternative is at least five years in which the capitalist world will have the power of life and death over us. I refuse to accept that we shall win this war only to lose the peace. From this moment an atomic bomb is First Priority.

"You"—he looked straight at Zhdanov—"will solve the insolvable."

☐

Anatoly Sheslakov thought to himself that it had been all very dramatic, but not very logical. If it was insolvable, it couldn't be solved; if it could be solved, it was not insolvable. The word game did not help very much. But he had appreciated the seriousness of the situation since two that morning, when everyone in the Atomic Division had been summoned from their beds and harangued by a white-faced Zhdanov.

Sheslakov leaned back in his chair, lit a cigarette, and watched the people walking past his door. He left it open for the occasional glimpse offered of Zhdanov's secretary, Tania, she of the wonderfully erect stance and lovely ankles. He harbored no amorous ambitions—in fact her personality rather grated on him—but he loved watching her; she had that physical arrogance of youth which he, and indeed his much-loved wife, had long ago lost.

He was approaching fifty, and most of his face bore the signs of his age. The eyes though were still bright and sharp, evidence of the undimmed intellect behind them. People had often said of him, sometimes kindly, sometimes not, that he had the perfect planner's brain, an ability to juggle an almost infinite array of variables into patterns of breathtaking simplicity that was matched only by his lack of imagination. He always replied that imagination was only the ability to stretch logic beyond what seemed, to lesser mortals, logical.

He had been twenty at the time of the Revolution, and had joined the Red Army in a fit of enthusiasm that he still found hard to explain. But it had paid dividends. His brilliance had outweighed his late arrival in the Party, and soon he was a commissar on the way up. After the Revolution he'd risen through the ranks of the state planning organs, prospering as they did with the adoption of a fully planned economy in the late twenties. The purges of the following decade decimated his colleagues but Sheslakov always survived; he had too good a brain for the Party to waste, too austere a brain for the Party leadership to feel threatened. He was a political neuter, a problem solver whose only demand of authority was that it should provide him with an endless supply of interesting problems. The outbreak of war and his assignment to the GRU and Atomic Division had changed the nature of the problems but not, fortunately, the scope they offered to his talents.

The First Priority was clearly a case in point. Sheslakov had all the relevant information—the military reports, espionage reports, industrial reports, scientific reports—scattered across his desk. Most of what they contained was now filed in his brain. He could see no reason to dispute Stalin's statement that they could neither make nor steal enough atomic bombs, but his intuition insisted that this was one riddle that had an answer. And intuition, he had always thought, was nothing more than logic making use of facts that were stored in the unconscious.

He lit another cigarette and closed his eyes. What were the arguments against the theft? He took a fresh sheet of paper and wrote, in neat capitals, "NOT ENOUGH CAN BE STOLEN." Not enough for what? For a possible war against the Americans? No, for deterring the Americans from starting such a war. The Americans would know how much of the Uranium-235 had been stolen, and consequently how many bombs could be made. A dead end, it had to be. So why didn't it feel like one? He could see no hidden assumptions. There had to be something else.

Sheslakov spent the rest of the afternoon attacking the problem from the other end, checking through the reports covering a possible acceleration of the Soviet program. He could find no hopes there. Feeling, for him, unusually frustrated, he ate dinner in the GRU canteen and went for a walk along the river. It was a warm evening for early May, the sky clear after the day's spring showers, and he surrendered himself to pleasant reveries, secure in the knowledge that parts of his mind were still carefully sifting through the problem.

It was just after eight when, sitting on an old capstan and staring across the water at a factory gutted by a German bomb, he found the hidden assumption he'd been searching for. And in the seconds that followed the pieces of an answer seemed to slip into each other like the parts of a matryoshka doll.

He lit a cigarette and sat for a few moments more watching the evening shadows lengthen. Then he walked briskly back to Frunze Street, collected a bottle from his office, and took the elevator back down to the floor that housed the GRU Secretariat. As expected, he found Olgarkov still at his desk, a mountain of a man surrounded by a mountain of paperwork. Seeing the bottle, Olgarkov produced two glasses from a drawer with a magician's flourish.

They drank each other's health and Sheslakov sank into the sofa beneath the window.

"Two things, Pyotr Alexeyevich," he said.

"First Priority, I assume."

"Word spreads fast."

"Words like those do."

"One, I want a report from Rosa, in Washington, as quickly as possible." He dictated the questions he wanted answered. "How long?"

"It will have to come out through Alaska," Olgarkov replied. "A week, perhaps ten days."

"That's quick enough. The other half won't be so easy. I want a man with experience in covert operations and the sort of loyalty rating that Comrade Beria would envy. Plus, he must be completely fluent in American English."

"And you need him tomorrow, I assume."

"Of course."

Olgarkov examined the bottom of his glass, then looked up. "Is the NKVD cooperating?"

"So I'm told."

"Then I know one possibility," he said, holding out his glass.

☐

After making the drop, the pilot wiggled his wings in farewell and disappeared over the trees.

"What the fuck do they think we're doing out here?" Kuznetsky shouted angrily, kicking the half-open crate. "Holding nonstop parties?"

Yakovenko groaned. "Not more vodka?"

"Enough to keep the brigade drunk for a week."

"Maybe there's food in the other crate."

The two men walked around the edge of the clearing, dousing the circle of fires as they went. The other crate had also broken open, spilling chocolate bars across the damp grass.

Yakovenko took the wrapping off one and bit into it. "Better than nothing," he said. "In fact it tastes good."

"Chocolate and vodka," Kuznetsky said disgustedly. "Moscow's idea of a balanced diet."

"Imported chocolate at that," Yakovenko added, passing him the wrapper. "Where's it from?"

"Made in the U.S.A.," Kuznetsky translated, "For Military Personnel Only."

"That's us. Should make you feel young again."

Kuznetsky grunted. "Come on, let's load this up. Plus a few bottles of vodka, say fifty. We'll leave the rest here." They picked up the crate and carried it across to their vehicle, a T-34 tank that had clearly seen better days. The bodywork was pitted with the scars of battle, the gun barrel was missing. But it still moved as long as there was gas in its tank.

"How are we going to carry the vodka?" Yakovenko asked as they lashed the crate behind the turret.

Kuznetsky's reply was drowned by the sound of another plane, this time unmistakably German, passing overhead at about five hundred feet.

"Good thing we had the fires out," Yakovenko said placidly, opening up another bar of chocolate.

"That's three tonight—"

"It's only the second."

"I was talking about German planes. There's going to be another sweep soon." He stared up at the sky. "The full moon's due in a couple of days. . . . Forget the booze. We're going back."

Driving the T-34 through the forest was a slow, nerve-racking business, but Yakovenko enjoyed the challenge, and Kuznetsky, on the rim of the turret, was left to his thoughts. He wondered whether it would be better to go back underground this time rather than move the whole brigade east for a few weeks. Surely the Germans couldn't spare that many men anymore, not with the offensive that everyone knew was coming in June. Yes, they should go underground and sit it out. In two months they'd be behind their own lines again. And he'd have to find a new job. *And* make a decision about Nadezhda.

The first light of dawn appeared through the trees ahead; the birds seemed to be clearing their throats for song. Kuznetsky loved this time of day: its sense of promise was indestructible, immune to human realities. He would miss the forest, *really* miss it. He'd have to join the bigwigs and get a dacha in the woods, somewhere like Zhukovka but farther out.

They were nearly home now, though no outsider would have noticed signs of habitation. The brigade, some eighty strong, lived in a connecting series of camouflaged dugouts beneath the forest floor; fires were lit only at night, and then only underground. Even the T-34 had a subterranean garage.

The lookouts, Kuznetsky noted with satisfaction, were as alert as ever, signaling them in from their perches in the trees. He was reminded yet again of the tales of Robin Hood, which he'd read as a boy.

Nadezhda was still sleeping, her long black hair falling across her face. As he lay down beside her, determined to get an hour or so's sleep, she snored gently and placed her arm protectively around his chest. He smiled and stroked her hair.

When he was her age he'd been playing hookey from school in Minnesota, bad-mouthing his parents, feeling up Betty Jane Webber in the hay loft, ignoring stupid questions like "What are you going to do when you grow up, Jack?" He had known nothing, experienced nothing, done nothing.

This sixteen-year-old lying beside him had seen her parents and brothers hanged, had killed at least three Germans, and had had at least one lover before him. It was only in sleep that she still looked a child. In sleep she almost had enough innocence for both of them.

He was wakened by Ovchinnikova less than an hour later. "We've got a visitor," she said.

It was a young girl, seven or eight years old, from a nearby village. She was sitting with Yakovenko eating a chocolate bar. "They've got an informer," Yakovenko explained. "They were going to string him up right away, but Mikhailova—remember her?—insisted that they follow all the proper procedures and have a trial. So Liliya here was awarded the fifteen-mile walk to fetch you."

Kuznetsky groaned.

"Breakfast?" asked Yakovenko, holding out a chocolate bar.

□

It was a beautiful spring morning, a bright sun warming the air and flooding the eyes with fresh spring colors. Swiveling his head around, Kuznetsky couldn't find a single wisp of cloud in the sky.

He was sitting on a piece of rubble waiting for the trial to begin. He'd given Morisov half an hour to put together the evidence, and it seemed like longer. He opened his pocket watch and was caught as usual by the beauty of the face that stared out of the photograph inside the lid. Anna, he called her, but he had no idea what her real name was. The only thing he knew about her was that the man who'd carried her picture had died in a ditch outside Lepel, with both hands vainly trying to stop the hole where his throat had been.

It was almost eleven. "Grigory," he shouted.

"Ready," Morisov shouted back. "Bring out the accused," he said to Mikhailova, who stood holding a pitchfork.

The man was brought out. He was about thirty, with a broad face that seemed ill at ease with his emaciated body. His face was covered in red welts; obviously not everyone had been prepared to wait for the proper authorities. He was clearly terrified.

The same old scene, Kuznetsky thought. The same circle of cottages, the same ring of onlookers, eyes bright with fear and lack of food. The crimes had changed, and the names of the criminals. Counterrevolutionaries, saboteurs, kulak profiteers, Nazi informers. His duty was the same. Liquidation. He listened to Morisov.

". . . the accused was seen entering and leaving the Fascist administrative headquarters in Polotsk. That afternoon a Nazi punishment detail arrived here, where they immediately discovered a clearing sown and cultivated against their orders by Comrade Poznyakov. After piling the clearing with loose branches and setting fire to it, they hanged Comrade Poznyakov, his wife, and two children. The accused returned later that day, feigning ignorance. . . ."

Why had he come back? Kuznetsky asked himself. What stupidity.

The accused sat on the ground, his head bowed, his right arm twitching. Kuznetsky wondered which of the stock explanations it would be.

Morisov had finished and was now joking with one of the village women. The other partisans looked bored; they'd seen this play too many times before. "Do you still deny collaboration?" Kuznetsky asked.

The man spoke without raising his head, a torrent of words. "I had to do it. They have my daughter in the brothel at Polotsk. She's only eleven and they promised to let her go. I only informed on Poznyakov, no one else. . . ."

The rush abated.

"I find the accused guilty as charged," Kuznetsky said. "Have the straws been drawn?" he asked Morisov.

"Yes."

Young Maslov walked forward, pulled the accused to his feet, and half dragged him off between two cottages. Why, Kuznetsky wondered, do we still have this need to execute in private? Who was the privacy for—the victim or the executioner?

The shot echoed through the village, silencing the birds for a few seconds. Kuznetsky walked over to the group of villagers.

"You'll be better off in Vaselivichi," he told them, but they knew better.

"Poznyakov wasn't the only one who sowed a clearing," they told him.

"Stenkin wasn't a bad man," one muttered. "He was right; he could have turned in the lot of us."

☐

Sheslakov arrived early at his Frunze Street office and found the NKVD messenger waiting outside his door with file in hand. He signed for it in triplicate, ordered his usual three cups of coffee from his secretary, and settled himself behind his desk. While he waited he studied the photograph that came with the file. Did the man look American or did he think that only because he knew he *was* American? Perhaps it was the half-amused expression on the face, not a common feature in NKVD portraiture. He put it to one side as the coffee arrived; faces were Fyedorova's speciality, not his.

The man's real name was Jack Patrick Smith; Yakov Kuznetsky was a literal translation of the first and last names. He'd been born in St. Cloud, Minnesota, in 1900 to second-generation Anglo-Irish immigrants. His father had been a cop and his mother a seamstress. There had been no other children.

Jack had joined the U.S. Army in 1918—"to see the world" he'd told his first Soviet interrogator—and had been posted to one of the battalions used in the American intervention. In August of that year his battalion was guarding the Suchan mines near Vladivostok, the only source of coal for the eastern section of the Trans-Siberian, a footnote helpfully pointed out. For several weeks the Americans and the local population had gotten on well, but when the Revolution reached the area the Americans sided with the Whites and the mining community with the Reds. The Americans occupied the mines. One day one of their officers was shot, and the Americans went out looking for a culprit. Smith and another man, O'Connell, were sent to search the house of a miner who lived some way from the village.

They didn't come back.

The Americans assumed they'd been captured by Red partisans and offered to exchange two arrested miners. They didn't believe it when the Reds told them Smith was not a prisoner, so a meeting was arranged between him and the American commander on neutral ground. Smith told him that O'Connell had attacked the Russian miner's daughter and that he'd shot and killed O'Connell. Smith told his commander he'd joined the Revolution and that was all there was to it.

Sheslakov put down the file, took the handbook of Siberian flora off the second cup of coffee, and watched the steam escape like a smoke signal. An apparently ordinary American boy "joining the Revolution," just like that. It didn't bode altogether well. The Mongols had always slaughtered deserters on the grounds that they'd shown they could never be trusted. Still, he mused, the current condition of Mongolia didn't say much for their judgment.

Sheslakov went back to the file.

After the Revolution, Smith—now Kuznetsky—had been thoroughly investigated. He'd come out clean, and since he'd already proved himself with the partisans, commanding his own group in the Chita area for over a year, he'd been snapped up by the Cheka in Irkutsk. Since then it had been all promotions and special assignments: head of the Chita NKVD 1931–34, commissar attached to special anti-kulak forces in the Saratov area, the West Ukraine, and the Crimea, 1934–37, administrative adviser in Spain 1937–39. He'd been sent back to the Far East in 1939 to a post in the Commissariat attached to Zhukov's General Staff, had still been there when the Far Eastern divisions were redeployed on the Moscow Front in November 1941. Finally, he'd volunteered for partisan duty and been parachuted into Belorussia in May 1942 as a replacement brigade commissar. For the last six months he'd been commanding the brigade, as the previous commander had been killed and not replaced.

Why, Sheslakov wondered, would a man with Kuznetsky's glittering record volunteer for partisan duty? The noble-gesture theory didn't fit with the rest of his career. Had he been trying to recreate his idealistic youth? And why, in twenty years of promotions, had he never gotten himself a position in Moscow? It wouldn't have been difficult if he'd wanted one. But he hadn't, and that was unusual.

Sheslakov took the fauna handbook off the third cup and took a sip. In all other respects the man was perfect, and choosing a more difficult life was no indication of disloyalty. The reverse, some would say. He lit his first cigarette of the day, watched the smoke wafting upward, then reached for the telephone.

He was on his third call when Fyedorova arrived. He

passed her the photograph without speaking, and she took it across to the window.

Fyedorova was his "administrative assistant," and had been since the beginning of the war. She was ten years older than Sheslakov, a small, thin woman who had worked for the GRU since its founding. Fyedorova drank to excess, cared nothing for authority, and did next to no work. Her only function, which both she and Sheslakov found self-justifying, was to act as his sounding board. For this she was perfectly equipped. Her intelligence was as purely psychological as his was purely logical; she had a wisdom, an insight into people, which he found as vital as it was irritating.

"First reaction?" he asked as he put down the phone.

"A wild card," she replied, pinning the photograph to the wall opposite her chair.

"Try this one," he said, passing across a picture of a young, dark-haired woman.

Fyedorova stared at it for some time. "This one tells me nothing," she said finally, "and that's unusual."

"A good start," Sheslakov murmured. "Put it up with the other one and I'll tell you who they are and what I have in mind for them."

He went through his plan, clarifying his own appreciation of it in the process.

"Ingenious," she said when he'd finished. "But you know that."

She looked up again at the two faces, both with the half-smile, as if they were looking at the same thing. "Even the best play . . ."

"Depends on good acting," he completed dryly.

"And one of our two leading actors has been forced on us by circumstance. Her file is about as useful as the people who wrote it."

"I've got Nikolai trying to trace the man who recommended her recruitment. Luerhsen, Josef. According to her file, he's in Moscow, but his file's disappeared."

She was still staring at the photographs. "Neither of them is Russian," she said. "Zhdanov won't like that."

"Zhdanov will like the alternative even less. Let's get the script right first, then worry about the actors."

He picked up the phone again and, after some playful banter with the switchboard girl, whose name he kept forgetting, was put through to Sergei Yanovsky, an old friend and the head of the GRU's German section.

"I need to talk to you, Sergei Ivanovich."

"I can't make it today or tomor—"

"First Priority. How about twenty minutes?"

"I'll be there."

"I must remember that for the bread line," Fyedorova said. "I assume you want me here."

"Yes, we have a long day ahead. Yanovsky is only the first." He picked up the phone again and made three more appointments, two in his office and one at a research institute outside the city. He'd barely put the phone down when Yanovsky arrived. The two men embraced.

"Right," Sheslakov said, sitting down and twirling his jade letter opener. "All you know of the German atomic program."

Yanovsky looked surprised for a moment. "There's none to speak of now, though there could have been. Their technical knowledge in 1939 was the equal of anyone's." He lit the cigarette offered by Sheslakov. "Tea?" he asked.

"When you've earned it."

"Okay. In 1939 the Nazis set up a Uranium Society, the Uranverein, and all the prominent scientists they had left after the emigrations were given particular tasks to do in solving the basic problem of how to make the bomb. Uranium exports from Czechoslovakia were stopped, a heavy-water production program was started. By 1941 the scientists reported that they could build a reactor that would make the U-235 they needed for a bomb. The problem—ours, too, as I understand it—was the deadline. Hitler wasn't interested in anything that would take a few months, let alone something that would need a few years, so the program wasn't given any priority. Our information is that the German scientists, most of them at any rate, were quite relieved about this and were quite happy to work on the theory knowing full well that their consciences would never be troubled by the practice.

"In the last year things have changed, though not that much. The Nazis are getting desperate, and all sorts of desperate solutions are being looked for. Atomic bombs are still seen as too long-term for practical use, but German atomic espionage in America has been stepped up. Fortunately most of their information comes from our Rosa, and she's been busy confirming their pessimism. That's about it. They have an atomic development program that might give them a bomb in ten years. Since they'll all have been hung within two years, it's completely irrelevant."

Sheslakov looked pleased. "But they have the scientific knowledge?"

"Yes."

"If they had the U-235, they could make a bomb?"

"Heisenberg actually told Speer as much. 'Give us the U-235 and we'll make you a bomb,' he said. You're not planning to give them any?"

"When did that conversation take place?"

"1942. June, I think. I can look it up."

"No need." Sheslakov stood up. "Thank you, Sergei Ivanovich. You've been most helpful. But," he added, seeing the other's expression, "I can say no more. And"—he looked at his watch—"I'm afraid there's no time for tea. Yelena is well?"

"Fine. Apart from worrying about our son Mikhail." He smiled ruefully. "You and Vera must come over. I'll telephone you."

Sheslakov closed the door behind him, thinking for a second about his own son, killed three years before in the war's first days.

"Well, no obvious problem there," Fyedorova said. "Tell

me, why are you bothering to visit Kapitza? There's no doubt concerning the scientific facts, is there?"

"I like to hear everything firsthand."

A knock on the door heralded their next visitor, a burly man with a sour expression. He sat down without being asked. "Well, Comrade Sheslakov, I am here as ordered. I would be grateful if this business took up as little time as possible."

Sheslakov sighed inwardly, smiled outwardly. "I know your time is valuable, Comrade Boletsky, but this is First Priority business."

Why, he asked himself, were there so many unmitigated bastards in the NKVD external sections?

"Comrade," he said "tell me about the U-235 trains."

"You have the report."

"Tell me anyway," Sheslakov said coldly, closing his eyes to help him keep his temper.

"They leave Oak Ridge on the first Friday of each month at around six P.M., arrive in Los Alamos on the following Tuesday morning. Each carries ten crates, weight approximately fifty pounds, each containing five pounds of U-235. Two military police accompany the train throughout, two state police are picked up and deposited at each state border."

"It seems an absurdly low level of protection."

"It is."

"Why so little, Comrade Boletsky, why?"

"Because the Americans have not considered the possibility of an attack. I think the two policemen are only there because of some instinctive desire to guard something that's important, not because they seriously think it needs guarding."

"Good, now the train. How is it composed?"

"What do you mean?"

"What does it consist of?"

"I don't have that information."

"Get it, please. I want to know how many railroad cars,

27

whether the engine is steam or diesel, where and when the engineers are exchanged, as they must be on such a long journey. I want the makeup of the train, the order of the cars involved, everything. Who is the source of information?"

"GRU," Boletsky said with ill-concealed distaste. "Melville, real name Aaron Matson, deputy chief of security at Oak Ridge. Rosa is his contact."

"Is she? What's his motivation?"

"Ideological."

"I want a full dossier on him too. Coordinate it with Barchugov. Also a complete timetable of the train's journey, where it is at all times. And I want to know why it leaves on Fridays at six P.M.

"Finally," he said, consulting his notes for the first time, "I want everything you have on the situations at Grand Falls and the Alaskan relay station. I particularly want to know the current situation regarding American cargo-checking procedures."

He stood up. "I realize most of this will have to come from America, but I would appreciate whatever urgency you can muster. This is First Priority."

"I've not forgotten," Boletsky replied stiffly.

"Why," Fyedorova asked after he'd gone, "does it matter what sort of engine is pulling the train?"

"Steam engines have to stop for water," Sheslakov replied as he looked for a particular file in the stacks on his desk.

Finding it, he passed it over to Fyedorova. "I'm going to see Petr Kapitza. That's all we have on Walter Schellenberg. When I get back you can tell me whether he's the man to be tempted by our bait."

□

After helping herself to the bottle of vodka that Sheslakov kept at the back of his filing cabinet, Olga Fyedorova settled herself on the old cot under the window and opened the file. Holding the German's photograph up to the light, she studied it for several minutes, trying to think herself behind the eyes that stared out at her. They were a boy's eyes, she thought, not unlike Sheslakov's.

A good beginning.

Her approach to an operation like this was completely different from Sheslakov's. He approached it like a diagram, she like the writing of a love story, weighing up the interactions in the diagram, the way the people concerned would respond to events and, most important of all, to each other. There would be no more than ten people intimately involved in the unfolding of the plan, and several of them would remain unknown to her. It was all the more crucial then that those she wove into the plot should be known quantities, and that their strengths and weaknesses should be written into the plan at the beginning.

Schellenberg was a special case. He had only one decision to make, and everything that was known about him had to be manipulated in the desired direction. He came from a well-to-do family, had been educated at a Jesuit *gymnasium*, had studied medicine and law at Bonn University. Soon after graduation he had enlisted in the SD, the SS Security Service. All plus points, Fyedorova thought. Intellectuals were always easier to predict, particularly those who chose subjects like medicine and law. If he had studied history or physics, she would have been much less sanguine.

The move from the Jesuits to the SS was equally indicative. To her it implied the need for an ideological father figure; the ideology itself would be the product of circumstance rather than conviction. In France before the first war she'd known Catholics who had become Marxists at almost the touch of a button; almost the same process, except, she thought with a smile, in that case it was a mother figure that was required. Anyway, Schellenberg's ideology was sufficiently vague and indeterminate to allow the free play of the sort of intellect that chose to study law and medicine. Neither would provide a driving force, and judging from his rise through the ranks, the man was not lacking in ambition. It couldn't be money that moved him, and she had a sneaking suspicion that power for its own sake did not attract him. Power for what, then? It must be for play, for the chance to play games at the highest level.

That would make him ideal.

She went back to the file. He had coordinated the intelligence from Austria before the Anschluss, then personally undertaken a spy mission to West Africa in the winter of 1938–39, checking out harbor defenses. And, she remembered it now, he had been the officer at Venlo in 1939 who had lured the two British agents into captivity.

Games.

From 1939 to 1941 he had worked under Mueller for the Gestapo and had reportedly been close to Heydrich. Then, in June 1941, he had been switched to Amt VI, the SD's Foreign Intelligence Service, as its new chief. With Heydrich gone, he had gravitated to Himmler, and was now thought to be the Reichsführer's chief political adviser. Early this year his organization had absorbed the discredited Abwehr to form a newly unified intelligence service. He was Hitler's spy master.

So much for his career: he hadn't missed an opportunity. He had a house off the Kurfürstendamm in Berlin, a country house at Herzberg. His office was built like a luxurious fortress, with a machine gun built into his desk and alarm sirens activated by photoelectric cells. When traveling abroad he "wore" an artificial tooth containing poison *and* carried a cyanide capsule in a signet ring.

That, Fyedorova thought, was particularly interesting. What kind of a man carried two suicide devices? An obsessive. In fact, the whole business about the desk reeked, not of paranoia—paranoids didn't go on spy missions—but of perverse perfectionism. The medical/law student again. Here was a man who believed passionately in details, and who would

probably have the two weaknesses typical of such people—
an inability to see the forest for the trees and, more damning
in a spy master, the compulsion to furnish from the imagination those details which were unavailable.

She got up and refilled her glass, fixed the photograph to
the wall in front of her, and lay back on the cot. "Will you
bite, Walter *tovarich*?" she asked the picture.

"I think you will."

☐

Sheslakov had found Professor Petr Kapitza supervising the
unloading of crates containing laboratory equipment. The
Institute was in the final throes of its return to Moscow and
chaos reigned. Kapitza's state of mind had not been noticeably
improved by the appearance of another interrogator from the
Atomic Division.

"As far as I'm concerned, the First Priority is saving several years' work from these vandals," he had exclaimed, taking in the removal corps with a sweep of his arm. "What the
hell are you talking about?"

Sheslakov had given him a telephone number to ring and
patiently waited in the Institute's spacious lobby, imagining
the swish of tsarist gowns in days gone by.

Eventually the scientist reappeared, motioning Sheslakov
to follow him outside. "We can talk in the gardens, where
we might conceivably hear each other."

Sheslakov set out to be disarming. "Professor, I know
your time is valuable, and I promise you that after this conversation the work can go on undisturbed. I have read the
report of your conversations with General Kostylov, and there
are just a few extra questions I need answered. First, if you
were given fifty pounds of Uranium-235, could you make an
atomic bomb?"

Kapitza looked at him sharply. "Is that a random figure
you've just thought up?"

"No."

"I thought not. The answer is yes, or at least the probability is very high. Two bombs, I would say."

"How quickly?"

The scientist spread his arms. "That is hard to answer."

"A month, a year, ten years?"

Kapitza looked up at the sky. "Two years, I would think. But I would not like to stake my life on it. The Fuchs diagram has no great surprises—the basic principles are clear. But there are always unforeseen problems." He looked at Sheslakov again, this time with something approaching a smile. "Of course continued access to the American development process would save us from duplicating their mistakes."

"How powerful would such a bomb be?" Sheslakov had no reason for asking the question save curiosity.

"Again, hard to say."

"A guess?"

"I would say powerful enough to raze a city the size of Novgorod."

It was Sheslakov's turn to look at the scientist. Kapitza couldn't possibly know that his questioner came from that city. A chill raced up Sheslakov's spine. He couldn't resist another irrelevant question.

"Professor, do you have any qualms about making such a bomb?"

Kapitza laughed for the first time. "Qualms? Of course not. Qualms have never stopped scientific development. We are on a roller coaster, as the Americans say, and the ups and downs keep getting steeper, and there's no way to get off. What use are qualms?"

The chill was still there, so out of place on a beautiful spring morning. Sheslakov reorganized his thoughts. "The Uranium-235—how easy is it to transport? How dangerous?"

"It won't explode if you drop it. It has to be kept in small quantities or a critical mass is reached. If that happens, radiation is released, and radiation kills."

"So the idea of carrying five pounds of Uranium-235 in fifty-pound crates makes sense?"

"You are well-informed. Is that how the Americans are doing it? Yes, the container for the U-235—a steel bottle probably—would be suspended somehow in the middle of the crate, keeping it an adequate distance from the other jars in the other crates."

"So there would be no danger in handling these crates, no time limit, temperature limit, pressure limit, anything like that?"

"Not that I can see. When can we expect these crates to arrive?"

Sheslakov smiled. "*If* these crates arrive, Professor, you'll be the first to know."

☐

"Yes," Fyedorova told him on his return to the office. "Or at least I see no reason why not."

Sheslakov sat himself behind his desk. "I think a drink is called for. In your case," he added, examining the bottle, "another drink. I'm beginning to distrust this operation. People keep saying yes to me, as if the whole thing is a foregone conclusion."

Fyedorova got up from the cot and took the proffered glass. "If it's difficulties you want, don't despair. They've found Luerhsen—in the Lubyanka. And they've lost Kuznetsky."

two

THEY had been underground for more than eighteen hours, and the strain of confinement was beginning to tell. The whispering grew louder, the accidental noises more frequent, the smell of the latrine buckets was becoming unbearable. Kuznetsky wondered whether it might have been better to send out scouts and risk the dogs picking up their scent.

There was a soft knock on the partition. He put down his book, extinguished the candle, and eased himself up off the bed. This girl would sleep through anything, he thought to himself as he fastened his belt. The knock was repeated.

"Coming," he whispered. Nadezhda turned over in her sleep, exposing one milky-white shoulder.

Yakovenko was outside. "Message coming in," he said.

Kuznetsky followed him through the maze to the radio room, watched the operator transcribe the message from the current code. "Colonel Kuznetsky required Moscow immediately. Pickup points 12 14 15 Tuesday Thursday Saturday. Signal required. Request receipt."

That was it. What the fuck did they want with him in Moscow? "Tell them the Germans are crawling all over the place and we're still hibernating," he told Beslov. "Diplomatically."

"Situation understood," came the reply. "Colonel Kuznetsky required Moscow immediately. Request receipt."

"Maybe it's a medal," Yakovenko murmured. "Though they could have dropped *that* with the chocolate."

Kuznetsky laughed. "Oh shit. Tell them—" He broke off at the sound of running feet.

Sidorova erupted into the dugout, mouthing the word "Germans."

"Cut the connection," Kuznetsky whispered to Beslov. "Make sure everyone's ready," to Yakovenko. He made his way to the periscope, squeezing himself between the roots of the tree that concealed it. The tube went right up through the center of the trunk, then into an artificial sapling that could be twisted where the trunk forked. Putting his eyes to the mirror, he could immediately see a single German soldier, a boy of about sixteen, walking slowly toward him, diligently scanning the ground for a sign. Gently swiveling the periscope, he could pick out the line of troops, spread out at around twenty-yard intervals, carefully advancing. Only the boy would actually pass over the camp. Kuznetsky prayed that he'd be nearsighted.

He seemed to be. He was already halfway across without pausing in his deliberate stride. Kuznetsky turned to check that his group and the other group leaders were all there, caught a glimpse of Nadezhda yawning in the background.

The boy stopped and reached down to pick something up, something small and red. A chocolate wrapper! *How the hell had they missed it?*

"Pretend it's not there," Kuznetsky silently pleaded. "Save your own and your comrades' lives. Just keep walking."

The German licked the paper, perhaps finding a last crumb of chocolate, and then he blew his whistle. Kuznetsky didn't dare turn the sapling, but he could hear the sound of running feet crashing through the undergrowth and, more ominously, the sound of motors revving. A lieutenant came into view, examined the wrapper, looked warily around. Then he strode off to the left, and Kuznetsky risked following him with the periscope. The officer was busily pulling dead branches away from the T-34's underground garage.

Kuznetsky climbed out of the roots, pointed to his watch, and held up one finger. The other group leaders scurried away through the interconnecting passages, counting seconds under their breath. He picked up the loaded antitank gun, checked that the automatic pistol was firmly in his belt, and continued counting.

Thirty-five, thirty-six. Everyone was ready. Forty, forty-one. And at least the light above ground was fading fast. Nadezhda smiled at him. Fifty-five, fifty-six.

Ever so carefully, he released the greased wooden peg that held the trapdoor and let it drop. A square of twilight appeared. Yakovenko placed the stump under the opening, and Kuznetsky used it as a launching pad to throw himself up through the square and onto the forest floor, screaming "Now" at the top of his voice.

Ignoring the nearby group of startled Germans, he picked out the approaching half-track and fired the antitank rocket. There was a whoosh of flame and the vehicle toppled forward like an elephant crashing to its knees. Yakovenko's machine gun seemed to be going off in his ear, but the group of Germans were all down or falling, and suddenly there was near silence, only the shouts of the Germans farther off and the rumble of other vehicles in the distance.

The partisans were pouring out of the hidden exits, forming themselves into their groups and moving away. Kuznetsky could see the nearest Germans moving back and knew why, having read a captured Wehrmacht manual. They were supposed to form a circle with a radius of three hundred yards.

He checked his own group and led them off at a run on their prearranged compass setting—due west. Fifty yards farther they found another half-track disgorging troops and he dropped to the ground with the rocket gun, felt Yakovenko load it as he took aim, fired. Another inferno and they were running again, zigzagging between the burning Germans, on

36

through the forest. Nadezhda was leading now, through a small clearing and down into a shallow riverbed as a burst of automatic fire shredded the leaves above their heads.

They must have gone three hundred yards by now, Kuznetsky thought, but there'd be a second line not too far ahead. With a supreme effort he managed to regain the front and pulled the group to a halt.

"Down! Quiet!" he ordered, and it was as if a switch had been flicked. There was heavy gunfire to the north, and they could see the flames of the burning half-tracks reflected in the forest roof. To both right and left the passage of vehicles was audible, but ahead of them, nothing.

It would be fully dark in an hour. Should they wait for the second line and hope to pass through it unseen? Kuznetsky was inclined to think so until he heard the dogs.

"Spread—no firing," he ordered, and they were on the move again, racing across the forest floor in a widening line, running into the enemy before either side had time to think. Kuznetsky's automatic pistol coughed twice as a silhouette loomed to confront him, and he pumped another bullet between the dog's yellow eyes as it broke free from its dead master's grip. To his right and left the forest was again full of gunfire. He kept running, the sounds fading behind him, conscious that at least some of the others were running parallel through the trees.

☐

It was not the first time that Sheslakov had visited someone in the bowels of the NKVD headquarters, but familiarity had not bred immunity. The grayness of the place seemed all-embracing, and this somehow seemed to emphasize the sharpness of each human touch. The people incarcerated, and their jailers, they all seemed like pieces of raw meat on an endless, uniform slab.

In the beginning, he thought, walking down another identical corridor, animality bred abstraction, the savage developed language. Now abstraction breeds animality, correcting some cosmic balance. Our rulers run the most perfectly devised system like savages, he thought, while the Germans, still animals, choose anal retentives for their leaders. He felt a surge of sadness.

The NKVD officer opened the door of Luerhsen's cell. "I must lock it behind you," he said apologetically.

"Too many mass escapes, eh?" Sheslakov said, unable to resist the gibe.

Luerhsen looked up at him with one of the most peaceful faces Sheslakov could remember. No one upstairs had seemed to know why he was imprisoned, and it had taken Sheslakov half an hour and several irate telephone calls to get his file released. The "antistate activity" with which he was charged—but not, as yet, convicted for—concerned remarks he had made in 1939, five years before. To be precise, he had called the Nazi–Soviet Pact "an error of judgment comparable only with that made by Judas." The NKVD officer in charge of the records had expressed surprise that the man had not been shot.

Sheslakov introduced himself and sat down on the bunk beside Luerhsen. "I wish to ask you some questions," he said, "about someone you knew long ago. It has nothing to do with your case. I can do nothing to help you in that respect," he added, suddenly deciding that honesty was the best policy with this man. "I can only say that the cause you served for thirty years needs your assistance once more. We need to assess how this woman will react in certain situations, and you are the only person in the Soviet Union who has actually met with her."

Luerhsen looked back at him placidly, a faint smile forming on his lips. "My loyalties survived many years in the enemy's prisons; they will doubtless survive a few more in the prison of my friends. Who is the woman you wish to know about?"

"Amelia Brandt, now Brandon. We understand from your

initial submission of her name as a possible GRU recruit that you knew her as a child and that you met again in Berlin in 1933."

Luerhsen smiled. "She was always called Amy, never Amelia. Our Berlin meeting was very brief, two hours at most. But yes, she made an impression on me, mostly, I think, because seeing her then, in those circumstances, was like seeing her mother brought back to life. They looked so alike, but it was more than that." He smiled inwardly, as if taken by a memory. "Hard to define," he said. "Do you have a cigarette?"

Sheslakov offered his package, watched the old man inhale deeply. "I need as complete a picture of her as you can give me."

"May I know why?"

"She's a key figure in an operation we're mounting in America. I can say no more than that."

Luerhsen looked at him, took another deep drag on the cigarette. "That pleases me."

"Tell me about when you knew her as a child."

"Her mother and I were lovers, you know that. We met in the spring of 1918. Her husband had been killed several years before, at Tannenberg, I think. She was totally committed to the Party—the Spartakusbund as it was then. It was what we called a 'comrades' marriage' in those days. Party work and bed and nothing much else. Amy must have been about seven—"

"She was born in August 1911."

"Six, seven. A lovely child, though I'm afraid we didn't have much time for doing things with her. You can imagine what it was like in Berlin in 1918—more meetings than there were hours in the day, more newspapers than there was toilet paper, which most of them got used as. Elisabeth Brandt's house was our center of operations; it was always swarming with people. Another woman, Anna Kaltz, also lived there, and she had a daughter the same age as Amy—Effi—so the two little girls looked after each other. One dark one, one blond one. They'd help out, too, making drinks, rolling leaflets off the printer, in fact they always seemed to have ink on their faces. They both worshiped their mothers, I do remember that. But so did a lot of people in Friedrichshain. They were remarkable women."

"Can you remember any specific incidents with Amy?" Sheslakov asked. Fyedorova had insisted on that question.

Luerhsen furrowed his brow. "Not really. I bandaged her knee once, I remember that. She'd cut it quite badly, should have had stitches, and it obviously hurt like hell. But she hardly shed a tear. She was a determined little thing. Once she started something she'd finish it. Really stubborn. I expect she still is. People don't change much, do they?" He gave Sheslakov a quizzical glance, accepted another cigarette.

"Then the roof fell in. January 1919. I was here in Moscow at one of those interminable conferences for setting up the Third International. Elisabeth was one of the Party leaders killed by the fascists, not that they called themselves that then. She was raped and beaten to death by a gang of them in her own house, and while it was all happening little Amy was sitting in the cupboard under the stairs where her mother had hidden her. She came out eventually and found her mother's body, then walked halfway across Berlin to her aunt's in the middle of the night. Imagine it! There was gunfire, gangs of thugs roaming the streets looking for Communists, everyone shut up tight in their houses, not daring to go out, and there's this little girl walking miles across the city. She didn't say another word for six months. The aunt married an American in 1921, and they all moved to America soon afterward."

"How do you know all this? You say you weren't there."

"From Anna Kaltz. She was in Kiel looking after her sick father during the week it all fell apart, and she didn't dare return to Berlin for several months. She's also the link with 1933, because she and Amy kept up a correspondence over the years—"

"With Effi too?"

"No. Strange. Or perhaps not. I think Anna was Amy's link with her mother."

"1933?"

"The terrible year. It was the summer, late July, I think. I'd been sent back to Berlin to organize the relocation of the *Pas Apparat*—the underground passport factories. The Nazis were well into their drive against us and we'd decided to move everything to the Saar. Effi Kaltz was the best forger we had—an amazing talent. Anyway, we were there, five of us I think, in this house in Friedrichshain, packing up all the stuff, the inks, papers, rubber stamps, everything. And there was this knock on the door and there stood this beautiful young woman in American clothes. Amy. She was in Germany for a holiday, a pilgrimage really, had tried to find Anna Kaltz and learned that she'd been arrested. So she'd somehow tracked down Effi.

"We didn't know what to do with her. We were expecting the Gestapo any minute, and for once we weren't wrong . . . but I'm getting ahead of the story. We had another couple of hours' work to do, and Amy said she'd wait, even though she must have known the risk she was running. I finished my tasks before the others and I talked to her for a time—twenty minutes, something like that. It was a strange conversation.

"At first I couldn't get over how much she resembled her mother—it was uncanny. Then I started noticing the differences. There was a reticence about her that Elisabeth never had, a feeling she was holding herself in, holding herself very tightly. Maybe it was just being in Berlin again, with all that that must have meant for her. But I think it was more than that—"

"She was unhappy?"

"No, not at all. On the contrary, she seemed very happy. She was wearing an engagement ring—"

"Are you certain of that?"

"Yes."

"But she never married."

"Engagements also get broken. No, it wasn't unhappiness. I sensed divided loyalties, and remember, it was my job to do just that for many years. You get a feeling for it, you know there's a split somewhere, sometimes even before the person concerned does. Amy was happy in one world but she still had at least half her heart in her mother's world. And I don't think she'd ever have been able to pull the two together. She had to choose."

Luerhsen paused, seemed to be examining the cell floor. "Or have the choice made for her, which is probably what happened that evening." He paused again.

"The Gestapo arrived," Sheslakov prompted.

"Yes. A crashing on the door. Those bastards even enjoyed hitting doors. But we were prepared. There was a tunnel from the cellar that ran under the house behind and up through a grating in the next street. The *Pas Apparat*'s houses were the eighth wonder of the world when it came to hidden exits. We got away down the tunnel and piled into the car that was waiting and half-rammed our way past a Gestapo car that was blocking a crossroads. It was like an American gangster movie. And Amy . . ."

He smiled at the memory. "In the car I said something to her, something flippant like 'Welcome home,' and her face— the reticence was all gone—she was the absolute image of her mother in that moment. It was that look that made me put her name forward, because I knew, I *knew*, that the German part of her life wasn't finished, and that sooner or later she would know it, too, and that somehow she would . . . not avenge her mother, but somehow justify her mother's death. Do you understand?"

"I think so. What happened next?"

"I know only from thirdhand sources. We had a routine in such circumstances. The passengers would get out one by one, so as to split the pursuit, and I was the first to leave the car that night. What I heard, months later, was that Amy and

Effi got out together, managed to shake off the followers, only to find the Gestapo waiting for them in Amy's hotel room. It seems likely that they'd been following her all day, ever since she started making inquiries about Anna Kaltz.

"They were taken down to Gestapo headquarters on Prinz Albrechtstrasse, put in adjacent cells. They could talk to each other but not see each other. At some time in the night some men came down and crushed Effi's drawing hand in the hinges of the cell door. Then they all raped her. Amy they left alone, probably because she had an American passport. She tried to comfort Effi through the rest of the night and in the morning they took her out and told her she was being deported. They put her on a train for Bremerhaven and must have held her there until the ship sailed. Effi died in Oranienburg a month later, killed by some pig of a guard for speaking out of turn. It was from one of her fellow inmates that we found all this out."

The two men sat in silence for a moment.

"I'm giving you facts, but it doesn't seem enough," Luerhsen said at last. "It's hard to imagine what it was like in those days, even for those of us who were there. We were Communists, disciplined Communists, but it was still an adventure. Does that sound crazy? But that's what I saw in her eyes that moment in the car—adventure. Is that what you're offering her?"

It wasn't a word Sheslakov used, but with this man it didn't seem out of place.

"You could say that," he said, getting to his feet. "Thank you, Comrade." He hesitated. "I'm very sorry there's nothing I can do for you."

Luerhsen shrugged. "There's nothing I want. When you've been at war for thirty years there's a lot to be said for the peace of a six-by-four cell. No," he said, refusing Sheslakov's package of cigarettes, "I shall only miss them more when they're all gone." He smiled his serene smile once more. "We never lose the discipline, do we?"

43

After finding his way out through the labyrinth of corridors, Sheslakov dismissed his driver and walked back to Frunze Street. Evening was coming on, the office workers pouring into the Metro at the bottom of Gorky Street. He felt profoundly depressed, as much by Luerhsen's tranquility as by Kaptiza's cheerful submission to the roller coaster. *Anatoly Grigorovich, you're getting old.* Car chases in Berlin seemed like echoes of another age, the romantic underground fighters of the Comintern dancing around the feet of the beast like . . . an appropriate metaphor failed him.

"There's nothing I want," Luerhsen had said. Well, there was something Sheslakov wanted—a problem to solve. The cogs were fitting too smoothly into place.

Fyedorova was still on the cot, glass in hand, staring at Rosa's photograph. Amy's photograph. He started to recount his conversation with Luerhsen, then realized that the bottle by the bed was empty. It could wait until morning. He sent her home.

Alone in the office, almost alone in the building to judge by the lack of noise, Sheslakov found a fresh bottle and put his feet up on the desk. He needed a name for the operation, something romantic he decided, something for Luerhsen and the past. Three glasses later he suddenly remembered a favorite book of his childhood, a tale of bandits in the mountains of the Caucasus. Their leader had been a woman called "Armenian Rose."

three

THE MOMENT he came through the door and breezed by her, she knew something was wrong. No hello, no smile, no kiss. He had that expression on his face that she hated, the righteous-child expression.

"What's the matter?" Amy asked, more sharply than she'd intended.

"Nothing," Richard said, in that tone of his that shouted "Something."

"All right," Amy said. She'd been through this game before.

He sat in the armchair and stared at the ceiling. She waited.

"Amy, I saw you with a man today," Richard finally blurted out. "Down by the river. Who was he?"

"Have you been spying on me?" she asked angrily, one part of her mind noting the irony of the question.

"Of course not. I was in the park—"

"He was a foreigner, a Czech, and he asked me for directions. His English wasn't very good so we started talking in German. He was a nice man. . . ."

"What did you talk about?"

"Oh, this and that. Living in America. The jealousy of the American male."

He turned back to the ceiling. She could tell that he believed her and was wondering how to climb down gracefully.

She would have to be more careful from now on. This might have been serious. What if he'd come up to her and Faulkner and started demanding explanations?

He was still sunk in thought. She and Faulkner had exceeded the usual meeting time, but there'd been more than usual to discuss. This sudden flood of requests from Moscow . . .

"What are you thinking about?" Richard asked.

"Nothing."

"Amy, I'm sorry. I do love you, you know." He held out his arms.

She couldn't lie to him this time, not with words anyway. She undid her dressing-gown cord, let it slip open. He pulled it off her shoulders and kissed her breasts. She didn't want to be kissed, not this time.

"Quickly," she whispered, and in moments they were on the carpet, he pushing inside her, his arms tight around her neck.

He came almost immediately. He hadn't done that for ages, she thought. Did something inside him know that she was feeling absolutely nothing? She kissed his cheek, put a finger across his lips to still the apology that she knew was forming. He really was a nice man in some ways.

My own hill of beans, she thought.

"I still can't decide whether your eyes are blue or gray," he said, gazing into them from a distance of about four inches.

Feeling suddenly irritated, she rolled over and sat against the sofa. "Richard, you're the only man in my life. If you see me talking to a man, it's not because I'm asking to go to bed with him."

"Amy, I've said I'm sorry. I know it's hard for you, but I can't leave my wife yet. I just can't do that to her."

"I know. I'm not pushing you." She wrapped her dressing gown around her, crossed the room, and turned on the radio. "Coffee?"

The newscaster announced the beginning of the Russian

attack on Sevastopol between sales pitches for new vitamin pills. Richard sat back on the sofa and looked around the room. Nothing had changed since the previous Friday; it still looked like no other woman's room he'd ever known. There were no pictures, no trinkets other than those he'd bought, no obvious keepsakes. It irritated him. Amy was so . . . so full of life, and her apartment was as exciting as a dentist's waiting room.

She came in with the coffee, now dressed in a green skirt and cream blouse. "Still redecorating my apartment?" she asked with a grin.

"You could make it look more lived in," he said reluctantly. They'd had this conversation before.

"It is lived in. I live in it, in case you hadn't noticed."

"It's not you."

"It is. How many times do I have to tell you? I like things unadorned. You native Americans can't understand that."

"The Indians are the native Americans. You're as American as I am." This mocking anti-Americanism was the one facet of her character which both annoyed and baffled him. "And, anyway, what's wrong with having nice things?" he asked belligerently.

She smiled sweetly at him. "Nothing, if you find them nice. Americans are brought up to care about their *things*. I wasn't. Come on, we'll miss the beginning of the movie. And don't look at me like that—if I was an ordinary American girl, you'd find me boring."

Perhaps so, Richard thought later, as he watched Marlene Dietrich throw chairs at James Stewart. He couldn't accuse Amy of being boring.

After the movie they had coffee in a diner, then walked through Dupont Circle, kissing each other good night under the fountain. Richard then went home to his wife, Jean, piqued at Amy's refusal to display any jealousy, angry at himself for wanting her to. Amy walked home slowly, trying to arrange her thoughts for the task at hand.

Back in her apartment, she made herself a pot of black coffee, changed back into her dressing gown, and retrieved Faulkner's instructions from behind the brick in the fireplace. They were clear enough: Moscow wanted a report on Wim Doesburg, everything she knew and guessed about him, and her opinion of the "relationship" between them. It should be short and comprehensive. Typical.

What relationship? she asked herself, switching on the desk lamp. And what on earth could be behind this request? She sat back in the chair, sipping coffee, wondering where to begin. The first meeting on the ferry, she supposed.

She began to write, describing the German's rotund appearance, his manner, recounting the gist of their conversation. It had been almost a year ago now, on a cold spring day. The whole encounter had seemed quite bizarre; several times she'd almost burst out laughing. He'd suspected nothing, thinking her just another patriotic German. Had she impressed him? She rather thought she had, almost too much so. She'd been too professional, too cool, and that, she knew, had slightly disconcerted him. But he'd responded in kind, and that had been the way of it ever since. She began to understand what Moscow meant by their "relationship."

"Our meetings," she wrote, "have always been conducted in a thoroughly professional manner, with little or no discussion of extraneous matters. He has never made any sexual advances, though he does seem aware of"—how should she put it?—"my femininity." Suitably neutral. "He has never asked any questions about my private life."

Funny, she thought, he seems more impressive on paper than he does in the flesh. Perhaps she had underestimated him. "He has never seemed concerned," she wrote, "at the possibility of exposure, and his confidence, in my judgment, is well-founded. His intelligence is hard to assess. He absorbs information quickly, but his sense of humor, on those rare occasions when it is displayed, is of a coarseness that does not suggest any depth of intellect."

Like Richard's, she thought unkindly, quick and shallow.

What else did they want? Doesburg had told her during one of their visits to the zoo that the giraffe was his favorite animal, but she doubted whether Moscow would be interested. They wanted an assessment of his motivation. Well, what made spies spies? Experience in her case, bolstered by conviction. She had no idea what Doesburg had experienced in his fifty or so years, and she found it impossible to believe that any man of his intelligence would work for Hitler on ideological grounds. A blind spot perhaps, but Doesburg didn't seem the ideological type. He wasn't even interested in the war. At their last meeting she'd mentioned some current battle and he'd not even heard of it. So for him it had to be money or excitement or both. She tried to picture his flat face, the expression in the pale blue eyes. It was probably both.

"I suspect," she wrote, "that his allegiance to the German cause is a matter of circumstance rather than conviction. From my limited knowledge I would guess that the possibility of material gain and the enjoyment of intrigue are more important to him."

Why did she think that? His clothes were always beautifully pressed; he seemed somehow at home in New York, at ease with its excess. Which was more than she could say for herself, particularly since that day with Fuchs. She shuddered involuntarily at the memory, forced herself back to thinking about Doesburg. "Bourgeois," that was the word that Moscow would understand. And pride too. He was proud, not of what he was doing, but of his skill at doing it.

"His mannerisms," she wrote, "are unmistakably bourgeois. This, given the nature of his work, is a help rather than a hindrance. He seems to take an unusual pride in his competence. On at least two occasions he has told me how pleased Berlin was with 'his' information. Since, as we know, the information passed on to Berlin has been consistently unhelpful to the German cause, these comments would seem to tell us more about him than Berlin's opinion of him. He clearly places much importance on the latter."

Was this getting too psychological? If only she knew why Moscow wanted this information. Faulkner would have told her if he'd known, she was sure. She pushed her hair back behind her ears and leaned her elbows on the desk, her hands cupped in front of her mouth. Why?

Suddenly it came to her. Moscow was planning to feed Berlin some false information through her and Doesburg, and they wanted to be sure that he would believe her and Berlin believe him. What could it be? That didn't matter for the moment.

"There is no reason to suppose," she continued, "that he considers me in any way unreliable. I have consistently supplied him with information that Berlin must know is scientifically valuable, albeit of no practical use to them in the current circumstances. Berlin presumably values him for the same reason. I have no reason to believe that he will question any information I pass on, or that Berlin will question any information he passes on."

That would do. She read through what she'd written, making only a few minor changes, and then spent the next three hours laboriously translating it into the month's prescribed code. It was past five in the morning by the time she finished, and by then both her tiredness and the sense of excitement had passed. Whatever it was that Moscow wanted passed on couldn't be that important; the Germans were already as good as beaten. It was just a matter of time.

Time. Her thoughts turned to the subject that was beginning to haunt her—the future. What would she do when the war was over? Carry on working against the wider enemy once her personal enemy had been ground under? Probably, but . . . if only they'd give her something important to do. Perhaps she'd leave it all behind, go somewhere like Africa, somewhere different. . . .

The sky outside was lightening. For the first time in many months she took out another man's photograph and sat by the window looking at his face. Three days they'd had once, three days on a floating palace. "I loved you," she said softly. And lost you, she thought to herself. Eleven years, a lifetime ago.

☐

Kuznetsky shifted the antitank rocket launcher from one shoulder to the other and stretched his cramped arm up above his head. Four days had passed since their escape from the German sweep, and the group's eight survivors were now more than thirty miles from their former home, still ten miles from their pickup point at Lukomskoye. From there he'd be Moscow bound, for whatever reason it was that they wanted him. He didn't really care, and that surprised him a little.

Nadezhda had been more upset than he'd expected, clinging to him fiercely with the tears pouring down her cheeks when he broke the news. He'd never seen her cry before. Since then she'd ignored him, a reaction which only reinforced the original impression. But there was nothing he could do. Orders were orders, the Party knew best or the Party knew nothing. How many times had he told people that? And there was only one passenger seat in a Polikarpov.

He looked at her now, striding ahead of him through the moonlit forest, her head erect, her black hair dancing on her shoulders. It had all been worth it, he thought, all the years of death, if a hundredth of the new generation were her equal. It was a comforting thought, and comforting thoughts seemed more important as the years went by. It was strange how the more impact a man had on the outside world, on other people's lives, the more the inner world clamored for attention. Perhaps she reminded him of himself at twenty, another orphan at war with the world, propelled by ideals rather than theory, with nothing to lose but life itself. Perhaps her generation would find a real dawn, perhaps not. History was never sentimental. And how many people had he told that to?

He could hear Yakovenko behind him munching noisily on yet another chocolate bar. The man was becoming an addict. A pawn of imperialist chocolate companies! He laughed out loud, and Nadezhda turned and smiled at him for the first time since he'd broken the news.

Up ahead Morisov was gesturing the line to a halt. They were close to the Ulla River, and the Lepel Bridge would be guarded. If necessary, they could ford it with a rope, but the waters would still be swollen with the spring thaw and extremely cold. Kuznetsky picked out Tolyshkin for a forward reconnaissance, watched him disappear into the darkness, and sat down with his back against a tree.

Yakovenko sank down beside him. "Well, Yakov?" he asked, "why do you think Moscow wants you?"

"I haven't the faintest idea," Kuznetsky replied, his eyes on Nadezhda. She came over and sat on his other side.

"I've decided to forgive you," she said only half jokingly.

He smiled and said nothing, slipping his arm around her shoulders and pulling her closer. Morisov was trying to read his map by the moonlight; the others were all propping up trees, looking exhausted. One thing he'd miss, Kuznetsky thought, was being called by name. In Moscow it would be "Colonel" again, complete with the looks of deference for the uniform and fear for the reputation.

Nadezhda, with her usual remarkable facility, had already fallen asleep on his shoulder, but Kuznetsky's head still whirred with thoughts when Tolyshkin returned. He eased her head gently onto the turf and joined Morisov.

"Good and bad," Tolyshkin said. "The bridge is guarded by only two men, but the light's very bright and there's at least a hundred yards of open ground to cover."

"That doesn't sound so bad," Morisov said.

"That was the good news. There's a German bivouac

another fifty yards down the road on the other side. About twenty tents, four half-tracks, one Panzer III. All the tents are dark, so I guess everyone's asleep, but they're close enough to be wakened by footsteps, let alone gunfire."

Morisov sucked his teeth and looked at the forest roof.

"How about the bridge," Kuznetsky asked, "along the girders?"

Tolyshkin thought for a moment. "Not too difficult—the trees go right down to the bank on both sides."

"How's the river look?" Morisov asked.

"Full and cold."

"What about the far side?" Kuznetsky asked.

"The Germans aren't holding their throats over the parapet. I'd say at least twenty yards of open ground between them and any cover."

"There must be more than a hundred of them," Morisov muttered.

Kuznetsky looked at his watch. "Look, it'll be getting light in a couple of hours, but the moon will be down an hour before that. The Germans will probably cross over in the morning and spread out, so we can't stay here. So it's either tackle the bridge or the river, and I don't fancy the river. Neither Anatoly nor Nadezhda can swim. Remember the last river crossing?"

Morisov and Tolyshkin grunted their assent. Four lost that time.

"So, we'll get under the bridge, wait for the Germans to cross, and then deal with whoever they leave behind after dark."

"And if they don't cross?" Morisov asked.

"Then we'll have problems, but we won't be any worse off than we are now," Kuznetsky answered. He got up to indicate that the decision had been made. Half an hour later he led the group down toward the river. They came out of the trees a hundred yards downstream from the bridge, whose upper structure was still reflecting the moonlight. Within minutes that light was gone, the bridge no more than a series of triangular shadows against the starry sky. The group edged their way along the bank, the sound of their breathing barely audible above the current.

□

Yakovenko stretched his legs and almost cried out with the pain of cramp. They had been sitting inside the underslung girders of the bridge for almost twelve hours, darkness had fallen, and Kuznetsky still showed no inclination to move. He sat there, ten yards away, legs crossed like Buddha, a poem on his knees, the one the Hungarian deserter had written out for him the year before.

It was written by a Communist, Kuznetsky said, but Yakovenko thought it sounded too melancholy for a *real* Communist. The poet's name was Attila Joszef. And the poem was called "Consciousness." The Hungarian had said that Attila threw himself under a train years before the war. A messy way to die, and not much fun for the railway workers who had to pick him up. Kuznetsky was always reading it; he had to know it off by heart now, Yakovenko thought.

Yakovenko massaged his calves, still thinking about Kuznetsky. They had been comrades-in-arms for more than two years now, and in that time his opinion of the commissar had changed only for the better. The man's qualities as a leader had become more and more apparent, but it wasn't just that. The man himself had changed, and not in the usual way. Yakovenko had seen any number of men—and women too—hardened by the partisan life, but Kuznetsky was the only person he'd known who seemed to have been softened, humanized by it. God alone knew what he'd done before the war—he never spoke of it, never hinted, ignored any direct questions—but whatever it had been, it must have taken a toll.

Yakovenko himself had been an office worker with the railways, had been called up, propelled to the front, and found himself left high and dry by the German advance, all in the space of a few days. For six months he had survived alone in the vastness of the Pripet Marshes, living off lichen and birds' eggs and whatever scraps he could beg from isolated villages. He'd been picked up by the brigade on the very day that Kuznetsky had been parachuted in as the new commissar and, like everyone else, had loathed him. He wasn't just hard— that would have been acceptable—but he also was pitilessly correct. If the book said show no mercy, he showed none. If the book said nothing, he still showed none. Yakovenko knew he wasn't the only one who'd toyed with the idea of putting a bullet through the new commissar's back.

But slowly and surely two things had changed. The brigade had been honed into a formidable fighting machine and Kuznetsky turned into a human being. Even a likable one. He still let little slip, but the rules themselves had changed: they were his now, not Moscow's, and they nearly always made perfect sense. He was still hard, but he now seemed aware of his own hardness, and somehow that made all the difference. Occasionally over the last few months Yakovenko had felt almost sorry for him, for the responsibility that seemed to bear a little more heavily each day. Nadezhda had made him happier but she'd also become one more responsibility.

He had watched Kuznetsky at the trial of that poor peasant bastard the week before. All the old self-righteous correctness had gone. Perhaps a man had only so many death sentences to give, even in times like these. If so, he guessed that Kuznetsky was near the end of his rope.

☐

Kuznetsky was not meditating; he was simply bored. It was too dark to continue with his task of memorizing the poem; he thought he had it all now but he couldn't see to check. *Like a pile of hewn timber,* he silently mouthed, *the world lies heaped up on itself, one thing presses and squeezes and interlocks with the other, so each is determined.* And here we sit, he thought, waiting to shake the pile. *By day a moon rises in me and when it's night outside—a sun shines here within.* It was more than a poem, more like a poem full of poems. He'd never read anything like it, never anything that seemed to speak to him so directly, as if he were already living out its lines. *Your wound is the world—it burns and rages, and you feel your soul, the fever.* Amen.

He folded the dog-eared sheets and replaced them in his tunic pocket, looked at his watch but couldn't make out the hands. It didn't matter; he'd always been able to judge the passage of time. Ten to eight, he reckoned, ten minutes more to the halfway point between sunset and moonrise. They had no idea what they would find up top; all five German vehicles had rumbled across that morning, making the girders creak alarmingly, but the occasional footfalls on the planks above told him that at least some men had been left behind. He thought he'd recognized six different voices but that didn't mean much. There could be fifty men up there.

His head said eight o'clock. "Okay," he whispered. The partisans stretched their limbs to the limits allowed by the confined space and precarious footholds, then climbed quietly along the inside edge of the lateral girders, four on each side of the bridge. At a hand signal from Kuznetsky, he and Morisov led the others up the abutments in a rush, firing from the hip before any target was visible, the noise of the machine guns shattering the peace of the evening.

Breasting the rise, Kuznetsky saw three Germans already falling in the hail of bullets. Fifty yards away, the rest were sitting around a fire eating their evening meal. He ran for the emplacement the Germans had set up to cover the bridge but the gun wouldn't turn far enough. Morisov zigzagged down the road still firing while the Germans scrambled for their weapons. "Down," he screamed, at the same time pulling Yakovenko with him off into the trees. The two men crashed blindly through the undergrowth for a hundred yards or so, the road invisible to their left, their passage rendered inaudible by the continuous gunfire.

Nadezhda had followed them, and Kuznetsky led his two companions to the left, moving more quietly now. They reached the road, concealed from the Germans by trees on a bend. "Grenades," he whispered, and they advanced stealthily toward the enemy's rear, Yakovenko and Nadezhda on one side of the road, Kuznetsky on the other.

The Germans had lacked the time or the sense to put their fire out, and their backs were lit by the flames. The grenades weren't very well aimed. Two overshot and one exploded in the pail of food, but the surprise was enough. The Germans leaped to their feet, their hands stabbing skyward in surrender.

Yakovenko looked at Kuznetsky, who nodded and resisted the urge to turn away as the machine gun cut them down.

There had been nine altogether, and only the sergeant looked a day over seventeen. All were spattered with blood and what looked like vegetable stew. Farther up the road, Morisov lay dead in a pool of his own blood. The only other casualty was one of Sukhanova's fingers.

"Pity about the food," Yakovenko muttered. "I could do with a change of diet."

Kuznetsky waited impatiently while Tolyshkin put a tourniquet on Sukhanova's hand, and then led the group off into the forest. They still had ten miles to walk.

□

The moon was high in the sky when the seaplane glided across the tops of the trees and gracefully splashed down on the surface of the lake. Nadezhda let go of Kuznetsky's arm to help douse the signal fire as the pilot brought the plane in toward the shore. He had expected more tears from her but there hadn't been any. She had asked him, simply, "Shall I look for you after the war is over?" And he, suddenly decided, had replied just as simply, "I'll be looking for you, my love."

Now he stood on the rocks by the lakeshore, waiting for the plane to come nearer, the group gathered above him on the outcrop. Yakovenko was in command now, and to Kuznetsky's astonishment he'd felt tears on his own cheeks as they'd hugged farewell. It was like leaving family, except that he'd not felt anything like that when he'd left his own back in Minnesota.

He waded out into the lake, feeling the icy water numbing his legs, and clambered aboard the two-seater. Christ, he was tired. The pilot grunted a welcome, revved the engine, and turned the plane back toward the middle of the lake. Kuznetsky thought he had a last glimpse of the group disappearing into the shadows as the craft gathered speed across the water and headed up into the moon. Now the tops of the trees were thirty feet below. He fastened the goggles, felt the bitter wind on his cheeks. The pilot shouted something about the German lines—Kuznetsky supposed they'd be passing over them in a short time. He didn't really care. What could he do about Germans four hundred feet below? Piss on them, that was all.

☐

Amy put the book back into her bag and got to her feet. She felt too restless to read, too full of suppressed excitement. The train was due in a few minutes, and she began to walk slowly up the platform, wondering again whether there could be any other explanation for the new instructions.

She couldn't think of one. Moscow was going to order her to "sell" Wim Doesburg something that Berlin would buy. Moscow's interest in the uranium train had been rekindled with a vengeance. Put the two together and it could add up to only one thing. She still didn't see how it could be done, but the idea itself was brilliant. And they wouldn't be able to do it without her because she was the only link with the Germans. This was *real* action at long last.

The train arrived, its locomotive belching black smoke into the clear blue sky. She took a seat in the front car, listened to the conductor's cries of "Manassas" reverberating down the platform, and checked her watch as they began to pull out of the station. Exactly nine minutes later she left her seat and walked back two cars, stopped for a minute to make sure she wasn't being followed, then continued toward the rear of the train. Another two cars down, she and Matson went through their fortnightly ritual, knocking into each other and exchanging dropped copies of *The Saturday Evening Post*. She had her usual glimpse of highly polished brown shoes, uniform, weather-beaten face, heard the Tennessee drawl intone "So sorry, ma'am" and her own voice say "It's nothing—really."

In the club car she took a seat at the bar and ordered a Coca-Cola. No problem, there never was, but still her pulse insisted on racing. She forced herself to sit there until the thumping had subsided, then locked herself in the washroom to examine the contents of the envelope left inside the magazine.

It was all there. A complete timetable, obviously copied from an internal railroad document, annotated with crew changeover points and watering stops. An explanation of the Friday timing—"an optimilization of clear paths," whatever that meant. A list headed "Locomotives Rostered for This Duty." And four photographs of the train itself, from different distances and angles, marked May 5 on the backs. That clinched it. Faulkner hadn't mentioned photographs, but Moscow must have asked for them, and there could be only one reason.

She put everything back in the envelope, the envelope back in the magazine, and caught sight of herself in the mirror as she turned to leave. "Yes," she told her reflection. "Oh yes!"

□

Thirty hours after leaving his group at Lukomskoye, Kuznetsky was driven down Lenin Prospekt toward Moscow's hub. It was his first sight of Moscow, actually of anything bigger than a village, for more than two years.

He had never liked Moscow, and had somehow contrived to spend only a few months of his twenty-six Soviet years in the capital. A homesick Muscovite had once drunkenly explained to him that his city combined the best of the West, its commitment to reason, with the best of the East, its spirituality, and therefore qualified as paradise on earth. Kuznetsky had always thought it was the other way around: the East's lack of reason allied to the West's lack of spirituality, a soulless bazaar.

He'd had a good night's sleep at the Partisan HQ on the city's outskirts, once he'd given up the bed for the more familiar texture of the floor. It was surprising how quickly one lost the knack of civilized living; he'd had problems with the cutlery at breakfast and the toilet had seemed almost obscene.

He'd also lost more weight than he'd realized. The NKVD colonel's uniform he'd left behind in 1942 now seemed several sizes too large, and it reeked of mothballs.

The Kremlin loomed across the river. The car swept across the bridges, past the Borovitsky Tower and across Marx Prospekt into Frunze Street, drawing up at the massive portals of the Defense Ministry. The driver opened his door and Kuznetsky climbed out. The guard at the door examined his pass and called for someone to escort him up to Sheslakov's office. On the way he consciously pulled himself together. He was out of practice at playing politics, but there was no need for anyone else to know that.

His guide knocked at the door, but Kuznetsky pushed past him and entered without waiting for a reply. Old habits die hard, he thought. Never surrender an initiative.

The man sitting behind the desk seemed unperturbed. He'd probably received the same training. Kuznetsky took the seat offered by the man's flourish of the jade letter opener and for several moments neither spoke.

His host, Kuznetsky observed, was a medium-built, middle-aged man with graying hair. He was dressed in civilian clothes, a well-cut dark blue suit, white shirt, and dark red tie. Most unusual, the shirt collar and tie were loosened at the neck, giving him a vaguely dissolute appearance. He had high cheekbones and deep-set dark eyes—Tartar blood probably—and a mouth that seemed on the verge of an ironic smile. The eyes contained the same air of amused condescension. Whoever this man was, Kuznetsky thought, he was sure of himself.

Sheslakov examined Kuznetsky with the same thoroughness. He was tall, over six feet, with thick, dark hair and the sort of profile you saw on hero-of-the-revolution wall posters. He *did* look American, but he could have passed for a Russian easily enough. The eyes—Fyedorova always told him to look at the eyes *first*—were quite extraordinary. Not because of anything intrinsic—because of the total contrast they offered to the rest of the man. The mouth, the posture, the sense of physical power, all shouted "Fighter"; the eyes whispered "Calm," the calm of killers and saints. He knew now what Fyedorova had meant by a wild card.

"Colonel Kuznetsky," he said, "you have been provisionally selected to lead an operation outside the Soviet Union. It is not an NKVD operation, nor a GRU operation. Both apparats are working together under the direct authority of the Atomic Division, which is itself responsible only to the Secretariat." He paused. Kuznetsky said nothing, only nodded slightly. "Your participation will be on a voluntary basis; you will understand why when you read this." He passed across a thin folder, the words "American Rose" stenciled on the cover in red.

Kuznetsky stared at the words. "The United States?" he asked.

"Yes."

He read for twenty minutes, increasingly absorbed, pausing only once to examine the old woman who came in and lay back on the cot under the window. Who the hell was she? And why was she staring at him?

Finally he closed the folder and placed it gently on the edge of Sheslakov's desk. "When will the bait be offered?" he asked.

"At the moment of maximum psychological impact. After the Allied invasion of France, which we expect on June 6, and before our summer offensive, which is set for June 22. The combination of a known disaster and an imminent one usually provides a potent mixture."

Kuznetsky looked amused. *Very neat* as the Americans would say. "And what if the Germans throw the Allies back into the English Channel?"

"That is unlikely."

"I wouldn't know. There are a lot of hopeful assumptions built into this. Maybe correct ones. But it *feels* like thin ice."

"There is very little margin for error," Sheslakov admitted. "But that is unavoidable when we have to be more concerned with avoiding detection and exposure than anything else. . . . You are willing?"

"I am not a believer in voluntary work, Comrade, but in duty. I will go for that reason." And, he admitted to himself, out of curiosity. What would America look like after twenty-six years? And how would it feel to be back there?

☐

"Come in, Anatoly Grigorovich," Zhdanov boomed, "sit down, tell me some good news."

Sheslakov took the proffered chair. "Thank you, Comrade Secretary. I do have good news—the First Priority is within our reach."

Zhdanov's ears pricked up almost visibly. "How?" he asked, offering Sheslakov the first Havana cigar he'd seen since the war's beginning.

Sheslakov lovingly applied the match, savoring the moment and taking an almost sadistic delight in the other man's ill-concealed impatience. "You recall your submission to Stavka on"—he consulted his notes—"April 28 concerning the possible theft of American Uranium-235. To summarize—you pointed out that the amount we could steal would be militarily useless even if we could contain the political damage."

"I have not forgotten."

"Both problems can be avoided." He took another puff on the cigar. If only Cuba was run by Communists! "The Americans, knowing how much material had been stolen, would know how many bombs we could make."

"That seems self-evident."

"Ah, but there is a hidden assumption, that our building of atomic bombs would necessarily be equated with the theft of the material."

"But it would be."

"Indeed, but the Americans need not know that. If we can both steal the material *and* convince the Americans that we have not stolen it, then the problem is solved. Our possession of atomic bombs will then be ascribed to our own domestic development program, and the Americans will have no idea how many bombs we *really* have."

"We'll still have only two, which the military say will be worse than useless."

"We will have only one. We must explode the first to show the Americans we actually have the capability. I'm afraid the military, as usual, is behind the times. They just don't understand that these atomic bombs are not ordinary weapons; the mere threat of using them will be enough. If both sides have them, no one will dare use them, and the calculations that matter will concern men and tanks and ships again. What is important is not actually having the atomic bomb, but instilling that fear into the Americans."

Comprehension dawned on Zhdanov's face, then swiftly made room for more furrows of concern. "Who else would steal it then?" It was such a stupid question that Sheslakov let Zhdanov answer it for himself. "A *ruse de guerre*. Soviet soldiers in German uniforms."

"No, no, nothing as"—he was going to say "crude" but Zhdanov was notoriously sensitive about his peasant background—"nothing as direct as that. The Germans themselves will steal the uranium. And we will help them."

Zhdanov looked at him as if he'd gone mad. "Explain," he said grimly.

Sheslakov did so, going over each point in his plan until he thought Zhdanov had grasped it. When he had finished the head of the Atomic Division leaned back in his chair and looked into space. "Very well," he said at last, "I can see the possibility. Put it in writing and find the people."

Sheslakov pulled the file out of his briefcase and handed it across the desk. "We already have the people," he said.

□

Stalin pushed the report to one side of his desk and closed his eyes. Why "American Rose"? he wondered. Only the Germans and the Americans made a habit of flattering nature and themselves by applying such names to human enterprises. Sheslakov was a strange man, an oddity. But for now an affordable one.

Would it work? he asked himself. It felt right. The Americans had the scientists and the money and a country that wasn't in ruins. And ambition. Unlimited ambition. But it wasn't a calculated ambition. Socialism might be weak now but it saw the way forward, it calculated, it planned. Capital, for all its power, was blind as a river. And what could be more easily bluffed than blind ambition?

There was only the one flaw—the number of foreigners who would know, who could expose the bluff. A German-born woman, an American-born man, the agents in America who would inevitably have been softened by the capitalist life. But that was a flaw that could be corrected at the end of the game.

He called in his aide. "Telephone Zhdanov. Tell him yes."

Four

"THE DIAGRAM was drawn by a German scientist who's now working at Site Y in New Mexico. He was apparently trying to impress his secretary," Amy told Wim Doesburg as they strolled through the small Manhattan art gallery.

"It will impress Berlin, I think," he replied, stopping in front of a canvas depicting a dark, almost ominous flower. "What do you think of this one?" he asked.

Amy forced herself to look at the painting. "Depressing," she murmured.

"Isn't it?" Doesburg agreed jovially. "But beautiful just the same."

They walked on, continuing their conversation in the spaces allowed by other visitors to the gallery. Amy couldn't remember ever feeling as nervous. At the meeting with Faulkner the previous day, he'd been almost unrecognizably tense, and once he'd shared what he knew with her, she wasn't surprised. Now the strain of listening to Doesburg's urbane chatter, observing the usual security precautions, *and* following Moscow's script was stretching her to the limit.

Doesburg was excited by the diagram—she knew that much. His face and steady stream of conversation might not betray anything, but his walk had become noticeably jaunty in the last few minutes. Now was the time.

"There's also some other unsolicited material," she said

casually at the next opportunity. "Of rather dubious value," she added. "Sigmund insisted on explaining it all to me despite the security risk, and he's included all the necessary information. You'll see what I mean." She paused to let a young couple meander by. "He'd just read the *Picture Post* article on Mussolini's escape to Germany, and, according to him, it gave him an idea. He says at first he thought it was ridiculous, but then he realized it was feasible. Apparently there's a train that takes the bomb material made in Tennessee to New Mexico for the bomb production process, and Sigmund has visions of Skorzeny dropping out of the sky and holding it up." Catching Doesburg's expression of amused incredulity, she said, "I thought the same, but he has looked into it all with great thoroughness, and the whole idea does have some lunatic logic to it. I can find no fault in his plan, but then I've no experience of planning such operations. Of course," she added almost wistfully, "it would be a spectacular, tremendous coup."

Doesburg said nothing for a moment, seemingly engrossed in a funereal painting. "I shall find the flaws for you, my dear," he said finally. "But we must humor Sigmund, if only to keep the flow of diagrams coming."

□

An hour later Doesburg was back in his Brooklyn home, spreading the contents of the envelope across the kitchen table. The diagram fascinated him—so much scientific advance represented on a single sheet of paper. His wife, Elke, looked at it over his shoulder. "Is that all?" she asked, unconsciously echoing his thoughts. "One page for a bomb that can destroy a whole city?"

It was only after dinner that he bothered to read Sigmund's report on the uranium train. He had to admit the idea was attractive, and read on expecting to find the point where fantasy took over from practicality. There was a timetable, a crew schedule, a map with the escape route plotted in, even photographs of the train. There was no mention of Skorzeny; Sigmund specified a long-range U-boat, even the precise class required.

Doesburg scratched his head, ignored Elke's attempts to interest him in the latest Victory Garden competition, and started from the beginning again. A U-boat drop-off on the coast of Georgia—simple enough. Two English-speaking German officers to be met by American operatives and transported to the hijack point. It was hunting country, so strangers hiring a lodge for a week would not seem unusual. The hijack itself seemed to present no difficulties, provided the information was all accurate. It was certainly comprehensive enough. Then a twelve-hour drive back to the coast for the pickup, with the FBI presumably in pursuit. But more likely in total disarray, Doesburg thought. Sigmund thoughtfully pointed out that the escape route crossed a state line in the first fifty miles, which would suitably complicate police reaction.

He walked out onto the backyard porch and lowered himself into his rocking chair. It was a beautiful evening, the distant towers of Manhattan silhouetted by the setting sun, the street full of children playing stickball. It was hard to believe that America was at war. In Tennessee and Alabama it would seem even more unreal. What a blow to American pride it would be! A coup.

And something of an opportunity. Doesburg knew only too well that when the Allies reached Berlin, as it seemed certain they would, there was every chance that they'd find a file with his name on it. He hadn't said anything to Elke— there was no point in worrying her in advance—but he had for some time been preparing in his mind for their discreet withdrawal from American soil. If the Abwehr could be interested in this operation, they would pay, and pay a lot. No one in Berlin, he knew from lucrative past experience, had any conception of how cheap espionage really was. He could ask for $10,000, and 80 percent of that, plus the proceeds from selling their brownstone, would set them up very nicely in Brazil or Argentina.

There was even the faint prospect of a successful operation altering the course of the war, leaving his file in safe hands. There were no risks involved that he could see; everything would go through Rosa, and she knew neither his real name nor his address.

He went back indoors, addressed an envelope to his contact in Rio, and enclosed the diagram.

"You must mail this tomorrow morning," he told Elke, "somewhere on Fifth Avenue. I must go to see Kroeger in Syracuse—there's something I want sent immediately on the radio."

☐

After her meeting with Doesburg, Amy took the train back to Washington and went to bed.

The next morning Richard was waiting in her office, looking no better disposed than he had on Friday.

"Good weekend?" he asked sarcastically.

"Yes, thank you," she said calmly. "You?"

"Wonderful. I listened to the radio Saturday night and listened to the radio all day Sunday—"

"Look, Richard," she said, suddenly feeling extremely angry, "I'm not obliged to give up my plans just because your wife takes it into her head to go away for the weekend. You don't own me—"

"I'm going to tell her."

She stared at him. "Why? To punish me?"

He grabbed her arm. "We had the chance of a whole weekend together. Is your father's family more important than that? You see them every month. They're not even real relations." He stopped, releasing her arm. "Is that where you really were?" he forced out.

"No, Errol Flynn invited me to his yacht."

"Don't joke!"

69

"What do you expect me to say? What do you think I am? Richard, if I wanted to start another love affair with someone, I'd do it in the open, and only after I'd ended this one with you. It's you who's in love with secrecy, remember?"

"Okay, okay, you've made your point."

"I just wish I didn't have to keep on making it. Richard, I know it would have been fun to spend the weekend together, but I am not, *not*, going to spend my life waiting around for you to be available. Some women might put up with it, but I'm not one of them. And I've never pretended any different, have I?"

"No," he said wearily. "I know you haven't."

"Good," she said, and kissed him on the cheek. "Now leave me alone. I'll see you Friday."

He went, leaving her feeling unsure of what she should do. Richard was a habit, one that she'd always considered distracting and harmless. One that helped fill the gap left by the impossibility of a real relationship. Now she was beginning to realize how dangerous a habit he had become.

☐

Twelve days after Wim Doesburg's trip to Syracuse, Obergruppenführer Walter Schellenberg sat brooding in the back of a limousine as it wound up the hairpin turns toward the Führer's mountain retreat. His interview with Himmler the previous day had proved less than satisfactory. Not only had the Reichsführer sprayed him with germs, occasioning his present sore throat and runny nose, but he'd also generously abdicated all responsibility for the matter.

"Take it directly to the Führer," Himmler had advised, the tone of his voice implying that nothing would persuade him to do so.

Himmler thought it too risky because it broke the infamous Goering Law—never offer the Führer anything that you don't already have at your disposal. Well, no one could accuse Himmler of a surfeit of imagination.

But the Führer would appreciate the plan, Schellenberg was sure of it. There really was no risk; it was merely the enormity of the prize that made it hard to believe. If they failed, it would cost them only two soldiers and a U-boat. If they succeeded, then at the very least defeat could be avoided. With an atomic V rocket they could reduce London to rubble in a single strike or, more to the point, threaten to do so. Then the Western Allies would come quickly enough to the negotiating table to talk about the real enemy, about saving Europe from Stalin's barbarian hordes. A few photographs of disemboweled German soldiers might wake Roosevelt up, and Churchill had always been an anti-Communist at heart.

There seemed no reason why success should elude them. The people in America seemed very efficient, the *Kriegsmarine* said there were no difficulties involved in the transport, the scientists had confirmed that they *could* make a bomb if they had the Uranium-235. There had been nine English-speaking officers to choose from with the necessary combat experience and firsthand knowledge of America. One of them had even been a physics teacher before the war. An omen, if ever he'd seen one. Himmler was a fool.

The car drew up outside the Berghof. Schellenberg was greeted by Hitler's adjutant, General Schmundt, and informed that the Führer was still involved in the afternoon military conference. This explanation was somewhat unnecessary: as soon as he entered the Great Hall, Schellenberg could hear Hitler's raised voice through the open door of the conference room. He sat down as far from the blazing log fire as possible and tried to ignore the suffocating perfume exuded by the myriad bowls of fresh flowers.

Hitler stopped shouting. Schellenberg could hear the obsequious tones of Jodl and Keitel taking turns explaining something. They obviously were not successful, for suddenly Hitler's harsh voice was echoing through the house once more.

"Rommel does not see the whole picture. The rest of them are cowards and fools. I try to make the orders so clear that even a child could understand them, and what do I get? Requests for authorization to do the exact opposite!" There was silence, then the Führer's voice again, this time sweet and reasonable, as if he were talking to a favorite young nephew. "I understand the military arguments for withdrawal, but war is more than a purely *military* matter. It is about people, individual soldiers, about their will to win. Retreat is addictive. It doesn't matter whether it makes sense *militarily*. It is psychologically disastrous. Always. Always."

Keitel and Jodl started talking again. Schellenberg could visualize the scene from past experience: the Führer leaning over the map, his arms rigid at his sides, while all the toadies murmured yes and shrugged at each other behind his back. Why did he bother with them?

The door behind him opened, admitting another perfume.

"Good afternoon, Herr Obergruppenführer," the woman said. "Or is it evening? I never know when one turns into the other. We haven't had the pleasure of your company for a long time."

Schellenberg rose from his seat and bowed. "Good evening, Fraulein Braun. I'm afraid the demands of the war leave little time for the pleasures of life."

She pouted. "If anyone knows that, I do." She looked around, as if, Schellenberg thought, she was wondering where she was. "I hope you have some good news for him," she said absentmindedly. "It's been so hard on him these last few months," she added, lowering her voice as if she were betraying a state secret.

"Of course," Schellenberg said sympathetically, wondering what else to say.

He was saved by the reappearance of Schmundt. "The conference will end shortly, Herr Obergruppenführer. The Führer suggests you wait for him in the upstairs study."

It was as hot in the study as in the hall, but like everyone else who entered that room, Schellenberg found his attention captured by the huge picture window and its breathtaking view of Alpine peaks fading into the distance.

An hour passed and the mountains receded into the gathering darkness as the stars brightened above them. He was beginning to feel vaguely hypnotized by the effect when the door finally opened to admit Hitler and his pet Alsatian.

"It's a wonderful view, isn't it? I designed the house myself, you know."

"Yes, my Führer."

Hitler sat down in one of the leather-covered armchairs. He looked pale, but there was none of the trembling that Schellenberg had heard about. There was a half-smile on his face as he stroked the dog's back and stared out into the night. "When there are difficult decisions to be taken," he said, "I often come and sit here by myself. I sometimes think that it is the majesty of all this"—he indicated the panorama of the outside world with a sweep of an arm—"that really makes the decisions. I am only its voice."

Schellenberg said nothing.

"I have studied your plan with the utmost care, Walter, and I have every hope of it succeeding. Of course," he added, turning to face Schellenberg, "it is doubtful whether we shall need atomic bombs for this war, but a leader has a duty to think ahead, and science never stands still. No, what excites me about your operation is its psychological dimension."

Hitler paused to pour himself a glass of distilled water from the decanter on the table. "Nations are wonderfully distinctive, and more and more I have been thinking about the resemblance each bears to a particular animal . . . yes, animals. It is no coincidence, Walter, that throughout history different nations have identified themselves, through flags, crests, emblems, whatever, with certain animals. The Russian bear, the English lion, the German eagle—these are only the most obvious examples. Note the differences—though each is a fine fighter the bear is stupid, the lion lazy, the eagle perhaps overprone to flights of the imagination. Yet within these nations one rule prevails. The strongest lion, the strongest bear, the strongest eagle—each assumes the leadership. It is the law of history."

Schellenberg restrained himself and merely nodded.

"Perhaps you are wondering what this has to do with the plan," Hitler noted calmly. "Tell me, what animal do you associate with America?"

Schellenberg's mind did not make the association.

"You see? You've confirmed it for yourself," Hitler said. "America is not a true nation, that is the point. It is a herd of disparate animals, a few eagles, a few lions, a few bears, and a host of inferior species. Herds, Walter, herds always, always, respond to the instincts of their weakest members. The German stock, the English stock will forever be at the mercy of the Jews and the Negroes because that is the law of the herd. It may be more numerous, potentially far more powerful than a single predator, but it only requires one member of the herd to take fright and there is general panic. Insecurity is the herd's strongest emotion. Now do you see the relevance?"

Schellenberg did. "This operation will create a panic that will far transcend the actual importance of the target."

"Exactly. Exactly. You do understand perfectly. We will put two eagles in among the herd, and the panic will spread around the world."

☐

The sun disappeared, slice by orange slice, into the distant horizon, its rays reflected in a thousand puddles. Major Gerd Breitner sat astride a rickety wooden fence on the outskirts of Beresino and drank in the splendor. At first he'd hated the Russian landscape, found it flat and boring, but after eighteen months he'd come to love its subtleties, its infinite variations on the same theme. A small compensation perhaps, but better than none at all.

The last slice slid away. Breitner lit a cigarette, looked once more at the moth-eared photograph of his wife. It was more than a year now, and the pain had lost its sharpness; like everything else, it had been flattened by the war. Only the irony remained: while he had survived countless brushes with death in France, Africa, and the East, she had been buried in the rubble of their safe Stuttgart home during an Allied bombing raid.

He put the photograph away and tried to picture her face. It grew harder with each passing month. Breitner felt the tang of tears forming and jumped down from the fence, angry with himself.

He turned and stared into the east. It was quiet, it seemed to get quieter each day. Intelligence put the attack four days hence, and they weren't often wrong these days. Four more days of sitting around, then all hell would break loose again. He wasn't sure which was worse. "Fuck you, Adolf," he muttered, "and all the other bastards."

He found his friend Paul Russman sitting on the running board of the derelict staff car with Burdenski, practicing his wretched cigarette trick. Paul placed the cigarette on his palm, pointed it away from his body, and brought his other hand sharply down on the wrist. The cigarette cartwheeled through the air, missed the waiting mouth, hit him in the nose instead, and dropped into the mud.

Burdenski was unimpressed. "Where did you pick up that stupid habit?" he asked.

"Africa," Paul replied, retrieving the sodden cigarette. "I watched an English prisoner practicing for hours in the compound at Mersa Brega. He said it helped to pass the time. He was right. And of course I couldn't let the English prove their superiority in such a crucial field of combat."

"I can see that," Burdenski said wryly.

"But there's more," Paul said. "The Englishman promised me the war would be over before I mastered the technique, so I reckon that mastering it will probably end the war."

"That's why I encourage him to practice," Breitner said.

"Clowns," Burdenski grunted.

Paul looked up at Breitner. "I have some rather disturbing news, Gerd," he said, lighting a dry cigarette. "We are shortly to receive an uninvited guest here at our summer residence— an SS colonel."

"Soldier or policeman?"

"That's the disturbing part."

Breitner felt a slight surge of panic. Absurd. "What can they want with us?" he asked. "We do nothing but fight wars."

"Perhaps it's the fact that we're losing this one," Paul suggested with a straight face.

"Paul, I hope you don't intend making jokes like that in his exalted presence," Breitner said. "It's possible that he may not share our sense of humor."

"He certainly isn't sharing our war," Paul observed.

☐

The SS colonel arrived at Beresino in the middle of the night, looking as shiny-smart as only an SS colonel could. A rather disheveled Russman and Breitner went out to greet him, and despite the lateness of the hour, Paul managed a "Heil Hitler" of such vigor that the black-uniformed officer was set back on his heels. Breitner concealed his laugh with a cough.

Sturmbannführer Rademacher was a man of few words. He declined schnapps, coffee, food, and small talk, all to the evident but unvoiced disgust of his escort. He simply withdrew two documents from his shiny briefcase and handed them to Breitner and announced that they should be on the funeral train leaving Baranovichi at ten that morning. The colonel then performed his own, more austere salute and climbed back into the motorcycle sidecar. His driver shrugged sympathetically at the two officers and opened the throttle.

"We must be neglecting our personal hygiene," Paul said.

"It's Russians he smells," Breitner muttered, glancing

through the documents. One was a release signed by Pan-zergruppe Command. The other was a summons to Berlin, to the office of Obergruppenführer Schellenberg, head of Amt VI, the external security section of the Reich Intelligence Services.

Paul was reading them over his shoulder. "How did nice girls like us get mixed up with a man like that?" he asked.

☐

Breitner flung the empty vodka bottle out the train window and into the Polish night. "Goddamnit, Paul, there must be English-speaking apes in the Waffen SS."

Paul shook his head vigorously. Both men were drunk, having chanced upon an enterprising Polish peasant selling homemade vodka in the middle of nowhere. Presumably the peasant had seen trains stop at the same place before, and the same type of train at that. He'd been disappointed but not surprised to learn that all his other potential customers were dead.

"There are no apes in the Waffen SS," Paul enunciated carefully. "Their hair is the wrong color." He pried the cork free from another bottle. "But to answer your question with the seriousness it deserves, I can only suggest our excellent record in the service of the Führer. Whatever they want done we'll have already done it on some continent or other."

Breitner smiled ruefully. "We've even survived a trip home in a funeral train. Unfortunately," he said, taking another swig from the bottle, "we are intelligent enough—not that it requires much—to know that this particular war is lost. Dying in a Russian ditch may not be everyone's idea of destiny, but it was one I was becoming almost fond of. Dying for the goddamn SS is something else entirely. It's—"

"It's not who that worries me, it's what. For all we know, they may have decided to kidnap the King of England."

"That's tame. I was thinking of Stalin."

"Easy. What about recapturing Marlene Dietrich?"

"I volunteer."

The train was drawing slowly to a halt, clanking over points. The lights of a city could be seen outside. "Where the hell are we?" Breitner asked.

"Posen, I think. Christ, look at this." Both men stared out on a panorama of ruin, pillars of masonry sticking into the night sky, empty streets choked with rubble. As the train chugged slowly forward they saw the body of an old woman lying beside the track, one arm rigidly extended upward, the light of the yard lamps reflecting off her spectacles.

"Who the hell would be bombing Posen? It's too far east for the Americans."

"Where there's a will there's a way," Paul murmured, suddenly feeling sober. He sat down heavily. "You know, sometimes I can't see how this war will end. It's just bitten too deep. There's more to forgive than there is forgiveness."

"They said that after the last war," Breitner said, pulling himself away from the window. "They'll probably say it after the next one."

Paul laughed. "You're an optimistic bastard, aren't you?"

"No. You know what really depresses me?"

"I'm not sure I want to."

"If we were winning, we wouldn't care."

□

Schellenberg stared through the peephole at the two officers waiting in the anteroom. Major Breitner, Hauptmann Russman. They looked younger than he'd expected; perhaps he was too accustomed to being around the old and the wounded who made up his staff. He went back to their dossiers on his desk. Breitner was thirty-five, Russman thirty-four. Well, perhaps the excitement of war had kept them young. He looked at his watch. It was time to let his two eagles in.

"Gentlemen," he said, still smiling as they seated themselves, "the Reich has a new need for your talents. An operation is being mounted by the external section of the Reichssicherheitshauptampt at the express instructions of the Führer himself. It has the highest security classification imaginable—only three men in the Reich are aware of its existence. When—"

"With great respect, Obergruppenführer," Breitner interrupted, "but before we are made privy to the nature of this operation, I would appreciate some clarification regarding our position. Are we still under the jurisdiction of the Wehrmacht or have we been officially transferred to your authority?"

Schellenberg's smile faded slightly at the edges. "Officially, this operation does not exist. To answer your unspoken question—I require volunteers, not conscripts. Though I must in all fairness add that if you decline this assignment, you may have to be temporarily detained. For security reasons, of course. There would be no imputation of disloyalty; you have both served the Reich with distinction in the past."

Breitner nodded and said nothing. Christ Almighty, he thought.

"I hope, however," Schellenberg continued, "that this operation will appeal to both your sense of duty and your spirit of adventure. This is no ordinary operation. It would hardly be an exaggeration to say that the fate of the Reich may rest on its success. You have been selected, after exhaustive inquiries, because you are not ordinary officers. You both speak excellent English, you work well together, and you, Major Breitner, have professional scientific experience. Above all, you have both lived in America."

The two men glanced at each other in astonishment. Science? America? What crazy scheme was this?

"As I said," Schellenberg continued smoothly, "this is not an ordinary operation. It is, however, a relatively straightforward one. You would be transported across the Atlantic to the state of Georgia by U-boat. You would then carry out a single, simple military operation of a kind you have performed in the past. You would then be transported back."

"And the objective?" Breitner asked.

"Ah, the objective. First I must fill in the background." Schellenberg explained the development of the new bomb, the state of German progress in the same direction, the significance of Uranium-235, the train itself, traveling through "thousands of miles of virtually empty countryside." He described the "wholly inadequate" American security precautions. "The Americans may not be stupid," he concluded, "but they are overconfident to the point of stupidity. To them the war is elsewhere. It would never occur to them that German officers might suddenly turn up in their own country. It would be a complete surprise."

Yes, Paul thought. That at least rang true. Perhaps this operation was less insane than it sounded.

"When?" Breitner asked.

"One thing we lack is time. The U-boat must sail from France, and regrettably the French ports may have to be sacrificed in the not too distant future. So we must aim for the August 4 train, which means a departure from La Pallice within the next three days. This of course will prevent any detailed advance planning. Our agents in America will have to brief you fully when you arrive."

There was a silence. Breitner looked at Paul and then turned back to Schellenberg. "We would like a few minutes to discuss the matter, Obergruppenführer."

"You may have the use of my office."

"We'd prefer to stretch our legs," Breitner said. "We've been on a train for the last thirty-six hours, and those gardens look most inviting."

"Very well."

Once outside the two men walked about fifty yards in silence. "Why did we have to come out here?" Paul asked eventually. "That was the most comfortable chair I've sat in for years."

Breitner lit a cigarette. "Christ, you're so naive sometimes. That office must be knee-deep in microphones."

"You think the garden isn't?"

Breitner laughed. "You're probably right. Okay, give me and the microphones a good reason for saying yes to this mad scheme."

Paul lit his own cigarette. "I'll give you three. One, if we say no, we'll at best end up back in the East."

"Good, but not very positive."

"Two, how does duty strike you?"

"Like the song says: My comrades and my sense of duty, they died together in the snow."

"Three, it's not such a mad scheme."

"Yes, you have to admire the nerve. Train holdups in America! In 1944!"

"And I'll give you a fourth. We're going, whatever we say. Like the man said, the U-boat leaves in less than three days, so they've decided it's us. And we've both still got living relatives."

Paul looked at him sharply. "You think they'd go that far?"

"Yes."

They walked in silence for a while. Paul was remembering another Atlantic crossing many years before, his first sight of her face across the smoky room, their first embrace on the promenade deck, surrounded by ocean and stars. Breitner was thinking that it had been American bombs that had killed his wife and son, and wondering why he felt no thirst for revenge.

He shook his head. "I don't suppose it'll be much different from holding up trains anywhere else."

"Gerd, what is this stuff? Uranium-235?"

"God knows. Atomic physics was taboo in my time. 'Jewish physics' they called it. Now there's an irony to savor." He ground out his cigarette. "I expect they'll enlighten us further before we go."

"We go, then?"

"As your superior officer, I strongly advise it. Let's in-

dulge our spirit of adventure. It's been so dull in the East."
Paul winced.

□

Three days later the two men stood on the conning tower of
U-107 as it eased its way out of La Pallice docks past groups
of sullen-looking Frenchmen. The crew, which seemed ex-
traordinarily young to the two soldiers, had just been told
that this was not to be a fighting voyage and were trying not
to express their relief too openly.

The young Bavarian captain had made less effort to hide
his feelings. "Welcome to the longest taxi ride in history,"
he had greeted them. Paul promised him a good tip if they
made good time.

EXECUTION

Five

AMY walked slowly across Battery Park, savoring the touch of the cool breeze blowing in from New York Harbor. She was early for the meeting, and the grass was still covered with office workers taking in the last minutes of sunshine from their lunch hour. At the café near the ferry dock she bought an iced tea and sat down in the shade at one of the outside tables. Across the bay she could see two ferries crossing. Behind them a troopship was moving out toward the Narrows and on to Europe.

When the clock showed five mintues to two she made her way across to the terminal, bought a ticket, and joined the crowd by the embarkation doors. Looking around, she could see neither Doesburg nor the young man from the Soviet Consulate.

Doesburg, arriving a few minutes later, recognized the dark-haired slim figure near the front of the line. He mopped his brow with an already soaked handkerchief, wondering if the heat was solely responsible for the sweat. He hadn't fully recovered from Kroeger's dramatic appearance the previous Friday night and Berlin's cavalier disregard of security that it implied. It might have been necessary, but he still found it hard to live with the knowledge that there was someone in America who could telephone the FBI and give away his address. But there was the money. Even $6,000 would go a long way.

The doors clanged open and the crowd surged onto the ferry. He found Amy in the usual place on the western deck, and for several minutes they stood side by side, staring at the New Jersey skyline and saying nothing. Then they went through the prescribed routine, exchanging pleasantries about the weather, her sitting down, then him, for all the world like a pair of strangers passing the time on a voyage that both found boring. Doesburg carefully placed his folded newspaper between them on the wooden seat.

"It's on," he said without changing his tone of voice. He wished she'd take her sunglasses off; he found her vaguely unnerving at the best of times, and with her eyes concealed the effect was multiplied.

Amy, her pulse racing, smiled sweetly at him. "When?" she asked, indicating with the slightest nod of her head that someone was approaching them.

"On August the fourth," Doesburg said, beaming at her. "Our relations will arrive late on the second, so they'll have two days sight-seeing before, and then they'll go back the next day. It's a long trip."

When they were alone again Amy asked, "Am I handling the operation from this end?" This was the big question, the one on which everything depended. If Berlin or Doesburg had dealt her out of the plan, then she'd have to use her only weapon—her access to Matson. She could try and cover the threat with patriotic zeal, but it would still be a threat, and she didn't think Doesburg would take it kindly. He wasn't the sort of man who'd like being dictated to by a woman.

"Not alone," he said, slightly raising his hand to avert her protest. "Berlin insists that a man be in charge, but you will be his girl Friday. The two of you will be busy enough."

"When do we meet?"

"I was about to tell you," he said with a rare note of irritation. "He'll be on the next ferry across, and you can go

86

back with him. He'll introduce himself by asking you if you know how many stories the Empire State Building has. Read the instructions before you meet, fix your arrangements, and Joe—that's his operating name—will report back to me. Any questions?"

She couldn't think of any. "Joe" might be a problem, but he might also be useful in establishing the German connection. The important thing was that she was in. Moscow could decide the rest. "No," she said coolly, picking up the newspaper. "I hope your wife feels better tonight," she said in a louder voice as she got to her feet. The ferry approached the Staten Island dock.

Amy made her way forward to the disembarkation end, passing the Soviet consular official with no more than an affirmative glance. Once ashore she went straight to a washroom and tore open the envelope. It contained three pages of neatly typed orders under the heading *Fall Doppeladler*. She took a deep breath and began to read.

The further she got, the more elated she felt. They had simply sent back the plan Faulkner had given her, and which she, attributing it to Sigmund, had passed on to Doesburg. There would be two German soldiers, and only two—Faulkner had been worried that someone in Berlin would decide to send a platoon, regardless of the difficulties involved in concealing them. The two would be put ashore off the Georgia coast at a quarter to midnight on August 2. The location would be checked beforehand by the "American-based operatives," and a list of possible reasons for changing it were attached. These included a Coast Guard station on the relevant beach.

The American-based operatives were also assigned other tasks. They were to check out the hijack location—Berlin had accepted Sigmund's choice, though on what grounds Amy couldn't imagine—and to observe the train on its July 7 run. That was this coming Friday. They were to hire "appropriate accommodation and vehicles" and acquire the necessary weaponry—another list. "Joe will deal with this" Doesburg had scrawled in the margin against the latter.

There was nothing else of significance. All in all the three pages, which must have taken a whole night to send in cipher, amounted to little more than an announcement of the soldiers' arrival and departure times, with a few pieces of advice thrown in. They'd bought it hook, line, and sinker.

Amy walked back to the dock, where the next ferry was already discharging its passengers. We're halfway there, she thought. The papers in the envelope would convict the Germans on their own, and if the man from the Russian Consulate had done his job, they'd soon have Doesburg's address.

She walked aboard, watched the water bubble and thrash as they got underway.

"Do you know how many stories there are in the Empire State Building?" a voice asked her.

"A hundred and two," she said, turning around. "Hello Joe."

"Rosa, I presume," he said, treating her to a display of perfectly even teeth.

He was not what she'd expected. If anything, the opposite. He was probably younger than she; his hair was light brown and wavy above a friendly face. He had the soft drawl of the South in his voice, and though he wasn't big, she felt he could take care of himself. Or at least thought he could.

He wasted no time on pleasantries. "We've got an outing to arrange," he began, and proceeded to tell her the arrangements. He had the car and the gas-ration coupons; he'd pick her up in Washington opposite the Library of Congress at 7 P.M. on Thursday. She must get hold of the necessary maps. He liked night driving. And then he left.

She watched him thread his way down the deck, the Manhattan skyline rearing above him, and remembered her feelings as a ten-year-old, seeing it for the first time. The Statue of Liberty, the amazing skyscrapers, the huge liners at their berths on the Hudson piers. The New World, which had turned out to be just another slice of the old.

☐

Joe picked her up in a black Buick at the appointed time, and within half an hour they were driving west through Virginia horse country, the mountains ahead a dark line against the sunset. He drove fast but well, a fact which impressed Amy, who had never liked cars and found no pleasure in driving.

He talked as he drove, an almost incessant hum. His favorite subject was war, the present one and all those that had gone before. As they crossed the foot of the Shenandoah Valley he treated her to a detailed account of Sherman's March, adding for good measure an analysis of its significance in the development of modern military strategy. She made what she hoped were appropriate noises on those rare occasions when he paused to draw breath.

He said nothing about the job at hand, and while he talked Amy occupied her mind writing an imaginary report to Moscow on his motivation. She was just concluding that the game alone was what interested him when he switched subjects and started talking political philosophy. She'd been wrong. He really did believe in the Nazi cause; it fit perfectly with his views on life in America. Miscegenation was the great evil, Roosevelt a Communist dupe, and Hitler a shining example to the white race.

"If Roosevelt wins the war," he said earnestly, "you know what will happen? All the goddamn liberals will make a lot of noise about world democracy and racial brotherhood and all that crap. And there'll be about two million goddamn niggers coming back from the war who've learned to use a gun, and their heads will be full of the same crap. The Klan will have a hard time keeping things under control." He looked at her briefly, a look of boyish intensity that almost took the sting out of his words.

"He won't win the war," she said. "Not if we're successful, he won't." The Klan, she thought. She suddenly felt as if they were driving into a foreign country. She'd always known it, but feeling it was different.

He was silent for a few minutes as he guided the car through the center of Harrisonburg. It was almost midnight now, but the main street was still full of people, most of them the worse for drink.

"Maybe," he said as they emerged into the country once more. "But the times are against us at the moment. This is a bad century to live in, I reckon. But we'll come back. Technology'll do it, you'll see. The machines'll get so good we won't need the niggers anymore. Then we can ship 'em all back to Africa, let 'em learn to look after themselves. See where democracy and equality gets 'em."

"But it's not just the . . . niggers," Amy murmured.

"True enough. But I don't rightly know where we can send the Jews." He laughed. "New England maybe. And put a wall around it. Let 'em *work* for their Friday bread." He looked at her again, his face so innocent of guile that she felt a shiver.

"It's cold in the mountains at night," he observed equably. "There's a blanket in the back—why don't you try and get some sleep? It's another ten hours yet."

"You're going to drive right through?"

"Maybe. I slept all day. If I get tired, I'll pull off the road somewhere and take a nap."

She took the blanket and closed her eyes, grateful for the silence even though sleep refused to come. She wondered why he'd said nothing about what her role was. Southern chivalry, she supposed. Marble columns and lace and happy black faces picking cotton . . .

It was light when she awoke, and they were parked by the side of the highway in a deep valley. Joe was asleep, snoring softly with his head against the window. She opened the door as quietly as she could and got out. In the near distance she heard a river and walked down through the trees toward the sound. Sunlight hadn't yet reached the valley floor but it was already getting hot, and the night dew was rising like steam from the ground, spreading the thick fragrance of fresh grass.

Amy relieved herself in the middle of a thicket, feeling foolish at needing concealment in the middle of nowhere, and then washed her face in the fast-flowing river. Looking around, she could see nothing but trees and, above them, the higher slopes of the valley. The highway was invisible and there was no sound of traffic. It was years since she'd been so physically alone, and it felt intoxicating. Her feet wanted to dance, but that, too, made her feel foolish for no good reason. She walked back up the slope, taking an almost furtive pleasure in the springiness of the turf.

Joe was awake when she returned, looking a lot less sprightly than she felt. "Okay," he grunted, and swung the car back onto the highway. "Let's find some breakfast."

They ate at a truck stop outside Bull's Gap and continued south through Knoxville, Athens, Cleveland, Chattanooga, the valley widening before them. Soon after eleven they reached Bridgeport, Alabama, found the railroad depot, and cruised the surrounding streets looking for a suitable hotel.

"That one," Amy said, pointing out a three-story white building.

They parked the Buick and went in. "Two rooms at the back, on the top floor," Joe told the proprietor. "We've got work to do," he explained, "and we need some quiet."

"Your secretary, I suppose," the proprietor said with a grin, looking across at Amy, who was studying a painting on the wall.

"If she wasn't, I wouldn't need two rooms," Joe said coldly.

"Okay, no offense intended." He led them up the carpeted stairs. "This is a decent house. You won't be troubled by any noise."

The rooms looked surprisingly comfortable. Amy went to the window and examined the view. "Fine," she told Joe. He went downstairs for their luggage, and a few minutes later he pulled two identical leather cases from his bag. "German officer issue, 1910," he said, handing her one and pulling the binoculars from the other. He studied the railroad depot through them. "Perfect," he muttered. "As long as Sigmund has his facts right," he said, turning to her.

"He hasn't been wrong yet," she said, joining him at the window. "What about the light?" she asked.

"There's yard lamps all over the place. No reason why they won't be on. I'm going to get some sleep."

"I'm going for a walk," she called after him.

It wasn't a big town, just the one main street petering out in each direction and about ten perpendicular roads on each side. The faces were mostly white; this was still hill country. She walked down to the Tennessee River, which looked narrower than she'd expected until she realized that the far shore was an island in midstream. The water had none of the blue-green purity of the mountains; it was a dull brown, rolling rather than running.

She heard giggling behind her and turned to see three black children staring at her over the trunk of a fallen tree. She smiled and walked toward them. They fled, laughing.

She suddenly felt a little dizzy, and cursed herself for not wearing a hat. The heat was stifling. Back on Main Street, she bought a Coke in a general store, aware that everyone was staring at her. "Where you from, honey?" the woman serving asked her. "If'n you don't mind me asking."

"Washington," Amy said, adding that she and her boss were driving down to Birmingham on business.

"Gadsden road would have been quicker," a man observed.

Amy didn't reply. What was she doing wandering about the town, hat or no hat? The less people saw her the better. She paid and walked out, feeling the looks aimed at her back.

□

From nine o'clock on they took turns at the window in Amy's room. While she watched he read a well-thumbed copy of a Civil War history; when the roles were reversed she tried without success to begin a Sinclair Lewis novel. As it grew darker the depot buildings grew indistinct, and there was no sign of the lights being switched on. The yard was bereft of activity.

"I'll have to go down there," Joe said, putting down the field glasses.

"Wait," she said. "It's not quite midnight yet." She looked at Sigmund's timetable for the twentieth time. "Bridgeport arrive 12:15, depart 12:25." She was about to agree that he go down when a car pulled into the yard, passed behind the shadowy bulk of a switching shed, and stopped, its headlights illuminating the side of the depot. Through the glasses they could just make out a figure disappearing through the door. The light inside went on, and a few moments later the whole yard was suddenly bathed in a yellow glow from the yard lamps. The car, they could now see, belonged to the state police. Two men came out of the office and stood by the car. Both lit cigarettes. One roared with laughter at something the other said.

A whistle sounded in the distance, and both men looked east down the tracks. Another man got out of the car and hitched up his belt. He took two rifles out of the backseat, walked over to the others, and gave one to his partner. They could now hear the train.

A couple of minutes later it drew smoothly into the depot and stopped, letting off steam, where Joe had predicted, alongside the wooden water tower. The train looked exactly like the one in Matson's photographs: the black engine and tender, the single long boxcar, and the caboose. The brakeman jumped down from the caboose and joined the state troopers while the engineer and fireman manhandled the hose into the tender. Four more men emerged from behind the train, having presumably come from the boxcar. The engineer left the fireman to turn off the water and joined the others. There were nine of them now in a circle, the low murmur of their conversation barely audible above the hiss of the locomotive.

The fireman, his task finished, walked out of sight of the others and urinated against the wall of the depot. He then moved down to join them, and for several minutes they stood together some twenty yards from the rear of the train. Then the gathering broke up. The two state troopers joined the pair in the boxcar, the crew returned to the engine, the brakeman to the caboose. The car swept out of the yard; the train, blasting smoke, began to move. The depot lights went out, followed by those in the office. Amy and Joe looked at each other.

"Couldn't be better," he said.

☐

Next morning Amy and Joe checked out of the hotel and drove another thirty miles down the valley to the larger town of Scottsboro. The realtor's office was in the center of town and Amy stayed in the car while Joe conducted their business inside. She could see him through the window talking to a gray-haired man, who then disappeared and returned with a set of keys. The two men shook hands, the realtor mimed the shooting of a rifle, and laughed. Boys will be boys, she thought.

"No problem," Joe said as he climbed back into his seat. "They're glad to have us. We're the first this year. Probably be the only ones this year. The war's not helping the hunting business."

"It is now," she murmured.

He laughed.

They took the Guntersville road along the banks of the newly created lake, another New Deal creation which Joe found unfortunate in principle but probably useful in practice. "Technology needs power," he told her.

After ten miles or so they found their turnoff, a dirt road leading up the side of a steep ridge. They passed through two shanty towns, seemingly empty save for staring groups of children in ragged clothes. Scottsboro was only an hour behind them, but it could have been centuries ahead.

Another hour and they'd left all signs of civilization behind. The road wound up and over the highest ridge, presenting them with a panoramic view of mountains stretching into the distance. A sign pointing drunkenly into the ground bore the legend "Jefferson Lodge."

"Nice name," Joe said, bumping the Buick onto a dirt track that made the one they'd left seem smooth as Pennsylvania Avenue. A quarter of a mile farther and they reached the lodge, a sprawling wooden cabin built against the ridge slope, flanked by enormous hickory trees. Above the door the skull of a deer gazed sourly down.

"It was built by some Birmingham big shot who went bust in '29," Joe told her. "He shot himself here. With a derringer, would you believe?"

There were six rooms and a kitchen. The furniture was minimal but clean, the kitchen well-enough equipped. A large pile of logs was waiting by the stove.

"It'll do," Amy said, sitting down on one of the bunk beds. "But that rough road worries me. There won't be any time for changing tires if we run into a problem."

"Not much we can do about that. We have a couple of spares for the car and I'll check out the road for sharp stones." He walked to the window, pushed back the shutters, and looked out. "Now *that's* America," he said.

She joined him. Far to the west the lower Tennessee Valley could be seen, a yellow-green swath framed by the dark green slopes of the forested hills. To the north there were only mountains, ridge after ridge fading into the blue haze of the horizon. In front of the cabin the dust-coated Buick looked like a bedraggled alien spacecraft.

"Yes," she murmured, turning away. That was one America. She didn't understand him and didn't want to. Though she loathed his opinions, there was something about him she found disturbingly likable, some boyish innocence that seemed far removed from the evil he represented. She took a conscious grip on herself. They were enemies, enemies at war, only that. In a few weeks he would be dead.

He went out to check the road, and she did another tour of the cabin, wondering which room the unfortunate "big shot" had killed himself in.

"Okay," he shouted from the door. "Let's move."

The Buick bounced its way back to the main road, where they turned north, motoring gently downhill across the plateau. A solitary peak—McCoy Mountain, the map said—loomed in front of them, but as they approached its base the road plunged down to the right, and before the pines engulfed them Amy could see road, river, and railroad tracks sharing the narrow valley below.

They hit bottom at the small town of Lim Rock, another group of shacks seemingly devoid of inhabitants, though rather more modern than those on the mountain. Following the valley westward, they reached their destination in less than a mile. Here the road and the main railroad line pushed on toward a gap in the ridge ahead, while the stream, a spur line, and another dirt track veered north up a narrow valley.

Joe stopped the car at the point closest to where the tracks diverged and they both got out. "Keep your eyes peeled," he told her, and she leaned back against the hood watching the road while he took the large iron key from the trunk and carried it across the tracks. She heard a click, a grunt, and a metallic thud. "No problem," he shouted.

"Nothing coming," she shouted back.

The noises repeated and he returned to replace the key in the trunk.

"A truck," Amy said, and they watched it approach and thunder past. The driver acknowledged Joe's cheerful wave.

He turned the car and drove it up the dirt road and into the narrow valley. It ran straight for half a mile, then took a bend that brought them out of sight of the main road. Joe drove slowly forward as they both surveyed the area.

"This'll do," he said.

"The bridge will do for a marker," she added, pointing forward to where both road and rails crossed the stream on a wooden trestle.

They continued up the valley to its head, turning the car in the space between some old abandoned mine buildings. On the way back they stopped again at the chosen spot. Visibility in each direction was about a quarter of a mile; the valley sides were covered in densely packed pines and already, in the late afternoon, the rays of the sun had departed for the day. The valley floor was no more than fifteen yards wide, leaving room for just the stream, the tracks, and the road. It was easy to imagine how dark it would be at night, even with the half-moon.

Amy took out her camera and took several pictures, making sure that at least one of them included Joe. He rolled the car forward to pick her up and they drove back to the main road.

"No problem, no problem at all," he said contentedly.

Neither of them spoke again until they reached Scottsboro, where they checked into another hotel, this time as brother and sister.

☐

The long drive back to Washington consumed most of Sunday, and by the time Amy reached her apartment she wanted nothing more than an early night. She stepped out of the elevator to find Richard sitting against the wall by her door, obviously drunk.

"The lady no longer vanishes," he said solemnly, pulling himself to his feet.

"The lady's tired," she said, more kindly than she felt.

"Then let's go to bed," he said, following her into the apartment and half-collapsing into an armchair.

She looked at him. He wasn't given to drinking, at least not to this extent.

"What's the matter?" she asked, sitting down in the other chair. She knew he wanted her to make some physical gesture, but for some reason the thought of touching him filled her with revulsion.

"Nothing's the matter. I've been celebrating. Why don't you keep anything to drink?" he asked, looking around wildly.

"Stop playing the drunk," she said acidly, "it's not your style. I'll make some coffee."

He followed her into the kitchen. "I said I've been *celebrating*," he said. "Don't you want to know *what* I'm celebrating?"

"Enlighten me." She sighed inwardly. Were all men in their late thirties just taller adolescents? "Has Jean kicked you out?" she guessed.

He laughed. "Oh no, it's much worse than that. She's *pregnant*. She's locked me in," he said, as if he was shocked by the discovery.

Amy had difficulty restraining the impulse to throw the coffee at him. "I suppose you had nothing to do with it," she said, brushing past him as she carried the cups into the living room.

He almost ran after her, and for a second she thought he was going to hit her. But his face relaxed and he sank back into the chair. Poor Richard, she thought, you can't even make it as a full-fledged bastard.

They sat for several minutes in silence. There had been a time, she thought, when this would have mattered to her, a time when she'd even flirted with the idea of giving up everything for him. It hadn't been for long, just a couple of weeks after they'd come together, when his kindness—and, she had to admit, his imagination in bed—had concealed his lack of character. But the romantic glow had soon disappeared as if it had never been, and she had settled for the sex, safe in the knowledge that Richard had nothing else to offer. Now she just wanted to be rid of him.

"Can I stay tonight?" he asked without looking up.

"No."

"Why not?" he asked angrily.

"Because I don't want you to."

"Amy, I love you. I—"

"No, you don't. You don't know the meaning of the word." She felt angry, angrier than she ought to be. She should be showing him that she didn't gave a damn about Jean's pregnancy.

It was too late. "I'm sorry," he said. "I didn't mean to hurt you. Look, I'll sort it out. I do love you. I don't love her. It's as—"

"No—no—no," she shouted. He looked at her with astonishment. "Richard," she said, her eyes closed, her fists clenched on her thighs, "will you just go?"

He didn't move. "Look, I've said I'm sorry," he said quietly.

"Just go."

"Is there someone else?"

"What?" She couldn't believe it.

"You heard."

She laughed. "You come here, tell me you've gotten your wife pregnant, and then ask me if there's someone else?"

"Is there? I need to know." He was looking straight at her, his voice completely calm. He might have been asking someone the time. She suddenly realized that he was holding himself together only by a thread.

"No," she said softly. "Satisfied?"

He smiled, an utterly meaningless smile. "Of course." He looked at his watch. "Time I was getting back," he said, and without another word walked out of Amy's apartment.

six

KUZNETSKY lowered himself through the hatch and dropped nimbly onto American territory. After almost four days in the air, frequently punctuated by stops at godforsaken airstrips in the middle of the Siberian wilderness, his mind felt like running a hundred-yard sprint, his body like collapsing in an exhausted heap. He compromised, leaning against the Antonov's wing and surveying the Alaskan landscape.

For a minute he thought they'd landed at the wrong location, then remembered what he'd been told about Ladd Field, that it was built underground. Above ground there were only the gaunt hangars and a few offices, and it was to one of these that the pilot led him. Inside, a flight of stairs led down into a brightly lit tunnel. "It's five miles long, in a circle," Brelikov told him. He tried to look suitably impressed.

"Welcome home, Jack," he murmured to himself as Brelikov led him along the tunnel toward the Soviet pilots' mess.

It was hard to believe they were in America; the only non-Russian speakers were conversing in Uzbek. The mess hall was crowded with fifty or so Soviet pilots, most of them washing down hamburgers with bottles of Coca-Cola. Kuznetsky asked an officer the way to Anisimov's office, and was coldly pointed farther down the tunnel. The local boss was apparently not popular with the masses.

It didn't take Kuznetsky long to understand why. Alexei

Anisimov, the Soviet head of the Lend-Lease Purchasing Commission, was a prime example of a particular NKVD stereotype—slightly built, elegant, with a supercilious air and an ascetic's face. He was probably younger than Kuznetsky, but the way he said "Welcome, Colonel" was nicely judged to emphasize his superior rank. Kuznetsky replied in kind, passing over his First Priority credentials with a condescending smile and making himself comfortable in the seat he hadn't yet been offered.

"Yes, Colonel," Anisimov said, offering him an American cigarette and lighting it with a contraption bearing a portrait of Mickey Mouse. "I cannot see any difficulties. I have of course been given advance warning of your requirements, but there is really nothing to it. We've been sending men into the United States for three years now without any trouble. They just hop off the plane in Great Falls, Montana, and catch a taxi to the railway station. No one has ever been stopped." He smiled contemptuously and carefully scraped the ash from his cigarette on the rim of the ashtray. "I sometimes think we could land a platoon of T-34s and they'd be halfway to Washington before the Americans delivered a mild protest."

Then any fool could do your job, Kuznetsky thought. But there was no point in antagonizing Anisimov, no point at all. "What about the return journey?" he asked. "There's still no inspection of outbound planes?"

"None whatsoever. Well, there was one incident in January. The American in charge at Great Falls, Major Jordan, he took it into his head one night to inspect one load, and he found quite a lot of . . . well, to call it diplomatic baggage was stretching the usual meaning of the term. Jordan was quite upset. He raced off to Washington and kicked up a fuss. Nobody took any notice of him. In fact we received an apology from the State Department, here. . . ." He pointed out a framed letter on the wall behind him. "Since then, no more inspections. We could probably bring out the Statue of Liberty."

Kuznetsky was glad that he'd already heard much the same in Moscow; Anisimov's complacency wouldn't have been very convincing on its own. Still, everything seemed okay.

"This First Priority business," Anisimov said cordially, "it must be of extraordinary importance."

"It is. I regret that I can tell you no more. Now I would like to get some sleep. . . ."

Anisimov hid his disappointment well. "Of course. You'll be on a plane at ten in the morning, if that is satisfactory?"

Kuznetsky nodded.

☐

Kuznetsky might have been tired, but sleep refused to come. He hadn't found it easy to fall asleep since leaving the forest. And Nadezhda. He'd had no idea how much he'd miss her; he still didn't understand it. Little things, like the way she put her hand on his shoulder and leaned against him. . . .

In Moscow there hadn't been time to think. For two weeks he'd been submerged in the affairs of his native country, memorizing political events, reading newspapers, watching Hollywood movies, reading radio scripts and comics. "Smooching" was the new dating game. "Well, cut off my legs and call me Shorty" was what the "drools" were saying to the "meatballs." In Florida they'd just built a drive-in church; the congregation listened through huge loudspeakers and honked their car horns, once for "amen" and twice for "hallelujah." Everyone was worried about Roosevelt's health, and the whole country had gone mad on vitamins. Most of the top baseball stars had been drafted and basketball had suddenly become popular. There was a national shortage of bobby pins!

If Nadezhda had a bobby pin, she'd probably stick it in a German. But after the war . . . he'd get her one, shortage or no shortage, a piece of America for his girl. . . .

He was awakened by a hand gently shaking his shoulder. "Comrade Anisimov wants you," a voice said. He opened his eyes and saw the man who'd shown him to his room. "Tell him I'll be there in a few minutes."

"I believe it's urgent, Comrade Colonel."

"That's why I said minutes."

The messenger retreated. Kuznetsky looked at himself in the minuscule mirror above the washbasin. He'd shave first, if only to keep Anisimov waiting. No, he wasn't worth it. Why was he feeling so petty?

There was another colonel in Anisimov's office whom Kuznetsky knew by name but not by sight. Colonel Kotikov was nominally in charge of the Soviet operation at Great Falls, though the real authority lay with Anisimov's NKVD surrogate, one Sergeant Vinogradsky. Kotikov was almost Anisimov's opposite in appearance—a big burly man with a wide smile; in years gone by he'd have been a prosperous Ukrainian kulak. Kuznetsky could see that he'd get on with the Americans, who'd fall for the hearty exterior and put down the bullying side to language difficulties. A real Russian, they'd think. Our gallant allies! Anisimov, on the other hand, would seem like a well-bred snake wherever you put him. These tunnels seemed ideal.

He did not, however, look so disgustingly self-possessed as he had the previous night. "We have a problem, Colonel," he explained between taking jerky puffs on his cigarette. "Colonel Kotikov will explain," he added, in a tone that implied his own blamelessness.

Kotikov shook hands with Kuznetsky and leaned back wearily in his seat. "I left Great Falls on Friday evening," he said. "I'm afraid the Americans have had another brainstorm. Comrade Anisimov tells me that you have already been informed of the nonexistent security. . . . Well, three days ago there was a meeting at the State Department in Washington. The FBI, Military Intelligence, Customs, everyone. They intend to demand a meeting with our embassy people and to tell them that in future the border and customs regulations regarding us will be strictly enforced."

Kuznetsky looked at Anisimov, who looked at the ceiling. "Of course this may be nothing but words," he said stiffly. He obviously found the whole business thoroughly embarrassing.

"It may be," Kotikov continued unperturbed, "and what the Americans know about security could be written on the edge of a kopek . . . but I have expected this for some time. Ever since the January episode. And since Jordan left, the atmosphere has changed considerably. On Friday the new liaison man made a point of showing me around the rooms reserved for the new inspection unit. Sooner or later the bastards are going to start checking everyone and everything going out. It may be later, but I don't think we can depend on that."

"No," Kuznetsky said thoughtfully. "How about entry? Will I have any trouble getting in?"

"Nothing is certain, but I will be very surprised if the Americans act that fast."

"Very well." He turned to Anisimov. "I presume you have already written a full report for Moscow. It must go direct to Comrade Sheslakov at Frunze Street, First Priority, and as fast as is humanly possible. I shall go in as planned."

☐

The flight to Great Falls took the best part of two days, each stretch of mountain or tundra culminating in an hour spent stretching his limbs at some small settlement airstrip. The American pilot fed the guardians of these lonely outposts with conversation, and Kuznetsky walked around examining the pinups of Betty Grable and listening to the vast Canadian silence. As far as the pilot knew, he spoke no English, and as such was treated as no more than a mobile piece of cargo whom it was necessary to feed but not to recognize as a fellow human being.

Great Falls was sighted soon after nine on Wednesday morning, a small but sprawling town where rivers and railroads converged. The airstrip, Gore Field, was perched high above the town on a plateau. Alongside the one lengthy runway Kuznetsky could see scores of fighters awaiting delivery to the Soviet Union, each one already adorned with its gleaming red stars.

He was met by Colonel Kotikov's wife, a petite, nervous-looking woman in her mid-thirties whom Kuznetsky would have thought more suited to Anisimov. She took him to the living quarters above her husband's office, provided a welcome breakfast, and left him to eat it in peace. He'd not yet seen an American, much less been challenged by one.

She came back as he was finishing his coffee, poured him another cup, sat down. "I suggest we make the switch between here and the station," she said. "I have a suitcase full of American clothes"—she pointed it out—"and there's an eastbound train at five this evening. You have to change several times, but it's all written out here. In English."

He inspected the paper. Minot, Fargo, Minneapolis. Familiar names.

"There's some newspapers here," she said. "Out of date of course. And there's the radio. Jack Benny's on at eleven. He makes $17,000 a program," she said wistfully. "Of course," she added quickly, "after the war our radio will be just as good."

"I doubt it," Kuznetsky said calmly. "There are some things Americans do well. Fortunately they're mostly things that don't matter very much."

"I'll leave you to rest then," she said, reverting to her nervous expression. She wasn't sure how to deal with this man. She wasn't even sure which nationality he really was.

"Thank you," he called after her.

At four they drove out of the airfield and down toward the town. The American guards on the gate merely saluted, and halfway down the mountain they stopped for Kuznetsky to change clothes. Kotikov's wife left him waiting at the station, sitting on his suitcase, leaning against the wall of the depot. The train was late, only an hour the clerk said, but Kuznetsky doubted it. He took out the copy of *The Grapes of Wrath* that he'd found and pocketed in the plane from Fairbanks. He'd never heard of the writer, but he'd just seen the film in Moscow and been grudgingly impressed.

A car turned into the station yard and two men got out. One pointed in his direction, and they walked slowly across until they were standing looking down at him. "What's your name?" one barked out in Russian.

"Uh?" Kuznetsky said, shielding his eyes against the sun as he looked up at them. "I don't get your drift, fella."

They looked at each other. The dapper-looking one smiled at him. "You're not a Russian, then?" he asked innocently.

"You a coupla smart guys? What's the game?"

The bulky one intervened. "Maybe we've made a mistake, mister. Do you have any means of identification?"

"No. Yes. Driver's license." He pulled the card from his inside pocket.

"Jack Tillotson. St. Cloud, Minnesota. Is that where you're heading?"

Kuznetsky showed him the ticket. "Who are you?" he asked. "Cops?"

"Something like that."

He snatched the ticket back. "Hey, this is a free country. Who the hell are you?"

The bulky one showed him a card. Military Intelligence. "Okay. Why pick on me?"

The dapper one smiled again. "Because you left Gore Field

with the Russian chief's wife, that's why, Mr. Tillotson. Or is it Tillotsky?"

"You're crazy. I'm as American as you are."

"So how come you seem so cozy with the Russians?"

"She gave me a lift, that's all. I didn't know she was Russian till I got in the car. They're our *allies*, aren't they?"

"Sure. How did you come to be up there?"

"I got a lift from Edmonton on a plane. One of the pilots is a friend of mine."

"Name?"

"Bob Simpson." Kuznetsky hoped that Simpson was on his way back to Fairbanks by this time. "Check at the airfield."

"What were you doing in Edmonton?"

"Visiting my sister. She married an oilman—they're prospecting up there."

"Close family, eh."

"Something wrong with that?"

"No. Would you mind if we checked your suitcase?"

"Would it make any difference if I did?"

"Nope."

They rummaged through the clothes, found nothing, and asked him to turn out his pockets. Kuznetsky blessed the inspiration that had told him to destroy Kolikova's note.

The bulky one looked relieved, the dapper one chagrined. "Okay, Mr. Tillotson, sorry to have troubled you. There's been a lot of Russians slipping into the U.S. of A. with trouble in mind. We have to be careful."

"Okay," Kuznetsky said, "sorry I got a bit ticked."

They started to walk away, then the dapper one said "Good-bye" over his shoulder in Russian. Nice try, Kuznetsky thought to himself. They'd obviously seen the same movie.

□

When Kuznetsky woke the next morning the mountains were gone, the sun was rising, and the train was clanking into

Minot, North Dakota. He was supposed to make a connection here for Fargo and St. Cloud, but after the business of the evening before with the American counterintelligence agents he had decided to wait for the through train from Moose Jaw to Minneapolis. If Simpson hadn't left, someone might be waiting for him in St. Cloud.

It was a slower train, and for most of the day it chugged across the plains passing through no towns of any size. On either side of the tracks the yellow-green, treeless country stretched toward a flat horizon, and every twenty miles or so a road would cross the tracks and arrow away into the distance. Occasional farms and occasional stations, dwarfed by grain silos, were all that broke the monotony.

It was hypnotic, and something more. For the first time Kuznetsky understood why so many Russians had preferred the labor camps to exile. Home was like a magnet, the more powerful the nearer you came. But you could step beyond the magnetic field, as he had, and cut yourself loose. It wasn't that they would miss Russia; what they dreaded was that they wouldn't, and that in some sense they'd then be forever homeless. Bravery and cowardice, hand in hand. They knew they could never go back, and Kuznetsky knew, even as he looked out on the Minnesota plains, as he came within the magnetic field, that neither could he. He longed to get off, to catch a ride to St. Cloud, see his mother and father if either was still alive, but he knew he wouldn't. It wasn't just a matter of duty, it was the way things were, the way the cards had been dealt. Regrets were the price of any choice; they couldn't be cashed in.

He changed again in Minneapolis, remembering the day in this station twenty-six years before. They'd taken the train west, forty men, boys really, all full of nervous bravado and curiosity. On to crisp uniforms and rifles that would feel strange in their hands.

He took the train east for Chicago, a forty-three-year-old NKVD colonel, immune to nerves, immune to bravado, not yet immune to curiosity. He lay back in his seat, drifting to and fro between sleep and wakefulness, between darkness and images of a young girl walking before him through a moonlit forest.

☐

"Amy looks as if she's got something on her mind," Harry Brandon whispered to his wife.

Bertha Brandon looked across the room at her niece. "She's always been like that," she replied. "It's just one of her moods. She might make more of an effort for James's sake."

Her husband laughed. "James isn't here."

"No, but that's not his fault, and we are celebrating his twenty-first birthday."

"James always adored Amy when he was a kid."

"What a romancer you are!" She patted him affectionately on the knee. "Amy, dear," she called across the room, "have you heard from James lately?"

"Not since he crossed to France, Aunt Bertha," she answered automatically. She couldn't seem to get Richard off her mind, though there didn't seem any real reason for concern. She hadn't seen him since the Sunday before, though on the next day he had sent her a huge bouquet of flowers with the message "Sorry about last night." Now he was halfway to New Hampshire to take part in a conference at Bretton Woods. He'd be gone all week.

Perhaps she was just getting tense about the operation and using him as a focus for her anxiety. The Russian—no, the American from Russia—would be arriving any day, might even be in Washington already. He was probably as anxious about her as she was about him. But he had to be good or they wouldn't be sending him.

Her aunt and uncle were now discussing, of all things, the recent spate of spy trials that had just ended in New York, and her uncle, noticing that she was listening, asked her, "What do you think, Amy?"

"Oh, I don't know," she said. "I suppose it's the motive that matters. If someone sells secrets for money, then they deserve all they get. But someone who does it because they believe in it . . . I think that's different."

"How could anyone believe in the Nazis?" her aunt asked sharply.

"Ah, but that's not the point," her husband said. "We're talking about morality. If it's wrong to spy, then why do *we* do it? Would you condemn a German who spied for us against the Nazis?"

"That's different, dear. This is a democracy."

"The land of the free," Amy murmured.

"Yes, yes it is," her aunt insisted. "We should be grateful. I don't care what they say. Anyone who helps the Germans should go to the electric chair."

"But that's what Amy's saying. We're fighting the Germans because they're wrong, not because they're Germans. It's the wider morality that counts, not the nation that happens to represent it."

If only you knew, Amy thought. She was fond, very fond, of her Uncle Harry, had been ever since her return from Germany in 1933, when he'd been so patient with her, so understanding, even though she'd told him hardly anything of what had happened. The fact that she'd worked through a lot of her pain in being like a second mother to his son, James, had brought them together. If she felt any regrets, they would be on his account. She knew how much he was going to be hurt by it all.

Her Aunt Bertha didn't matter. They had never liked each other, never really pretended to. Amy thought it was jealousy, not of her but of her mother, Bertha's sister. Elisabeth had died young, a heroine to some, leaving her memory to hang like an unliftable pall over Bertha's more mundane existence and Amy to serve as a constant reminder. Now she might live to see her niece strapped into the electric chair. The chill of the thought couldn't quite obliterate an almost pleasurable sense of irony.

Amy had thought about such consequences, not often, but she knew the possibility lay there at the back of her mind. Every time a German spy was caught and paraded across the newspapers and newsreels she pictured her own face in his or her place. People would spit on her picture, would press their ears to the radio for the details of her execution.

She knew it was real, but it didn't seem so, not really. Fear, yes, an underlying fear, a subterranean darkness. But she could cope with it, she knew that much; she would hold herself together to the end. She had promised her mother, promised Effi. She was only offering up her life, like so many millions of soldiers, like James in France. The manner of the death was neither here nor there. What mattered was to be true.

□

"One more time," Fyedorova asked him, "what's wrong with Vladivostok?"

"I'm not convinced it's the best solution to our problem," Sheslakov muttered, tracing his finger across the Pacific on the wall map.

"But it is a simple answer."

"Yes, it is," he conceded.

"And that's why you don't like it."

"No. It's more than that." He filled both their glasses with vodka and walked to the window. The streets were empty, but he thought he could make out a lightening of the sky above the cupolas of the Kremlin. A whole night they'd been going around in circles. A decision had to be made, but he felt too tired to make it.

Fyedorova swung her legs off the couch and leaned forward. "Right. Let me assume *your* usual role. Fact one—the earliest we can get a ship to Seattle or Portland is August 12.

Fact two—the earliest we can get one there by the safe route is August 20. Fact three—if the Americans find one of our ships in mid-Pacific . . ."

"It's a big ocean."

"It's still possible, and would be highly suspicious. Fact four—an August 20 arrival would leave our people and the material stranded in America for almost three weeks . . ."

"And then find the ship surrounded by American customs. If they're tightening up at Great Falls, there's no reason to suppose they aren't tightening up everywhere . . ."

"Which is why we ruled out the Atlantic convoys."

"Yes."

"Well, we've still got to cross an ocean."

"Apparently." Sheslakov rubbed his eyes. "So, the short route or the safe route?"

"The short route," she said.

"Zhdanov will want to play safe," he said morosely.

"Zhdanov . . ." Fyedorova's eyes suddenly lit up. "Oh yes, yes!" she said.

"What?" he asked irritably.

"I was talking to one of the secretaries at Trade about a year ago. Do you know how Zhdanov gets his Havana cigars?"

☐

Kuznetsky's train from Chicago pulled into Union Station early the next morning. He checked into a nondescript hotel on Massachusetts Avenue, shaved, and went out to shake the long train journey out of his limbs. He'd never been to Washington when he was young; in fact he'd never been farther east than Chicago, and the sights, familiar from school textbooks, seemed almost artificial, like life-size versions of photographs. At noon he put through a call to the prearranged number and informed the unknown answering voice that Rosa's brother was in town. "Five o'clock," the voice said, and the connection was cut.

He then walked to the Capitol, past the White House, and to the Lincoln Memorial. The sun seemed to get hotter by the minute, and he sat in the shade listening to the sightseers talking about Lincoln. He could tell that most of them seemed to come from the South, and few of them had anything complimentary to say.

Yakovlev arrived precisely on time, looking as hot as Kuznetsky felt. He was dressed American style, loose trousers, shirt unbuttoned at the collar, jacket thrown over one shoulder, a jaunty hat hanging on one side of his head. "Well, Comrade," he said in thickly accented English, "how is Moscow?"

"Same as ever," Kuznetsky replied. "Not as hot as this."

"Ah, Washington was built on a swamp, you know."

"Yes."

Yakovlev took the hint. "It's better we complete this quickly," he said. "I won't see you again—any problems, you have the telephone number. Call any hour, day or night."

"We already have problems," Kuznetsky said. He explained the situation at Great Falls.

Yakovlev swore in Russian, thought for a moment, and then shrugged. "That's for Moscow to sort out," he said. "Today is July 16—there won't be any word for at least a week. Start telephoning on the twenty-fourth. As for this end, everything is going as planned. The Germans arrive on the night of August 2, and all the advance work has been done. The July train ran as scheduled and the plan was checked through by Rosa and her friend from the Abwehr. They're picking up the weapons Tuesday night. You meet her tomorrow, at the Tidal Basin, just west of the Jefferson Memorial, at six o'clock. She'll be wearing a white blouse, burgundy suit, and carrying an orange."

"I've seen her photograph."

"Of course. Attractive, don't you think?"

"So's Ingrid Bergman," Kuznetsky said dryly.

"I don't think you'll find Rosa lacking in other qualities,"

Yakovlev noted with a trace of irritation. "Now, what do you need?"

"A gun. Preferably a Walther automatic. A reliable car and enough gas coupons to run it."

"There's no difficulty there. The car is ready. It was hired in the Abwehr agent's name last week. It will be left outside Union Station tomorrow morning at nine. The number, key, and coupons will be delivered to your hotel tonight. With the gun."

Kuznetsky told him the address and got up to leave.

"Good luck," Yakovlev said.

□

Kuznetsky had an enormous steak for dinner and then went into the first movie he could find. He got back to his hotel at around eleven, was handed a package by the night clerk, and persuaded the man to dig him out a bottle of ersatz whiskey. Once in his room, he inspected the gun, took off his clothes, and lay down on the bed with a glass of the amber fluid. It tasted awful, but he assumed it would eventually relax him.

He thought about the movie, had to admit that it had been an enjoyable enough piece of propaganda. The hero had not only discovered his sense of duty, but he'd also won the beautiful heroine as well. "You do know how to whistle, don't you?" she'd asked him. Kuznetsky laughed. A partisan who didn't know how to whistle wouldn't last long. He remembered Bogdanov, who'd claimed he could imitate thirty-seven different species of birds. Dead now.

Amelia Brandt, alias Rosa. He'd read the file in Moscow, listened to Sheslakov's account of his talk with Luerhsen, and for some reason he'd been filled with a deep sense of foreboding. He couldn't put his finger on it. Perhaps it was just that her life had been so different from his own, almost the reverse in fact. Perhaps it was her being a German, perhaps being a woman. What he wanted to know, he told himself, feeling the alcohol beginning to loosen his body, was whether she was ready to die. Like Nadezhda. How could she be?

Yes, she'd known tragedy, she'd met the enemy face to face, but only fleetingly—the rest of her life had been, no, not easy, but . . . removed. Espionage was a fantasy world, a game played out on the war's margins. How could she, how could anyone in America know, really know, what thirty years of war had done to Europe, how thin the civilized crust had grown, how utterly cheap a mere life had come to seem?

He emptied the glass Russian style, feeling it sting his throat. No, he didn't think he knew how to whistle anymore.

□

Amy sat on the edge of the basin with her legs dangling over the side and watched him walk toward her around the rim. He looked American, dressed in chinos and a checked shirt, but she knew it was him. She took the orange out of her bag and absentmindedly tossed it from one hand to the other like an impatient baseball pitcher waiting to be relieved.

He bought a Coke and sat down about fifteen feet away, separated by a fat man, watching, she knew, to make sure he hadn't been followed. They'd done a good job in Moscow. The haircut was perfect, the army boots looked as if they'd seen a few Pacific Islands. She wondered how good his English would be—twenty-six years was a long time.

After about ten minutes the fat man got up to leave and Kuznetsky took out a cigarette, patted both shirt pockets, and discovered that he had no matches. "Would you like a light?" she asked, taking her cue. "Thanks," he said with a flat Midwestern twang. He moved closer and casually took the matches and offered her a cigarette. As he lit hers their eyes met.

The last thing he'd expected to see was her half-veiled amusement. Nervousness yes, cold efficiency perhaps. She was either very right or very wrong for this sort of work, and he wasn't in an optimistic mood. She looked so young too. You could go from one end of the Soviet Union to the other and not find a thirty-three-year-old that the years had treated so kindly.

"I'm sorry," she said in a soft, almost accentless English. She picked up the orange. "The absurdity of things like this . . ." He was a remarkable-looking man. Not in a purely physical sense, but he seemed to radiate . . . power, that was the only word for it. His eyes had seemed to look straight through her, utterly clinical. And yet, as he walked around the basin, even as he'd sat not five yards away, she'd had an almost opposite impression, a sort of bearlike shambling. . . .

He seemed to relax. The eyes switched to neutral, gazing blankly across the water. He was thinking about something that woman with Sheslakov had said. "She will be driven, she will drive herself. . . ." Now that did sound absurd on a day like this, in a place like this.

He told her, slowly but precisely, what he had told Yakovlev about their problem with the escape route. She didn't interrupt, merely asked whether it was still on.

"Until we hear otherwise, and I doubt whether we will. The Party will have us cross the Pacific on a raft rather than let this chance go by."

She was pleased, he could see that. That was something. "All I need for now," he said, "is a good look at your German friend."

"He's American. He'll be picking me up outside the Library of Congress at six on Tuesday evening and dropping me at the same place later, I don't know how much later." She reached into her bag, brought out the photo of him she'd taken on their trip. "That's him. Joe Markham is the name he's using."

"No trouble with him?"

"Not yet. He's not the type to have doubts, but he's not a fool. And he's an excellent shot, or so he tells me."

"I'll bear that in mind."

She got up, leaving the cigarette pack. "You can keep them," she said.

He watched her walk away past the memorial, cursed softly under his breath in English, and then started off in the opposite direction.

Back in his hotel room, he removed the tightly folded rice paper from the cigarette package, memorized the address and telephone number it contained, and flushed the paper down the toilet at the end of the corridor.

SEVEN

SHESLAKOV watched the streets of Gothenburg roll past the open window of his limousine. The drive from Stockholm had taken most of the day, but he'd spent much of it asleep, recovering from the previous night's flight across the Baltic. Perhaps it wasn't really necessary for him to deal with Lorentsson personally, but he knew he wouldn't have trusted such a task with an underling.

They drove through the city center now, old buildings and young blondes, so many blondes, a nation of not-quite-Garbos. Sheslakov recalled the film he'd watched with Kuznetsky a few weeks before—*Ninotchka*—and smiled at the memory. Garbo had been so beautiful, and the bright young NKVD men watching had been too busy expressing their ideological outrage to notice. What did they expect from Hollywood—*Alexander Nevsky*?

"We're nearly there," the driver told him.

They had left the city behind, were close to the sea, and every now and then a gap in the trees would reveal the waters of the Kattegat bathed in the gold of the setting sun. Houses were few and far between, but they made up in size for what they lacked in numbers. It was a fitting place for a shipping magnate to make his home.

Lorentsson's mansion was built like a castle, complete with stone walls and crenellations, perched above the rocky coast. Sheslakov was admitted by a butler and ushered into a reception room that, from the sensuous depth of its carpet to the exquisite workmanship of its chandeliers, reeked of affluence. There was no doubting that capitalism worked for this capitalist.

There he was left to his own devices for more than half an hour, a little lesson, he told himself, that Swedes don't like the thought of being pressured. In his younger days Sheslakov would probably have been annoyed. Now he found such stratagems amusing.

The butler returned and led him up through the house to a study that overlooked the sea. Lorentsson sat behind a polished mahogany desk, a big man with blond hair and beard, fifty-five years old, according to the NKVD file in Sheslakov's pocket. The shipping magnate didn't rise to greet his visitor, merely gestured him to a chair. Another little signal.

Sheslakov sat down, savored the comfort of the chair, and smiled at the Swede. "We can speak English, yes?"

Lorentsson nodded.

"It has been made clear to you that I represent the Soviet Government, and doubtless you have made certain that this is so. . . ."

Lorentsson nodded silently again.

"Good, I will come straight to the matter. We understand that an agreement exists between the British, the Germans, and your own government permitting four Swedish ships to travel, unmolested, between Gothenburg and transatlantic destinations. Is that correct?"

Lorentsson nodded again, looking a trifle more wary.

"And this agreement is still honored? We understand there were some problems in January but that since then everything is fine."

"You are well-informed. . . ."

"There is no reason to expect problems in the months to come?"

"Not that I know of. What is the point of all this, Mr. Sheslakov?"

"I am coming to it. We understand you are the owner of two ships involved in this arrangement, and that one of them, the *Balboa*, is due to dock in Maracaibo, Venezuela, in the next few days. . . . ."

"The point?"

Sheslakov smiled. "The Soviet Government wishes to give you some business, Mr. Lorentsson. We want that ship to call at Havana, Cuba, on August 12 and collect something for us."

"What is the cargo?"

"For your information, it will be two naturalists, two *German* naturalists, and their crates of specimens. I am assured by our own shipping experts that such a diversion would not add many miles or days to the homeward journey, and you will of course be generously paid."

The Swede's expression had gone through surprise, amusement, and anger. "How much can two German naturalists possibly be worth to the Soviet Union?" he asked.

"We will pay a million Swedish krone on delivery in Gothenburg," Sheslakov said dryly. "As far as your company—and your ship's Captain Torstennson—are concerned, this is a request from the German Government, a humanitarian request."

Lorentsson stood up. "I'm sorry, Mr. Sheslakov, but Sweden is a neutral country."

Sheslakov didn't move. "I'm aware of that. I can assure you that this transaction has nothing whatsoever to do with the current war, and cannot therefore in any way compromise your country's neutrality."

"You'll have to do better than that," Lorentsson said. "Who are these 'naturalists' really? What are their 'specimens'?"

"I am also obliged to inform you," Sheslakov said quietly,

"that a refusal to accept this contract will be considered a most unfriendly act by the Soviet Government."

Lorentsson stared at him, and for the first time seemed unsure of himself. "Am I being threatened?" he asked incredulously.

Sheslakov remembered Fyedorova saying that the Swedes had not known terror since the Middle Ages. "Mr. Lorentsson, I will be perfectly honest with you," he said, looking the other man straight in the eye. "I do not know who these 'naturalists' are, nor the nature of their 'specimens'. The fact that half the Politburo smokes Havana cigars may have some relevance. I have no need to know, and neither do you. My government is willing to pay you well, very well, for collecting them. Where is the problem?"

The shipping magnate stared out of the window, seemingly engrossed in the embers of the sunset. "What if I refuse?" he asked without turning his head.

"Why even consider it?"

"I'd like to know."

Sheslakov sighed. "You'll be dead within a month."

Lorentsson whirled around, seemed on the verge of an angry outburst. "For a few crates of cigars?" he half-shouted.

"I understand," Sheslakov said matter-of-factly, "that the Swedish people take a pride in being practical, and nonideological. You had nothing to gain and much to lose from entering the war, so you stayed out. You have nothing to gain and much to lose from refusing this contract, so why not accept it? No country, no person, is free of pressures."

Lorentsson still said nothing, but Sheslakov knew he was beaten, knew from the blinking eyes, the turned-down mouth, the slightly sagging shoulders.

"You have no choice," he said gently, "because, like most people, you want to live."

Sheslakov stood up, took the envelope from his pocket and placed it on the desk. "It's all written down. When we hear from our people in Venezuela that your instructions have arrived, you will receive half the payment."

And your death will be ordered, Sheslakov thought as he descended the stairs. Outside, a red moon was hanging low in the eastern sky, edging the trees with blood. As they drove back toward Gothenburg he felt a profound sense of anticlimax. His part was over. All that remained was the waiting and hoping.

□

Kuznetsky wiped his brow for the hundredth time that day. He was used to heat, but of the dry variety. This damn humidity was something else entirely; it was like floating in a steam bath. His shirt and trousers clung, his feet squirmed inside his shoes. The end of his cigarette was sodden with sweat.

He tossed it out of the car window and sat back, watching the denizens of Washington going home for their supper. He still wasn't accustomed to the new fashions, particularly the women's. All these skirts tight around the hips and the broad belts with buckles. All the legs on display! He smiled as he imagined the reaction of the Party bosses back home—bunch of hypocritical prudes. It had been so different in the Revolution years; maybe this war would have the same effect. There was nothing like death for breaking down the mystique of the human body.

The atmosphere in Washington was difficult for him to judge. He'd known America was a long way from the war, but it was at war, and yes, there were some shortages, the casualty lists, the newsreels, and the radio programs full of letters from the boys at the front. But it didn't *feel* like a nation at war. It felt more like a nation engrossed in watching a war movie. The faces walking past were free of strain, smartly dressed and made-up, unconcerned. . . .

His fellow Americans. An alien species, yet somehow achingly familiar. It was the physical gestures, the way they moved their arms, tilted their heads—those were his gestures, *American* gestures.

He looked at his watch. A minute to go and, sure enough, there she was, walking toward the pickup point. He studied Amy's walk, wondering if there was anything particularly Germanic in the graceful, upright stride. Everyone else, all the Americans, seemed to be slouching in comparison.

She had just reached the library steps when a black Buick drew up alongside the curb. He watched Amy feign surprise, say something with a smile, and get into the car. She was a good actress if nothing else. The driver's face was in a shadow; as expected, he'd have to wait for their return and then follow the man home.

The Buick made a U-turn and headed west at the next intersection along Independence Avenue. Kuznetsky took out a cigarette, and as he did so noticed a red car, a Pontiac, draw away from the curb and into the Buick's slipstream. It might be coincidence, it probably was, but a little alarm bell went off in his mind. It would do no harm to make sure.

□

"Who are these people?" Amy asked Joe as they drove the Buick deeper into the Maryland countryside.

Joe thought for a moment, an impish look on his face. "Let's call them our Axis partners," he answered.

So it *was* the Mafia. Faulkner had thought it would be. "What do they know?" she asked.

"Nothing. Only that we want the guns and have the money. A simple business deal."

"What's the connection?"

He ignored the question. "Have you ever noticed," he said, "the similarity between the Mafia and the federal government? They both love competition so much, they spend all their time trying to kill it."

She grinned in spite of herself. "And the connection?"

"There's no need for you to know," he said flatly.

"Okay. But since I'm here in this car, I'd like to know how you're so certain we can trust them."

He stretched his right arm in front of her and sprung open the glove compartment. A fearsome-looking Colt revolver was clipped to the inside. "You'll stay in the car with that," he said. "But I don't expect any trouble. They have a code of sorts. They like doing business properly—makes them feel like upright American citizens."

"I hope so," she said, slipping the gun out of its clips and feeling its weight.

"I assume you know how it works," he asked.

"An American's birthright," she replied in the same tone. "It's heavy," she added. The GRU training hadn't included Colts. She looked out of the window at the flat country surrounding them. The sun behind them was still bright but its shadows were lengthening, and the fields, thick with grain, seemed to emit a golden haze.

"We're nearly there," Joe said.

Ahead she could see a truck stop, a large diner surrounded by parking spaces. He turned the car in, making for the far corner of the lot where a long gray sedan waited under the trees.

☐

Kuznetsky saw the Buick turn in and followed the Pontiac past. A quarter of a mile farther and his last doubts were removed. The red car pulled onto the grass turnout, and Kuznetsky, passing at speed, watched it make a U-turn in his rearview mirror. He continued on around a bend and made one himself. Passing the truck stop again, he saw the Buick in the distance, the Pontiac sitting by the diner a hundred yards away.

He drove on, wondering what to do. They would be returning to Washington once the deal was done, and there was no point in him interfering. He drove another half mile and pulled off into a side road, reversed the car, and settled down for another wait.

□

There were two of them. Joe shook hands with the younger one, a slight, dark-skinned man in a smart blue suit. The older man, who wore a light gray suit that was too tight for him, seemed to be staring straight at Amy, though it was hard to be certain through his sunglasses.

"Your partner doesn't walk?" he asked Joe.

Joe grinned at him. "She's nervous. It's okay." He lifted his arm to indicate the paper bag in his hand. "Here's the money."

The young one took it and disappeared into the car. Joe and the older one stood there smiling at each other. "I'll bet she has a gun, your partner," the Italian said conversationally. "Don't you trust us?"

"Like I said, she's the nervous type."

The Italian looked at Amy again. "Rather you than me," he said to Joe. "I like low-strung women, if you know what I mean."

"I like ones who can hit what they aim at."

The younger one had finished counting the money. "Okay, Paolo," he yelled through the window.

Paolo opened the sedan's trunk and took out a long canvas bag. Joe put it on the ground beside the Buick and examined the contents—three gleaming black tommy guns. He took one out, checked the action, and peered up the muzzle. "Needs greasing," he muttered to himself.

"Okay?" Paolo asked indifferently.

"Fine, it's been a pleasure doing business with you."

"Are you planning a war?" the young Italian asked sarcastically.

"There's one on already," Joe said, throwing the bag onto the backseat. "We just collect guns, that's all."

Paolo shrugged, stared at Amy once more, and climbed into the sedan. His partner pulled away with a squeal of tires. *"Mama mia,"* Amy murmured.

☐

Kuznetsky watched the black Buick sweep past and, a moment later, the red Pontiac. He pulled out of the side road and concentrated on keeping the second car in sight. As they entered the Washington suburbs he shortened the distance between them, preferring discovery to the loss of his quarry.

The Buick stopped outside the Library of Congress, let the woman out, and continued on its way. The Pontiac didn't move. Kuznetsky cursed; whoever it was, he was following Amy, not the German agent.

She succeeded in hailing a taxi and the procession resumed, this time heading west. Presumably she was going home. Kuznetsky took a chance and let the distance between himself and the Pontiac widen as they turned up Connecticut Avenue. He was right. Arriving at Amy's home, near the zoo, he saw the Pontiac park opposite her apartment building, its occupant get out on the sidewalk and light a cigarette. Kuznetsky stopped and watched. The man looked up, looked at his watch, and looked up again. As he did so the light went on in Amy's apartment. The man threw the cigarette down, causing a cascade of sparks, and got back into his car.

He drove straight toward Georgetown, down Wisconsin, and stopped in front of a seedy-looking building near the Potomac. After exchanging a few words and a laugh with the building security guard, he disappeared inside. Kuznetsky watched until a light went on in a sixth-floor window.

He got out of his car, crossed the street, and slipped into an alley that ran behind the building. In back he found the fire escape, raised out of harm's way, but managed without much difficulty to climb a drainpipe to the first floor, then took the fire escape up. At the sixth floor he forced the sash on a window overlooking the fire exit and clambered inside.

The building seemed empty; there were no sounds at all and the only visible light came out from under the door at the end of the corridor. A panel on the door announced that the office belonged to James Duncarry, Confidential Investigations.

Kuznetsky listened but could hear nothing. As far as he could tell it wasn't locked—why should it be? Slipping the Walther from his shoulder holster, he opened the door, stepped inside, and closed it behind him, all in one fluid movement. Duncarry sat behind his desk, pen in hand, a glass of whiskey in easy reach.

"What the hell . . ."

"Shut up," Kuznetsky said softly. "Let me make something crystal clear to you. If you make any unnecessary noise or movement, I will kill you. Understand?"

The man tried to look defiant but failed. He nodded.

"Couch," Kuznetsky said, gesturing with the gun. He moved across the room to where he could see both the man's side of the desk and the door.

"Well, Mr. Duncarry, tell me why you were following that woman all evening."

The detective's face visibly relaxed. "Ah shit," he said, "is that what all this is about?"

Kuznetsky searched the desk drawers. "I'm waiting," he said.

"I can't give you the name of my client. It's—"

"Would you rather give me the name of your undertaker?"

The voice was so matter-of-fact that Duncarry shivered. "This guy came in last week—"

"Name?"

"Lee. Richard Lee. He wanted me to follow this woman—his girlfriend, I guess, he didn't tell me—while he was out of town. Find out if she was sleeping around with some other guy, I guess. That's all."

"And what happened tonight?"

"She met a guy all right, and they went for a drive. Met some other car at a truck stop on the Annapolis road—he was doing some sort of deal, I guess—and then they drove right back. He didn't even take her home. That's all." He was regaining his confidence. "And what the fuck's it gotta do with you? She your sister or something? Waving guns around . . ."

"If you have to drivel, do it quietly," Kuznetsky said. The evening's events might not mean anything to Duncarry, but they'd probably mean something to Lee, whoever he was. Therefore Duncarry must not pass the information on. There seemed no way around it. Why was he looking for one? "Where are your case notes?" he asked.

"They're all on the desk."

"No file?"

"Not for this sort of job." The tone was contemptuous.

Kuznetsky put the detective's notepad in his pocket, glanced quickly through the other papers. Three more sheets followed the notepad. "We're leaving," he said.

"What? Where to?" Duncarry asked, the tremor back in his voice.

"You can tell the lady what you told me."

"Okay, okay."

They walked down the corridor toward the elevator, and as they approached the fire-escape door Kuznetsky brought the Walther down on the back of the detective's head. He opened the door and looked down into the alley six stories below. There were no lighted windows, no sign of life at all. He pulled Duncarry out and levered him over the railing and down into darkness. There was a distant thud as the body hit the ground.

Closing the door behind him, he descended the steps. At the bottom he made sure that the detective was dead, then walked back to his car. He lit a cigarette and stared out through the windshield. *The world lies heaped up on itself.* He started the engine and headed back downtown.

It was past midnight when he reached Amy's apartment. There was no light showing. It was several minutes before she responded to his soft rapping on the door, and when she did he walked straight in, holding his finger against his mouth to signal the need for silence.

She closed the door and stood with her back against it, her arms crossed over her breasts, a half-questioning, half-accusatory look on her face. One part of Kuznetsky's mind took note of how desirable she looked, sleepy-eyed, her dark hair falling across her face. The other part took charge.

"It's all right, I'm not here for your body," he said with a thin smile.

"What is it then?" she asked, inadvertently acknowledging her suspicions.

"Do you know a Richard Lee?"

She felt as if she'd just taken off in a high-speed elevator, leaving her stomach behind. "What about him?"

"Who is he?"

She shrugged. "My boyfriend, I suppose. Or I'm his mistress. Call it what you like. He knows nothing—"

"I'd call it incompetence," he said flatly, sitting down on the sofa.

Her eyes flared. "I've been working ten years in this city. You've been here less than a week. How the hell—"

"You were followed this evening," he interrupted without raising his voice.

"I thought that was the idea."

"By someone other than me."

"What?" She was astonished. "But Richard's in New Hampshire. . . ."

"He hired a private detective to make sure you weren't cheating on him."

"Oh Christ," she muttered, sitting down and pulling the dressing gown across her legs.

Kuznetsky offered her a cigarette and lit one himself. Would she accept the obvious? For some reason, he wanted to share this decision. She looked at him silently, a bleak expression etched on her face.

"When is he coming back from New Hampshire?" he asked.

"Friday, probably. He calls me up most evenings. To check up on me, I suppose," she added bitterly. "But the detective may call him there."

"He won't."

She looked at him again, an expression on her face that he couldn't read. "Faulkner said you'd be thorough."

"I do what has to be done," he said calmly. "There's no pride in it. No shame either." In his mind's eye he saw Duncarry's body plummeting down into the dark.

She didn't seem to hear. "So Richard will come back, go to collect his report, and find out the detective's been killed."

"There's a chance the police will think it's suicide. A thin chance."

"Is that a chance we can take?" she asked, looking him straight in the eye. Her voice was hard, her eyes bewildered.

"No," he said gently, replying to the eyes rather than the voice. "How long have you and he. . . ?"

"Two years, more. . . ."

"A long time." He'd known Nadezhda for half that.

"He's married. We met only once a week. He's not . . ."

"Ah." He lit another cigarette, wishing it was Russian. These American ones were like smoking thin air.

"He might not go to the police," she said. "I don't think his pride would let him admit that he'd had a woman followed. And there's his wife as well—she might find out."

"Can he risk not going? He won't know what the police have found in the detective's office."

"And Richard is suspicious," she said, almost as if she were talking to herself. "I've been away so often recently. He kept thinking it was another man, but this will make him consider other things. He's not a fool." She looked down at her bare feet, wriggled her toes. "There's no alternative, is there?" she whispered.

"No. If he's eliminated"—the word seemed curiously out of place here—"will the police come to you? How secret is your. . . ?"

"Probably," she said. She seemed calmer now that the issue was out in the open. "No one really knows, but people at work, they guessed long ago." She gave him a wintry smile. "This is the point in the movie where someone says it'll have to look like an accident," she said, taking another cigarette from his package, her hand visibly shaking. "I'm sorry," she said between puffs, "but I've never killed anyone. I think I should tell you that."

"I will do it. Do you accept that it has to be done?"

"Yes." She did. It surprised her how easy it was.

"I'll need his address. A photograph if you have one. And you'll have to find out the details of his return trip. He'll be flying, I suppose?"

"No, he hates flying. He's taking the train. He was going to call me from Union Station." She rummaged through a pile of books. "Here's a photograph. That's him," she said, pointing out a tall man in his late thirties standing at the back of the group.

"Who are the others?"

"Colleagues. It was a State Department picnic, last summer. He gave me the picture." She was businesslike now, her hands steady, her eyes devoid of expression.

He got up, feeling sorry for her, wondering why. She stood by the door, hugging herself tightly while he let himself out.

□

Rafael Soto threw the remains of his lunch into the water and started to make his way along the dockside to the empty berth. He'd spent the last hour watching the Swedish freighter inch its way through the San Carlos narrows toward Maracaibo; now it was so close that he could make out the captain's face on the bridge. Gustav Torstensson. Soto's comrade at the post office had let him see the cable, and Torstensson would soon be learning that he had an extra week for loading the mountains of coffee beans. Doubtless the Swedish crew would be pleased to discover that a fresh consignment of virgins from the interior had just been delivered to the whore-houses on the Ramblas.

Soto took up position some fifty yards from the gangplank and waited for his quarry. He had a description of Sjoberg, but it seemed to fit every seaman he could see. It didn't matter though. There wasn't a customs official in Maracaibo who wasn't willing to help for an extra peso or two.

It was several hours before the crew came ashore, and as they went through the customs shed Soto received the nod he needed. His Swedish comrade was in a group of four men, and he followed them into the town, to a restaurant in the Cathedral Square. After an hour of drinking, the visits to the lavatory began, and Soto introduced himself to Sjoberg as they stood side by side above the stagnant trough. A proper meeting was arranged for the next day.

☐

Kuznetsky watched the passengers from the Boston train stream out into the Penn Station concourse, recognized Richard Lee, and followed him into one of the bars. Richard ordered a whiskey, and from his gestures and the slight slur in his voice, Kuznetsky knew that it wasn't his first drink of the evening. He ordered one himself but didn't touch it, smoking a ciga-rette and taking occasional glances in the bar mirror at his intended victim. He had as yet no idea of how he was going to do it, but that didn't worry him. *It's for nothing that I seek something more sure than the throw of the dice.* That was one thing he hadn't needed Joszef to teach him.

Richard ordered another, looked at the clock, and swigged it down in one gulp. Good, it was the 9:30 train to Washington. Kuznetsky followed him out, across the concourse and onto the platform. As expected, Richard headed straight for the club car. He ordered another whiskey, took a seat, and picked up a used copy of *The Washington Post*. It was the previous day's copy, the one with the short report of Duncarry's demise. "Detectives investigating the case would neither confirm nor deny foul play." Very conscientious of them, Kuznetsky thought, watching Lee turn the pages.

He found the piece about Duncarry just as the train eased its way out of the station. His hands gripped the newspaper, crumpling the edges; his eyes were wide with the shock. Well cut off my legs and call me Shorty, Kuznetsky thought.

Richard quickly ordered another drink, and once he returned to his seat seemed to stare blankly out of the window, perhaps at his own reflection. Judging from what the woman had said, Kuznetsky could guess what was going through the man's mind. The detectives "admitted that they are looking into the dead investigator's recent cases." That must have given him a jolt.

The train emerged from the tunnel under the Hudson into the New Jersey night and gathered speed. Richard still sat motionless, the half-empty glass in his hand, the newspaper spread across his knees. The train rushed through Newark, its whistle shrieking, on to Philadelphia, and then out into flat open country.

Midway between Philadelphia and Baltimore, Kuznetsky went to the bar himself, less for a drink than for a look at Richard's face. The man's eyes were closed, but he wasn't sleeping, for one hand was beating an invisible tattoo on the arm rest. Kuznetsky wondered what Amy had seen in him. He was good-looking enough, but the mouth was weak, and there was something vain about the neatly trimmed mustache. He looked younger than his age, but not in a good way.

The clink of Kuznetsky's glass on the bar seemed to rouse Richard from his trance. He gulped down the rest of his drink, rose from his seat, and walked down the car toward the toilet.

Kuznetsky followed, stood outside the door listening to the sounds coming out and watching the doors for other passengers. He heard the toilet flush, saw the latch begin to move, and threw his full weight against the door, the Walther in his hand.

There was no need for it. The impact had thrown Richard back, hitting his head against something, probably the washbasin. He was out cold.

Kuznetsky examined the window. It was large enough but he couldn't get it open. It would have to be the door outside. He eased the toilet door open, found the vestibule empty, and dragged Richard out and into an upright position. Just in time. Someone passed by on his way to the club car, taking only a cursory glance at the two men standing in apparent conversation by the door.

Kuznetsky let Richard slide to the floor and jerked open the outside door. The force of the train's passage blew it back, but he managed to push the folding steps out and down, jamming it open, and then, with both arms and a leg, to scoop Richard out. For a few moments Richard's feet were trapped in the steps, his head bouncing on the rushing tracks, but then the body was gone, sucked into darkness. Kuznetsky pulled back the stairs, let the wind close the door, and stood there, his pulse racing, his mind a jumble of deaths.

eight

THE CHURCH emptied its flock as Joe and Amy drove into Scottsboro, the men in their best string ties, the women in their pastel frocks. If the coattails and the hem lines had been longer it could have been a scene from *Gone With the Wind*. There were even a few horse-drawn buggies mingling with the farm pickups and rusty Cadillacs.

Joe pulled the car up outside the realtor's house, climbed out, and walked up to the door. An elderly black woman ushered him inside. Amy examined her face in the rearview mirror; she looked as tired as she felt. This time the drive had seemed longer and felt different; this time she was leaving Washington, her family, the few friends she had forever. Soon she would be leaving America, her adopted home for more than twenty years. She would miss her uncle, James if he survived.

She wondered if Kuznetsky—she must remember to call him Smith—if he had such feelings. She couldn't make him out. He seemed a reflection of the world rather than one of its inhabitants, like a force of nature—no, like a force of the opposite, of human order. . . .

She had once read a novel, an awful novel called *Orphans of the Storm*, and, being a fourteen-year-old orphan at the time, had romantically identified herself with its title. But Kuznetsky really did seem to fit the words, he seemed to carry the storm within him, to live in it, to deal it out in controlled bursts. And that was why, she realized, she felt no fear of him. There was nothing irrational in his actions, nothing at all. He would succeed in this operation or die trying, would kill or die without hesitation.

She could see Joe through the window talking to the realtor. Why was he taking so long? He'd hardly spoken during the long journey and seemed to have lost his cockiness. She guessed that he'd suddenly realized that it wasn't a game, that the master plan might go wrong, that the Feds he so despised might strap *him* into an electric chair. But he would come through, she was sure. His pride wouldn't let him back out. It was a pity that such determination should be wasted on such a twisted morality.

And you? she asked the mirror. *Where are you going?* What would the Soviet Union be like? Once she had longed to see Moscow, Leningrad, the other side, her side, but now she felt almost indifferent. The thought of a new life seemed unreal, anticlimatic, not so much a beginning as an end.

Joe came out of the house, keys in hand, and climbed back behind the wheel.

"What took you so long?" she asked.

"He wouldn't stop talking. Nothing important."

An hour later they reached the lodge, and while he unloaded the supplies they'd brought from Washington, she lit the wood stove and made coffee. But by the time it was ready she found him fast asleep on one of the bunks. She drank her own cup, smoked a cigarette, and stared at the three shiny tommy guns leaning against a wall. She felt more tired than sleepy, and after concealing the guns under a bunk, went outside.

It wasn't so hot under the trees, and she found herself walking farther and farther along the side of the ridge, taking a sensual pleasure in the play of colors, the panoramic views, and the feel of the forest floor. After half a mile or so she spotted a clear green pool in a hollow below and walked down to it through the pines. Looking at the water, she felt twice as sticky. "Why not?" she murmured to herself, looking around to make sure that the silent pines were the only witnesses. She stripped off her clothes, piled them on a rock, and waded into the water. It was only a few feet deep at the pool's center, and for several minutes she floated on her back, wallowing in the delicious coolness.

Lying on the rock to dry herself, she felt a sexual tremble run through her body. She touched herself, at first tentatively, then with a pleasure she had not known for years. His face was clear in her mind, the ivory light shining in through the porthole, the feeling of not knowing where the one ended and the other began.

She opened her eyes. Physically satisfied, she had never felt so alone. The trees towered over her, both graceful and threatening. She sat up, feeling suddenly cold, tears gathering in the corners of her eyes.

☐

Joe was awake when she got back to the lodge, seeming more like his normal self. Perhaps he'd just been tired.

"Where are the guns?" he asked. "Found a swimming pool, I see," he added, noticing her wet hair.

"Under the bed in the middle room, and yes," she said, brushing past him. "I'm going to try and sleep now."

"If you hear gunfire, it'll be me testing them," he called after her.

She took the room farthest from his and lay down, feeling tired and confused. The tiredness triumphed, and when he woke her the light had gone and the lodge was full of the smell of cooking. "Just some canned goods," he said as she entered the kitchen. "I didn't see anything to shoot."

"The guns are okay?"

"Yep."

They ate in silence, and washed down the meal with strong coffee. "Do you play checkers?" he asked. She nodded and got up to wash the dishes while he set up the board. They played several games, and he won all but the last. She was convinced he'd lost it on purpose, a thought that almost brought back the tears. What was the matter with her? She suddenly had a picture of jailers playing such a game with the man in the condemned cell, the man feeling sorry for the jailers. It was too much. She had to be alone, physically alone.

He watched her leave the room and felt slightly worried. The whole business was obviously getting to her. He'd hated the idea of working with a woman from the beginning, but had reluctantly conceded to himself that in her case he'd been wrong. She knew what she was doing, and until now she'd shown no trace of nerves at all. Perhaps she needed some comforting, physical comforting. She wasn't his type—he preferred women with more flesh on them—but . . .

He knocked softly on her door, put his head around it. "Don't suppose you want some company?" he asked softly.

"No," she replied coldly. "Thank you," she added more gently, "but no."

"Just thought I'd ask," he said cheerfully. "Sleep well."

He lit a cigarette and went outside. Her part was almost over in any case. He and the Germans would do the rest—give all those fucking Yankee liberals a jolt they'd never forget. Two more days.

□

And then, as I stand up, the stars and the Great Bear glimmer up there like bars above a silent cell. The poem was beginning to haunt him, to follow him around like a running commentary on his life. *In the goods station yard I flattened myself against the foot of the tree like a slice of silence. . . .* Well, that had been a Hungarian goods station yard, not this one. There were no trees in this one, no *gray weeds . . . lustrous, dew-laden coal lumps.*

Kuznetsky had checked into the hotel in Bridgeport late that evening and been given, without knowing it, the same room Joe and Amy had used for their earlier vigil. He'd walked down to the station, awakened the sleeping clerk to inquire about the next day's trains, and familiarized himself with the layout of the yard. A tree would have been useful, but the decrepit boxcar in the siding adjoining the main line would serve the same purpose. Everything seemed as Amy had reported it.

Now, back in his room, he sat by the window, staring across at the darkened yard, wishing he had a Russian cigarette. He thought he could detect the first hint of moonlight; five days hence it would be earlier, making this end of the operation harder, but the other end easier. *The cat can't catch mice inside and outside at the same time.* True. And somewhat facile in this context. It was time he got some sleep.

Next morning he took his car in for a final checkup, arranged to collect it that evening, and walked down to the station. Waiting for his train, he again checked the layout of the yard, measuring distances in his mind, calculating the safest angle of approach.

The train was on time, a good omen, and almost empty. A group of boys in uniform, presumably on their last leave before going overseas, were good-naturedly pestering a solitary young woman. She seemed to be enjoying the attention. Kuznetsky took a window seat and set out to memorize the route. For half an hour they chugged down the valley, mountains to the right, the river occasionally visible several miles away to the left. The train stopped at every country junction, though no one seemed to get on or off. The conductor inspected his ticket, tried in vain to start up a conversation about some circus fire in Connecticut, and took out his irritation on one of the young soldiers who'd had the temerity to soil the upholstery with a dirty boot.

After stopping in Scottsboro, the train climbed away from the main valley and up into the hills. It stopped in Larkinsville but not at Lim Rock, which looked like a ghost town. A few minutes later it passed the point where the old mining spur diverged, and Kuznetsky had a brief glimpse of the narrow Coon Creek Valley stretching north toward a high ridge.

Thirty-five minutes later the train pulled into Huntsville. Kuznetsky got off, had some lunch, and spent several hours sitting on a park bench with nothing but his thoughts. He remembered how, when he'd first lived with Russians, their slowness, their ability to sit doing nothing for hours, had infuriated him, partly because they could, partly because he couldn't. Since arriving back in America he'd had the opposite sensation: everyone seemed so impatient, so determined to be doing things, so incapable of just being. It was sad. Amusing as well.

He walked back toward the station and was about to cross the road outside when a familiar black Buick cruised past. He and Amy exchanged indifferent glances.

□

Amy felt relief at seeing Kuznetsky. She had no doubts about his efficiency, but it was still good to be certain that he was around. That morning she'd suddenly imagined his being killed in some ridiculous accident and Joe coming back to the lodge with the Germans. What would she do then?

She checked in the mirror to see that the camper Joe was driving was still following her as she took the Scottsboro road. Everything was going so smoothly, it was almost too good to be true. She and Joe had spent the day driving to and from Birmingham, where they had picked up the camper, complete with fishing rods, hunting rifles, and enough food for a businessmen's sporting holiday. Unknown to Joe, Amy had also been checking out their eventual escape route, making sure that there would be no unexpected impediments to their flight. According to the radio, some bridges along the route had collapsed in the summer storms, but the road to Birmingham was clear.

They arrived back at the lodge as the last rays of the sun cleared the ridge, and Joe started preparing supper. He obviously enjoyed cooking, if only from cans. Amy pulled some water up from the well and washed herself. In thirty-six hours the Germans would be here.

"Where are you headed when it's over?" Joe asked.

"Back to Washington."

"It'll be a bit tame after this, won't it?"

"Joe, what are *you* in this for?" She hadn't meant to ask, hadn't wanted to know, but the question came out just the same.

He stirred the corned-beef hash thoughtfully. "Funny you should ask that," he said finally. "Don't get me wrong—I believe in the German cause, but it doesn't take a genius to realize that they've lost this war. Maybe what we're doing will change things, but to be honest, I doubt it. It's a mixture, I guess. Idealism, adventure, getting my own back . . ."

"Own what?"

"My family used to own a farm up the valley, near Louden. It wasn't big, but it was beautiful. My folks just lived their life, hell, my pa was even good to the niggers, lot of good it did him. Then one day, just like that, man from Washington knocked on the door. It was 1935. Told us that in a coupla years time our land would be at the bottom of a lake. Nothing we could do about it. Pa just gave up, died rather than see the land drowned. And Ma died because she couldn't live without him. Government killed them both, men in Washington who didn't give a damn about people."

Amy couldn't think of anything to say.

"And you?" he asked.

"I'm a German."

"Yeah, but there's a lot of Germans fighting for the U.S. of A."

"Not *real* Germans."

"Maybe."

"And my father died in the first war."

"Where?"

"Tannenberg."

"It must be worse dying in a battle that your side's won."

"I doubt if he knew."

"No, I meant for the relatives. Seems more of a waste somehow. Crazy, I know. Tannenberg was a fascinating battle. . . ." He went on to discuss the merits of Ludendorff's strategy, stirring the hash, completely oblivious to the fact that Amy might find the topic distressing.

She wasn't even listening. He died rather than see the land drowned. She couldn't understand a person feeling like that. She'd lived in big cities all her life. She looked at Joe, suddenly seeing him as a farm boy in city clothes. They shared a need for revenge if nothing else.

After supper they played checkers again, but this time she didn't win a single game and there was no tap on her bedroom door. She lay in bed and tried to consciously relive the past, those dreadful nights in Berlin that now seemed so long ago. But the anger that had lain so long so close to the surface had either burrowed deeper or been eroded by time; she wasn't sure which. Images of Effi kept interrupting her thoughts, images of her as a seven-year-old, happy, laughing, running through the Tiergarten with her socks around her ankles and one pigtail half-unraveled.

☐

Forty miles up the valley, on the stroke of midnight, Kuznetsky called the number in Washington.

"Yes?" the voice asked.

"American Rose."

"Melville says that train will do fine."

He put back the receiver, walked along the corridor to tell the night clerk that he wanted an early call. Tomorrow— no, today—he would kill Joe Markham. *Only what will be is a flower, what is crumbles into fragments.*

☐

By midmorning Joe was driving the Buick south toward Atlanta. He knew the road well, having spent two vacations visiting the old battlefields where Johnston had fought his brilliant rearguard campaign against the butcher Sherman. Kennesaw Mountain, Marietta, Peach Tree Creek—rolls of glory reflected in the road signs. Confederate flags still fluttered on flagstaffs in the gardens of suburban Atlanta.

He didn't feel the slightest bit nervous or tense, which surprised him. This was by far the most dangerous part of the operation; it needed only one pair of unwelcome eyes to spot the surfacing U-boat and the FBI would be pouring into Georgia like Sherman's army. But Rosa had said the spot was well-chosen, and she hadn't been wrong yet. She was quite amazing, though about as human as a block of ice. He wondered how the man in New York had found her. Or had she found him? Not that it mattered.

Beyond Atlanta he followed Sherman's route to the sea. He imagined the smoldering barns, the blazing fields, the women raped in the plantation mansions while the torches were laid. But he had to admit that militarily it had been a brilliant move. If Lee had shown such ruthlessness, things would have been different. Might have been, anyway.

The Buick purred onward. He loved driving, was proud of his skill behind the wheel. In his late teens he'd entered dirt-road car races as far away as Memphis and won quite a few of them. Trouble was, there were too many kids who didn't care whether they lived or died, and though you could outlive them, they were hard to beat. He'd never been able to understand kids like that, kids who just ignored the odds.

Savannah lifted his spirits with its beautiful buildings. It was how a city should look. He stopped by the old harbor, checked his watch and odometer. Just over four hundred miles in under nine hours, and Rosa had been worried he'd be late! He had a doughnut and coffee in an empty diner and took to the road again. Another sixty miles.

At Richmond Hill he took out the map she'd marked and perched it on the dashboard. Turning off the main highway, he followed the route toward the coast, crossing the long trestle bridge that connected the mainland to Ossabaw Island. There was hardly anything on the road, and the island's only town boasted few vehicles or people. The final stretch of road to the sea was hardly a road at all. The coastline was an unspoiled wilderness, heavily vegetated low cliffs and a rocky beach pummeled by the Atlantic waves.

He parked the Buick under the trees and took the signal lamp out of the trunk. The sun had almost set; there were four hours to wait. He clambered down the cliff and settled himself in a comfortable niche between two large rocks. Remembering the extra doughnut in his pocket, he devoured it with relish, the jelly oozing out over his fingers. Still feeling stiff after the day's driving, he lifted himself out of the niche and went to wash his hands in a tidal pool. Leaning forward to splash his face, he caught a momentary glimpse of a shadow crossing the sky before the bullet exploded through his brain, knocking his body forward into its reflection.

☐

Kuznetsky dragged Joe's body out of the pool, across the rocks and up the bluff. Markham wasn't heavy but it was still hard work. At the top he stopped to get his breath back, then pulled the body through the trees, past Markham's car, and well into the woods. Then he returned for the car and brought it forward to the same spot. He got into the backseat and fired a single shot through the windshield above the steering wheel, hoisted Markham's body into the front seat with the head pushed down on the wheel, resisting the temptation to close the staring eyes. After checking the car's visibility from twenty yards away, he lightly camouflaged the chrome bumper with vegetation. He looked again and was satisfied. Anyone looking for it would find it, but it was unlikely to be found by accident.

It was quite dark now, and he had some difficulty in picking out the spot where he'd concealed his own car. He moved it out of the trees and onto the flattened area where the road reached the cliff. Judging by the empty bottles littering its perimeter, he guessed it was used as a picnic area.

He next eased the crate out of the backseat and carried it across to Markham's car. There he jimmied it open and, using his weight, cracked one of the sides in half. It looked convincing enough, provided that Matson's description of the uranium crates was accurate.

Clambering back down to the beach, he took up position in the niche Markham had found. It was a quarter past eight—three and a half hours still to go. He lit a Lucky Strike, leaned back against the rock, and inhaled deeply. He'd killed three men in America, two he'd never even spoken to, but his conscience remained untroubled. He supposed that most people would consider Duncarry and Lee innocent victims, but as far as he was concerned, innocence had vanished with mass newspapers and the radio. No one could claim innocence anymore. Except children and animals perhaps. Everyone else had been free to choose sides, consciously or not.

The evening star was sinking toward the ocean. He guessed it would be dawn in the Russian forest, wondered if Nadezhda was still faithful to him. The thought didn't disturb him; if she wasn't, it wouldn't change anything.

He sat up suddenly, listening to the sound of an approaching car, then ran nimbly across the rocks to the base of the low cliff, watching the light from the car's headlamps illuminating the air above the rim, and flattened himself against an outcrop.

He heard a door open, the last indistinct words of a conversation. Footsteps walking toward the cliff's edge, a silhouetted figure above him appearing and disappearing.

"Who the fuck is it?" It was a young voice, a boy of fifteen, sixteen.

"No one local. It's got D.C. plates." A young girl, a Georgia peach of an accent.

"Shit."

"C'mon, Jeff, there's no sense in gettin' fired up. Let's go somewhere else."

"Like where?"

A giggle. "Well, we can't do it here, can we?"

"I'll flatten the bastard. This is *our* place."

"There might be more than one of them."

"Umm."

"C'mon, I've got to be home by ten."

"Okay, okay."

The footsteps receded, car doors slammed, a revving motor. The headlamps drew a circle of light as the car turned and headed back inland. Kuznetsky put his gun in the shoulder holster. What had he been thinking about children and animals? If they'd found the other car . . . He hoped they were the only young couple who thought they owned this trysting place.

But there were no other interruptions as the hour hand on his watch crept slowly forward. At 11:30 he started flashing the signal lamp at five-minute intervals, straining his eyes for a sight of the submarine. Several times he thought he glimpsed a periscope slightly to the north, but it must have been something else for, at precisely a quarter to midnight and directly ahead, U-107 broke surface with disconcerting abruptness. He flashed the light again, and thought he could glimpse figures climbing down from the conning tower onto the hull.

☐

Breitner and Russman shook hands with the captain and launched the inflatable raft. Paul eased himself in and held it fast for Breitner to follow. Conscious of the U-boat descending behind them, they paddled for the shore, a dark wall that gradually resolved itself into a forested line of cliffs. The light blinked again and they shifted direction toward it.

"There's not many who're going to be able to say that they took part in the Wehrmacht's invasion of America," Gerd whispered.

"Or the strategic withdrawal."

"Optimist."

When they were nearly there they could see the man waiting on the rocks. He waded out into the surf to help them beach the dinghy and indicated that they should follow him. He'd dug a hole for their boat and all three shoveled the sand back in on top of it.

"The clothes will do," he said after looking them over. "I'm Jack Smith. Call me Jack," Kuznetsky said in English.

"Gerd Breitner, and this is Paul Russman," Gerd said, holding out his hand. The stranger's grip was brief but strong.

"My German's not very good," Kuznetsky said, "but we speak English only from this moment in any case."

"Understood."

Kuznetsky led them up the cliff to the car. Gerd took the seat beside him, Paul the back. As they drove inland Paul watched the strange shapes of the foreign trees silhouetted against the sky. Here they were, he thought, casually driving through the American night, two officers in an army that was losing battles almost everywhere else. The whole business was absurd. Daring, perhaps, but if the Führer and his friends hadn't yet learned that daring had its limits, then they were even madder than he'd thought.

Paul looked at the back of the stranger's head. Who the hell was he? An Abwehr agent obviously, but he wasn't a German. What reasons could any non-German have for supporting the Nazi cause? There were enough Germans with doubts. He didn't suppose it mattered—the man seemed to know what he was doing. There was an air of authority about him that was almost chilling. And most un-American. Paul closed his eyes and listened to the purr of the car.

He was awakened by a prod from Gerd. They had stopped outside a hotel. Kuznetsky handed him a collection of documents: driver's license, military deferment, there were about ten of them. "Memorize them," he said.

"Where are we?" Paul asked.

"Savannah," Gerd replied.

"We're staying the night here," Kuznetsky said.

He led them into the hotel, where rooms had already been booked. A sleepy clerk showed them up, explaining that he got a tip for carrying the luggage even if there wasn't any. "It's the principle," he said. Kuznetsky gave him one, pointed the two Germans into one room and disappeared into the other.

They didn't bother to undress. "Very strange," Paul murmured, looking down from the window at the empty street.

"*Ja*. Yeah."

"Very good. And him?" Paul indicated the next room.

"We're here."

"He's not what I expected. He's no amateur." He lay back on the bed. "I wonder how he's avoided the Army."

"Too old," Gerd answered. "The Americans have still got some young men to spare."

"It feels really strange wearing these clothes. Do you know how long it is since we were out of uniform?"

"Too long, Paul. Go to sleep."

□

It was a blazing hot morning, the heat of Africa wrapped in a clammy Georgian blanket. Paul was glad to see that their driver was sweating as profusely as he was, and that he'd had the sense to place a case of beer on the backseat.

Smith didn't say much though. They learned that he'd had military experience in South America and Spain, but beyond such bare facts he offered nothing. He refused to discuss the operation until the fourth member of the unit—a strange name for it, Paul thought—was present.

148

"We have to know everything each other knows," Kuznetsky said.

They asked him about the fourth member. He was a she. A German woman who'd lived twenty years in America. It was at this moment that Paul wondered if it were possible, only to dismiss the idea as ridiculous. She would never fight for Hitler's Germany. "How old is she?" he asked.

"About thirty-five."

That fit. But it couldn't be. "What's her name?" he asked.

"Rosa, as far as we're concerned."

Rosa. She'd had a doll called Rosa. "Is she attractive?"

"I suppose so. Why do you ask?"

There seemed no reason not to explain. "I knew a German girl who lived in America. She'd be about that age now. Just curiosity. It couldn't be the same woman."

"Why not?"

Was he imagining it, or was there an edge in Smith's voice? "She had no reason to help Germany, rather the opposite."

"What did she look like?"

"Slim, dark-haired, a lovely face. Full of life." It was funny, he could see her so clearly, even after all these years.

"Amy," Paul murmured.

☐

Kuznetsky could hardly believe his ears. His mind raced. How could this have happened, how could something so vital have been ignored? Question followed question. When had they known each other? How much did he know about her—was her cover blown? The German might be talking about a chance meeting at a party when they'd both been in America. He might be talking about a love affair lasting months. He knew she had "no reason to help Germany." What did he know? Christ, what a mess.

What could he do? There was no way of warning her—they'd just come face to face at the lodge. He'd have to play it off the cuff. But could he and she do it on their own? He unconsciously tightened his grip on the steering wheel.

"She is slim and dark-haired," he said, measuring his words. "I wouldn't say she was—what did you say?—full of life. But people change. It could be the same woman. But there are a lot of Germans in this country who support Germany without loving the Führer. How well did you know her?"

"Oh, I don't know. We knew each for only a few days. A long time ago. 1933."

"Not a memorable year," the other German said ironically.

Kuznetsky breathed an inner sigh of relief. That was before her recruitment; the German couldn't know anything specific. But . . . if there was one complication they hadn't needed, it was something like this. He wondered how she'd react. Coldly, he supposed. The death of a current lover hadn't seemed to upset her that much, and eleven years was enough to kill off any emotion, certainly anything generated by a few days' romance. If that's what it had been. And what else could it have been? He pulled the car off the highway and drew up outside a diner.

"Lunch," he said calmly.

nine

AMY spent the morning trying to read, and constantly found her mind wandering off in other directions. The tension in her body seemed to grow by the minute, and she doubted if the endless cups of coffee were helping. She felt like a real drink, but Joe had sensibly decided against bringing any.

She crushed out her cigarette, retrieved one of the tommy guns from their hiding place, and walked west along the lee side of the ridge. Under the trees it was cool, and even on the stretches of open ground the breeze made the heat bearable, even pleasant. She passed above the pool feeling no communion with the woman who had lain there two days before. Her body today felt like an alien attachment, just a means of transport for her mind.

After she'd walked a mile from the road, she unslung the gun from her shoulder, took aim at a line of hickory trees, and fired a short burst. The gun was a good one; the action was smooth, the recoil minimal, and it was not as loud as she'd expected. Her marksmanship was good too; she'd always been an excellent shot. Three of the trees had been hit, and at an even height. If there turned out to be a need for her to use the gun, there'd be no problem.

She walked back to the cabin slowly, feeling more relaxed than she had. A few more hours and they'd be here. Two

German officers, two of her fellow countrymen. She hoped they'd be SS, real Nazis.

The afternoon dragged. She lit the stove, mixed a stew from an assortment of cans, and left it to simmer. Then she sat by the window, staring at the forested ridges receding into the haze. This is it, she told herself, the moment of commitment. From today there would be no turning back, no more choices. The thought comforted her. No more choices. And no more deception. The debt would be paid in full.

The light had begun to fade when she heard the approaching car. She walked out front, shielding her eyes from the glare of the setting sun. Her first concern was the driver, and she felt immediate relief on seeing Kuznetsky's profile behind the wheel. The German in the front got out, then the one in the back, and her heart did a somersault. Eighty million Germans to choose from and they'd sent *him*.

Her heart thumped, her mind whirled. She had just a few seconds to change her story—he would never believe she was a simple German patriot. With an enormous effort, she propelled her legs forward out of the shadow to greet them.

"Hello, Paul," she said quietly.

"It *is* you," he said. "It's been a long time."

"Eleven years," she said automatically, suddenly conscious of the expression on Kuznetsky's face. He knew, was hanging back, waiting for her cue. Oh God. "Let's get inside," she said cheerfully, turning back toward the door. "There's some food almost ready," she called back, disappearing into the kitchen and praying that he wouldn't follow. He didn't. She heard Kuznetsky showing them their rooms.

The shock was wearing off slowly, ever so slowly. After all, the number of Germans of his age with the necessary experience of America was bound to be limited—it shouldn't have been such a surprise. And she'd been anti-American even when she knew him. That would have to do: patriotism and anti-Americanism outweighing her hatred of the Nazis. It was thin, but what reason would he have to doubt it? She was here. Eleven years was a long time; she could have changed. She had changed, if not in that direction.

What would Kuznetsky be thinking? First Richard, now this. Hearing footsteps, she turned, thinking it was him, but it was the other German. "Gerd Breitner," he said, offering his hand. "We weren't introduced." They shook hands, and he ambled over to inspect the stew on the stove. "Smells good," he said. "Anything would smell good after four weeks in a U-boat. Rather a surprise, yes?" he added.

She knew what he meant. "Yes, it is."

He looked at her with a steady, not unfriendly gaze. "For a moment I thought Paul had seen a ghost."

She returned his gaze. "We were close once. Things got in the way. I never thought I'd see him again, and I suppose he thought the same. But," she continued, turning away to stir the pot, "it won't make any difference to the operation. It was all a long time ago."

"Eleven years," he muttered.

The four of them ate at the trestle table. The two Germans talked incessantly to each other, Kuznetsky said nothing, and Amy concentrated on feeding a nonexistent appetite. As soon as they were finished she cleared the dishes away and disappeared into the kitchen, refusing any assistance.

She returned to find Kuznetsky placing a large map across the table. He went through the plan, first running through the intended chain of events, then the emergency procedures devised to cover conceivable failures. He showed the Germans the photographs of the train and Coon Creek Valley, produced a diagram he'd drawn of the attack itself. Tomorrow they would see the valley for themselves.

"There can be no survivors," he said impassively. "The train will be missed at Huntsville, that's one hour. They won't be able to contact Scottsboro or Bridgeport, that's another. If they start looking immediately, they could find it in one more. That's three hours. We won't be a third of the way to the coast, and if anyone's alive to identify us or the vehicles, we'll never reach it." He looked questioningly at the two Germans.

"Agreed," Gerd said grimly.

Paul said nothing, but gave an infinitesimal nod.

"Delivery," Kuznetsky continued. "Rosa—Amy—and I will take the crates in the camper. A woman will arouse less suspicion, and as an American I'm the best qualified to deal with any unforeseen trouble. You two will take the car. We'll take different routes"—he indicated them on the map—"and meet at Ossabaw Island the following evening."

"So we're just here for the shooting," Gerd said.

"You're here as soldiers. Any suggestions?"

"No, it seems tight enough."

"Are you coming back with us?" Paul asked, not looking at Amy. "We weren't told, and neither was the U-boat captain."

"Not unless something goes wrong. We plan to be back here next morning, continuing our vacation," Kuznetsky said, treating them to a rare smile.

Paul turned to find Amy looking at him. He held her gaze for a second. She broke the contact, saying she'd make some more coffee. He watched her carry the bucket out to the well, thought of following and decided not to. Since seeing her, since hearing in the car that it might be her, he'd been experiencing an apparently inexhaustible variety of emotions. She was as beautiful as ever, he thought, but harder, much harder, at least on the surface. Yet she didn't want to look him in the eye.

He wanted to tell her about the letters, but this obviously wasn't the time. There probably never would be a good time. The past was better left as it was. They'd both changed, and though he knew it was unjustified, he couldn't help feeling a deep resentment. He wished she'd been anyone else, leaving his memories intact, unsullied.

☐

Amy and Kuznetsky sat on the only chairs; Gerd had found the checkerboard and played with Paul, the two of them sitting against the wall with the board between them on the floor. Two oil lamps were burning but the light was still dim, and the room seemed full of moving shadows.

Amy was trying her novel again, but every now and then she couldn't resist a glance across at Paul, who was sitting, purposely she guessed, with his face turned away from her. He seemed so unchanged in some ways: there was still the physical reticence complementing the withdrawn eyes, the feeling that he was watching the world rather than taking part in it. There'd been flashes of the old sense of humor, the thread of irony that seemed to run through most of his utterances. His companion's too. The boy was still there in the man.

But there'd been one change, one that was both subtle and all-embracing. Each of the characteristics seemed to have been exaggerated: the eyes were more withdrawn, the humor more bitterly manic, as if the parts of his being were straining at each other, as if the boy and the man were finding it harder to get along with each other.

His partner was quieter, more watchful. He seemed as diffident as Paul, but she knew he was taking in everything. Gerd had noticed her glances at Paul. Physically he was heavier set, but in some manner he reminded her of a big cat; there was the same blend of self-confidence and constant wariness. And she could almost feel the protective mantle he threw around Paul. In fact the relationship between them seemed almost symbiotic. She felt a twinge of jealousy, then laughed at herself for being ridiculous.

Kuznetsky was doing nothing, just sitting there smoking cigarettes and staring into space. "I'm going to bed," she announced, getting up. "Sleep well," Gerd said. Kuznetsky and Paul said nothing.

"Where've you seen combat?" Kuznetsky asked after she was gone.

"Almost everywhere," Paul said, moving one of the black pieces.

"France, the East, Africa," Gerd answered.

"Where in the East? I've taken a particular interest in the Russian campaign."

"So have we," Paul muttered.

"The march to Moscow. Almost to Moscow. Kharkov, Kursk, Vitebsk."

"Which division?"

"Seventh Panzer."

"The Ghost Division."

Paul looked up. "Yes," he said ironically. "Nothing but ghosts now."

Extraordinary, Kuznetsky thought. The four people in this lodge, like intertwining threads of the twentieth century. First her and the German, now this. They'd fought in the very division his Siberians had faced on the northern outskirts of Moscow in the last days of 1941. Wonderful, terrible days, when every mile recovered had contained a thousand frozen German corpses, when everyone knew that Hitler had been halted in his tracks. It had felt like spring, a blood-soaked frozen spring. Each morning the drop in the temperature had been announced, and his Siberian troops had cheered, knowing that each degree colder would kill another division of the Nazis.

And yet the Germans had fought on, most of them still clothed in denim, many of them half-crippled with frostbite. It had been pathetic, wonderful, beyond reason, beyond humanity. And these two had been through it. He'd known before they answered. It showed in their faces, seeped out through their humor. *I have heard the iron weep.* In those days there'd been nothing else to hear.

☐

"Lovely day," Gerd said, stopping by the window to examine the view. Outside, he could see Smith giving the vehicles a final check.

"It'll get a lot hotter," Amy said. She turned to Paul, the list in her hand. "Right, what's your name?"

"Paul Jablonsky."

"Date of birth?"

"August 5, 1908. Milwaukee, Wisconsin."

"Army record?"

"One Hundred and Thirty-fourth Division. Purple Heart and medical discharge after Battle of Kasserine."

"Present employer?"

"General Motors. War production consultant."

"That'll do."

"Am I married?"

"No."

"I wonder why."

"You never found the girl of your dreams, perhaps."

"Or found her and lost her."

Kuznetsky came in at an opportune moment. "Everything's ready."

He drove, Paul beside him, Gerd and Amy in the back. There was nothing on the road down the mountain; between Lim Rock and the valley they passed only two trucks. Paul had forgotten how vast America was, remembered Schellenberg's remark about empty territory, which no longer seemed quite so absurd.

They drove up the narrow, claustrophobic valley, stopping just short of the trestle bridge. "It's going to be very dark," said Paul to no one in particular.

"Our eyes will get accustomed," Gerd said.

"Yeah." Paul walked across to the area assigned to him, imagined the train pulling to a halt, the doors opening. . . . Another graveyard. The place reminded him of one of those narrow valleys in the Ukraine—where had it been. . . ?

"Outside Rzhavets," Gerd said, reading his mind.

"The day I drove the T-34," Paul said, smiling.

"The day you *tried* to drive a T-34," Gerd corrected him. Paul didn't respond. He was looking at Amy, sitting on her haunches by the side of the stream, noting the vivid contrast between the raven hair and the cream blouse.

"Memories," Gerd murmured.

Paul wasn't sure whether he was referring to the T-34 or her. "This is going to work," he said thoughtfully.

Gerd grunted. "Seems almost too easy. Someone in Washington's going to suffer," he added. "And deserves to."

"We've still got to get home, and the problems won't end when we reach the U-boat. *If* we reach it. They'll be scouring the Atlantic for weeks."

"Big ocean."

"The approaches to the ports aren't so big."

"Well, one step at a time."

They walked back to the car, where Kuznetsky was already waiting. Amy followed, carrying a posy of small white flowers in her hand. Flowers from a graveyard, Paul thought with a shudder.

☐

At the end of the lodge road the two Germans got out, and Smith wished them good luck with one of his rare smiles and drove himself and Amy off toward Scottsboro. Paul and Gerd ambled along the track, the former engrossed in his own thoughts, the latter wondering how to broach the subject. Straightforwardly, he decided.

"How does it feel to see her again?"

Paul grunted. "How indeed?"

"Why did you never mention her? You've talked enough about other women."

"Good question." He kicked a stone into the undergrowth. "The one I've been asking myself in a way. What made her so special? Gerd, this sounds crazy, but maybe first love really doesn't die. Or maybe it was just the time. It was 1933, and I was coming back to Germany, a different Germany, and my father was dying—it felt like a moment between two lives. We met on the ship, had three wonderful days together, and then never saw each other again. . . ."

"Why not?"

"Oh, a series of accidents really. It doesn't matter. What I'm trying to say is that we, the two of us, those few days, they seemed—not at the time but afterward—as if they'd existed outside normal time, as if they had nothing to do with this world. Again, it sounds crazy, but it was like a moment of innocence—of *adult* innocence—and everything since has semed corrupt in comparison. . . ."

"Not only in comparison."

"True. And she and I were outside all that."

"But no longer. I'm sorry, my friend."

"So am I. Maybe she is too."

□

"And you never saw each other again," Kuznetsky repeated. "Regrets?"

"At the time."

"Now?"

"No." She didn't want to talk about it with him, because all he cared about was whether it would affect the operation. And it wouldn't. The Germans would be left for the FBI to pick up as planned, and that was that. Her feelings were irrelevant. But . . . it was cruel. She felt as if she was being tested, tempted almost, as if some malicious fate had decided to find the one person she'd least like to sacrifice. . . .

They drove through Scottsboro. She looked at the bunch of white flowers on the dashboard, already beginning to wither in the heat. "Are you married?" she asked Kuznetsky.

"In a way," he said. "What's the old word? 'Betrothed.' " He smiled at some unspoken thought, looking for a moment almost vulnerable. What a life he must have led, she thought. Or was she just romanticizing?

"Tell me about the Soviet Union."

He was silent for a while. "It's a place where the present hardly exists," he said finally. "The past and the future are both very real, but the present—you have to steal it piece by piece."

She hadn't expected this somehow. "Where do you live, before the war I mean?"

"In a lot of ways we hardly noticed the war. There was no one moment when peace turned into war. There's been no real peace since Kirov was shot, ten years ago. I've lived all over, wherever my work was."

"I don't think you can have been a propagandist."

He smiled. "You don't hear people saying how wonderful breathing is. It depends on what inspires you. We have crammed two hundred years of development into twenty, and most of it will have to be done all over again when the war ends. All the children have schools, there are no famines, everyone has work and purpose, sometimes too much work. You should go to Siberia. There the past is weakest, the future strongest. And it's beautiful, beautiful beyond imagining."

"Moscow?"

"Just another city."

Another country boy. But she felt like a child with this man. He couldn't be more than ten years older than she, but it was like what she'd always imagined talking with a father would be like. Stern, distant, wise, sure of himself, above all, sure of himself. The way adults were supposed to be, the way so few seemed to be.

They were coming into Bridgeport. He stopped a block down from the hotel and got out. "Take care driving back," he said as she slipped across behind the wheel. "I'll see you later."

"Good luck," she said, not sure that he'd consider luck relevant.

He was already walking away, turning into the shambling bear once more. She turned the car and headed back out of town. It was four o'clock—nine hours to go. She'd often wondered how soldiers felt waiting to make an attack and now she knew—a mixture of impatience, terror, and curiosity.

And in nine hours she'd say good-bye to Paul again. Siberia, she'd go to Siberia, where the past was weaker.

☐

At ten o'clock Kuznetsky put a call through to a hotel in Knoxville. The telephone rang only once. "How is Rosa's uncle?" he asked.

"Fine. She took the train this evening."

"And her cousin?"

"I'll be seeing him tonight."

"Good."

He went back up to the familiar room, studied the yard through Markham's binoculars for the last time, and then hid them under the mattress, taking care to leave the cord visible. He left by the fire escape and followed the preplanned route through the darkened back streets and alleys to the perimeter of the freight yard. There was no sign of life. He climbed through the rail fencing, under a couple of Pullman cars, and found himself forty yards from the solitary boxcar. Still nothing. He darted across the open space and took up position underneath it. It was 10:20. If everything went well, they'd be at sea in just over twenty-four hours.

Kuznetsky felt intense relief at the thought. Was it only two weeks ago that he'd been considering espionage one of the lesser forms of endeavor? Well, he'd be glad to get back to where the enemy wore a different uniform and openly challenged you. Deception was a tiring business, and, he thought, probably as self-damaging as anything he'd ever done. He didn't know how Amy had held herself together all those years. With people like Richard Lee, he supposed. And a capacity for self-delusion.

The noises of the town slowly died down and the lights finally went out on Main Street. It must be the war—Friday nights in St. Cloud had never been so quiet. He had a fleeting image of Nadezhda at a barn dance, smiled to himself in the gloom. America! So much energy so ill-directed. He was glad he'd come back, glad he'd seen the Minnesota plains again. It seemed like an end, a welcome end. The war would soon be over, and they could start to build again, this time with the people as one. Taming the wildernesses, the one outside and the ones within.

He heard the sound of a car approaching. He mentally ran through the sequence of events Amy had written out, watching the state troopers, both of them this time, walking across to the depot. He heard the rap on the door, the greetings, a laugh. The lights went on, brighter than he'd expected. Three men came out, lit cigarettes, and gazed hopefully down the track. The train was late. They sat down on the edge of a loading platform, their voices sounding unnaturally loud in the overall silence.

Then the toot of a whistle, the distant chuffing of the engine. Kuznetsky watched it pull around the curve into the station and stop at the predicted place. *Damn.* He had miscalculated the length of the train: the caboose didn't cut off his line of approach from the group of men. He would have to cross the first ten yards in clear line of sight.

The fireman stood atop the tender, holding the hose as the water glugged through. As he disappeared over the other side, the meeting began to break up. Now or never. He crawled across the rail, out from under the cover of the boxcar, and wriggled his way across the first ten yards. There were no shouts. He got to his feet and sprinted the remainder, drawing the Walther as he did so. Hauling himself up the cab steps, he found himself face-to-face with the fireman, who had just lifted a sandwich to his mouth.

"Silence or you're dead," he whispered harshly. The sandwich dropped as the man lifted his arms, shock giving way to indignation on his face.

The engineer was coming, shouting something back to the

men he'd left. "I mean it," Kuznetsky said, maneuvering himself into position for the driver's appearance. At least the engine was making enough noise to half-drown a shot. But the fireman's face relaxed; the moment of immediate danger for him had passed.

"Keep coming," Kuznetsky said, holding the automatic a foot from the engineer's face as he climbed into the cab. "Now let's go," he said, moving back to where he could cover them both.

"Hey . . . !"

"Do it. Your life is hanging by a thread, mister. Believe me."

The two men stared at him, found nothing in his eyes to doubt. The engineer opened the regulator, and the engine began moving forward. "There's easier ways to get a ride, bud," he muttered.

"Just drive the train. Normal speed, normal everything."

"Can we talk?"

"Just drive the train." Kuznetsky shifted position to allow the fireman to shovel some coal while he watched the engineer's actions. "Now slow down slightly," he ordered. The man did so. "Okay, back to the usual speed."

"What sort of game are you playing, bud?" He sounded curious rather than belligerent.

"No games. I wanted to know how to slow this thing down if you two happen to meet with an accident."

The two men exchanged glances. The train rattled across a bridge. Kuznetsky lit the cigarette he'd been wanting for two hours.

"Where are you heading, bud?"

"Down the line. Shut up."

Behind him, as if in pursuit, the half-moon was rising.

☐

Fifty feet farther back, and considerably closer to the ground rushing by, young Bob Crosby was tightening the strap that held him to the girders beneath the boxcar. He'd run away from home that evening and was already beginning to regret it. The noise was unbearable, his mouth seemed choked with dust, and he felt as if his bones were all being wrenched loose from their sockets.

He'd boarded the train at Chattanooga, more from desperation than choice. He'd expected a long train of boxcars with straw-filled interiors and sliding doors, not this strange short train with one car and a cargo that seemed to consist solely of policemen. But he'd had to get away before his father alerted the local cops, and at least he'd done that.

There were probably better places to travel; he'd learn as he went, he supposed. God knew where that guy at the last stop had ended up. He'd watched him crawling, then running toward the locomotive. There must be places to hide there too. He'd have to find out. There was lots of time: he was only fourteen. He'd go back home in a few years, when he was big enough, and show his father what a beating was really like. The bastard. He couldn't understand why his mother stayed with him.

☐

The train approached Scottsboro. "We stop here," the engineer shouted over his shoulder.

Not according to Melville's information, Kuznetsky thought, and there'd been no other way of checking. If the driver was telling the truth, and they went straight through, then the wires would start humming, to the north at least. If they stopped, and the driver was bluffing, the guard and the troopers would get suspicious. He had to trust Melville.

"We go straight through," he shouted over the noise of the engine.

The engineer turned to protest, but Kuznetsky could see the bluff in his eyes. "Straight through," he repeated. It was the correct decision: Scottsboro station was dark and deserted.

164

The driver spat over the side, an empty gesture of defiance. "Huntsville, then," he shouted.

"Okay. Huntsville." The train climbed away from the valley floor, bellowing smoke across the stars. Another ten miles. The road on their left was devoid of traffic, the houses dark. Kuznetsky felt a sense of rising exhilaration, swaying with the passage of the train, feeling the warm gusts of air from the firebox whipping past his face.

□

At the spur turnoff Amy stood by the car, straining her ears for the sound of the approaching train. Her eyes had grown used to the darkness since their arrival an hour before, but even so she could barely make out the line of the main road two hundred yards away. Paul and Gerd had taken the camper up the valley. The switch had been thrown.

She gripped the tommy gun in one hand, hoping that she wouldn't have to use it. If Kuznetsky had failed, if the train failed to slow down, there was every chance that it would come off the rails at the turnoff, and she alone would have to take on the occupants, at least until Paul and Gerd arrived. And it would all be in full view of the main road. Only one car had passed in the last hour, but it needed only one at the wrong time. That car had swept past only seconds after Paul had finished cutting the wires above the road.

An orange glow could be seen in the distance, climbing the valley toward her. For a moment it disappeared, sheltered from sight by the invisible buildings of Lim Rock, and there it was again, growing larger and brighter. Now she could see the long, moving shadow that was the train, now she could hear it above the natural sounds of the night.

□

"Slow down," Kuznetsky said.

"On this grade—you're crazy!"

Kuznetsky moved forward, immediately behind the engineer, jamming the Walther into the back of his neck. "We're taking the spur. Slow down."

"We'll have to throw the switch."

"It's already thrown."

At least he hoped it was. There was a sudden movement behind him; he ducked by instinct, glimpsed the shovel flash past his head. Straightening up, he put a bullet through the fireman's face, reached out too late to catch his body as it tumbled from the cab, and turned the gun quickly enough to stop the engineer in his tracks.

"Slow it down," he screamed, and the driver, his mouth hanging open, turned to obey.

It was almost too late. The locomotive's wheels screeched as they hit the points and the whole train swayed alarmingly. Beneath them the trestles of the river bridge creaked and snapped, but they were across, moving up the narrow valley.

☐

Amy watched the train rock its way through the points and the bridge, saw a silhouetted guard emerge from his lighted sanctum and apply himself energetically to the hand brake on the rear platform. Blue-white sparks flashed across the valley as the braked wheels ground against the rails, but the train kept moving away as the engineer overrode the hand brake. The noise seemed deafening. She looked up and down the road—nothing.

☐

Half a mile ahead Paul and Gerd heard the train, stamped out their cigarettes, exchanged grim smiles, and moved to their positions. Soon they could see it rounding the bend in the valley, first the glow from the locomotive, then the sparks from the wheels at the rear. The train's shape slowly swam into focus, and two figures were visible in the engineer's compartment. And one on the roof of the boxcar! Someone was going forward to see what had gone wrong.

Suddenly the boxcar door slid open, throwing light across the road and the valley. The train pulled to a halt, and as the engine subsided into relative silence, the noise of the man running along the car roof mingled with shouts from the men hanging out of the boxcar door.

The first rattle of Paul's tommy gun blew the man off the roof and out of sight; simultaneously Gerd sprayed the open door, knocking at least two troopers back across the car.

Out of the corner of his eye he saw the engineer kneeling as if in prayer, Kuznetsky standing above him, holding the gun to his head and pulling the trigger.

Paul and Gerd reached their positions on either side of the open door. They could hear talking inside, frightened, bewildered talking, then the rasp of the other door being pulled back. At a signal from Gerd they moved forward in unison, firing as they went. Two bodies plummeted out through the far door, thumping into the gravel. Kuznetsky stepped past them, pulled himself up into the car. Inside, one man was dead, another whimpering from wounds in his thigh and chest. Kuznetsky walked behind him, placed the gun to the back of his head, and fired. The man slumped forward across the makeshift table of crates, scattering cards and quarters.

His face blank, Kuznetsky turned to look down at the Germans. "Check the others," he said.

Paul walked around the train muttering *"Ja, mein führer"* under his breath. The two other troopers were dead, and so was the guard, lying face down in the stream, the rippling waters pulling his hair above his head. Murder most foul or an act of war? Paul was damned if he knew.

Amy pulled the car up by the camper, walked across to the scene of carnage. Kuznetsky and Gerd were already moving the crates to the door, easing them down to the ground.

"Thrown the switch?" Kuznetsky asked her.

"Of course," she replied coldly.

"Open the camper doors," he ordered.

She walked across, passing Paul, who smiled bitterly at

her. She slammed the doors open, the sound echoing from the valley sides. Gerd staggered across with the first of the crates, and she helped him load it.

☐

In the darkness under the boxcar Bob Crosby watched the unloading. *Who were these people?* They sounded like Americans, but the thin one had muttered something in German. And they had killed everyone, everyone but him.

Not three feet away from his hiding place, within reach of a lunge, one of them had placed a fearsome-looking machine gun, leaned against the rail beneath the door. The shiny metal had an almost hypnotic appeal lying there, just lying there, but he silently fought the desire to make that lunge. What business was it of his? But he liked guns, had always been fascinated by them. . . .

No, they'd soon be gone—"One more" someone had just said. Then he'd be gone, too, far away from all this. He could see the upturned face of one of the troopers lying by the track, the hole where his left eye should have been.

They were standing in a group now, over by the camper, talking. Eight legs in all. Perhaps they'd forgotten the gun, would leave it behind, and he could try it once before taking off. He could even sell it—no, that was stupid. There was movement now: one pair of legs had disappeared. He wriggled his body around to get a better view and his leg slipped off the girder. For a second he teetered, thought he was going to fall, but with a supreme effort managed to lower himself to the ground, causing only a soft thud as his legs dropped onto the ballast between the tracks.

They'd stopped talking. Had they heard anything? His breathing sounded too loud. *Shit!* One pair of legs walked back toward the train; he had to do something fast. He squirmed across the rail and took the gun in his hands. The legs stopped their approach; the stream gurgled in the silence. He got to his feet, leaned against the side of the boxcar, wondering how to do it. He remembered the Marines training film—run, roll, and fire. Surprise was everything. He could do it.

Taking a deep breath, he took off, rushing along the back of the train, conscious of shouts and other feet running after him. Bursting into the field of light at the rear, he threw himself into a perfect roll, just the way he'd practiced in the garden at home, and pulled the trigger. He had a flashing glimpse of people falling, could have cried out with exaltation. Run, roll, and fire. His chest seemed to burst with burning pride.

□

Gerd walked over to the body, rolled his victim, face up, with his foot. A freckled adolescent face stared past him, an obscene smile creasing its lips. "Jesus," he muttered, "Jesus Christ."

"Gerd." It was Amy's voice, soft, shaking. He ran across to where she and Paul had collapsed against each other. She was holding her right side, just below the breast, blood trickling between her fingers. Paul was unconscious, and for a second Gerd feared the worst, but he couldn't find any bullet wounds. Gerd pulled him forward, found a lump still growing on the back of his head. Something had hit him but good.

"Is he dead?" she whispered.

"No, just unconscious." He moved on to Kuznetsky, who was lying a few feet away. A bullet had plowed a furrow across the side of his head, just above the left ear. It had probably thrown him back against the camper door, and it was the door, Gerd guessed, that had hit Paul. Some luck, but it could have been worse. None of them was dead—yet.

He got the flashlight from the car and went back to Amy. "He's out cold too. Let's look at you." He gently pulled her hand away and lifted the blouse. It was a nasty flesh wound, but not serious.

"There's a first-aid box in the front," she said.

He found it, soaked a cotton ball in disinfectant, and

applied it to her wound and then to Kuznetsky's. Then Gerd wound bandages around his head and her lower chest. Time to go, he told himself, and it looks like I'll be driving.

She was on her feet, somewhat unsteady; the blood was already seeping through the bandage. "Get in the front," he said.

"But . . ."

"Get in the front. I don't want to carry three bodies."

She seemed to smile at some private joke, then did as she was told.

He lifted Paul into the back, laying him out alongside the crates. He then pulled Kuznetsky up on the other side, folded the steps up, and closed the doors. "Jesus," he muttered again. Now for the car. He took off the emergency brake, turned the wheel, and shoved. It stuck against the near rail; he'd have to use the motor. He climbed in, switched on the ignition, and forced the car back over the rails, too far almost— the rear wheels were left spinning in space above the stream. But the road was now clear.

He clambered aboard the camper. Amy didn't look too bad; her face was pure white, but there was life in her eyes. He pulled away down the valley, trying to remember the route. Left at the end.

"Turn right at the end," she said.

"No, left."

"Just do it," she said with an effort, "I'll explain as we go."

He glanced at her, knew she wasn't rambling, that there was something here he didn't know about. He swung right onto the main road, waiting for the explanation.

Amy tried to get her thoughts in order, to override the pain in her side. For one terrible moment she'd thought Paul was dead, had wanted to die herself, but he wasn't, and she couldn't, and it had to go on. Since climbing into her seat she'd thought more quickly than she could remember, and it seemed foolproof. If only she could be sure she was thinking straight.

"You and Paul weren't told the truth," she said.

"Go on."

"The crates were never meant to go back to the U-boat. Berlin wanted the U-boat, and you and Paul, to be unwitting decoys. You were meant to be caught, and the U-boat sunk. You see, the crates contain only enough material for two atomic bombs at most, which is almost useless to the military. We'd need dozens of bombs to turn the Allies back. So it had to look as though this uranium never reached Germany, that the eventual German bombs were made from German-produced material. . . ."

"But they'd never find the crates."

"They'll find one identical empty crate on the beach at Ossabaw Island. Smith left it there when he picked you up."

"Wonderful," he said bitterly. "And the U-boat?"

"A telephone call to the local FBI. The U.S. Navy will sink it, and they'll assume the rest of the crates have gone down with it. Even if it escapes, there'll be no one looking for us."

He sighed. "Makes sense, as Paul would say. Just where are we going?"

"South. Mobile, than a boat to Cuba, then a Swedish freighter to Gothenburg."

"We're coming into a town," he said, his mind whirring at what Amy had told him.

"Huntsville. Go left at the . . . Farley road, I'll tell you when."

The streets were empty. As they passed the station Amy could see lights but no sign of activity. The train was now half an hour late; soon someone would be picking up the telephone to find out that the lines east were dead. Then the police would be called, then a search back up the line, then . . .

"Turn here," she said. They passed an empty police car parked by a house whose lights still shone in the upstairs windows. Soon they were back in open country, a large lake to the right, a line of low hills to the left, the road pointing straight and south.

"How far to the coast?" he asked.

"About four hundred miles, but we didn't plan to do it in one go. The idea was—is—to spend the daylight hours in the Talladega Forest, which is about halfway. We should be there by dawn."

"And by the time we leave for Cuba, the U-boat will have been sighted by your conscientious citizen."

"That's right."

He admired her for not expressing any contrition. "How's your side?" he asked.

"The bleeding's stopped, I think."

"Give me the map," he said, "and try and get some sleep."

She passed it over and leaned back in the seat, a faint smile on her lips.

ten

THE ROAD unfolded before Gerd Breitner, an endless pool of lighted asphalt slipping under the camper's wheels. It was the first time in many weeks that he'd felt alone, the first time since that afternoon he'd spent mourning—yes, that was the word—mourning Johanna on that fence outside Beresino. And for some reason he felt strangely at peace with the world. Happy just to be alive, perhaps, but he thought it was more than that. The boy's face, the death grin. It had ended in that moment, he realized. The war was over for him.

He was thirty-five years old, and he'd seen a lot of men die younger. He'd loved and been loved, always had friends. He'd seen four continents. And here he was, driving down a foreign highway on a moonlit night, a lovely woman asleep beside him, two wounded comrades in the back. Who could ask for more?

He grinned and lit another cigarette. Paul would ask for more. They were so alike in some ways, yet deep down they were so different. Yin and yang, the Buddhists called it. Paul would always look back, regretting, or at least reexamining his choices, imagining that things could have been different. It might be illusion, but it gave him his strength, that crazy refusal to bow down before what others considered inevitable. Paul didn't believe in fate, it was as simple as that. For Paul there would always be choice, and so there could never be total satisfaction—the future would always be open, uncertain.

Gerd had no regrets. Sadnesses, yes, but the good had gone with the bad. Johanna and little Paul were dead, and so were those Russians in the little village outside Vitebsk. It was funny how the two always went together in his mind, as if the one had been a punishment for the other. Perhaps it had. They'd gone mad that day with blood lust—three years ago now, though sometimes it seemed like a century, sometimes like yesterday. The war had done away with coherent time, broken it up and thrown it together. It was all part of the same madness.

He remembered the conversation with the Arab in that room in Tobruk. A sufi, that's what the man had said he was, some kind of holy man. They'd talked for hours in broken English, but all he could remember was the one proverb: *People fall in love with each other because of what time has made of them both; tribes fall in madness with a moment, because of what time has made of them.* He and Johanna. Germany and the twentieth century.

Gerd thought about what the woman had told him. They should have expected the deception, or something like it. It made perfect sense, provided you didn't mind sacrificing a U-boat full of boys and a couple of soldiers. And who would? The Russians, the British, all of them would have accepted the same logic without batting an eye. If you were prepared to kill thirty million people, what difference did a few more make?

The camper rolled on, climbing and descending ridge after ridge, swooping across fast-running streams that glittered in the moonlight, tunneling through pine forests, rumbling through one-street towns where no lights shone. It was in one of these that the front tire went flat, jerking Gerd from his reverie and slewing the vehicle across the street.

Amy woke with a start and gingerly climbed down from the cab. Gerd was already unbolting the spare tire from the chassis, letting out a long and imaginative string of German profanities. She looked up and down the street, lit only by the now-sinking moon, which threw shadows across the silver-gray surface. No lights had gone on in the houses.

"How long?" she asked.

"About twenty minutes."

As he answered they both heard footsteps, way down the street but coming in their direction. Two people, she thought. He put a finger to his lips and gestured her back into the camper, but before she had moved more than a few paces, the footsteps stopped. They heard a door close, distant voices, saw a faint glow that indicated a light had been turned on.

"Is there any way I can help speed it up?" she asked.

"No."

She leaned against the hood, listening for any further activity while he finished taking off the punctured tire. The glow down the street seemed to be brightening as the moon shadows lengthened, then suddenly it blazed and a door slammed and there was laughter. More doors, car doors this time, and then two headlights were shining straight at them, illuminating the whole street. The car, a convertible, rolled toward them and stopped alongside the camper, its headlights now pointing away, down the street.

"Trouble, folks?" the man sitting next to the driver asked.

"Just a flat," Gerd replied.

"You folks from up North?"

"Yep. Just tourin'. Saved up our coupons a year for this trip."

At that moment a flashlight beam stabbed out of the convertible's rear seat, flooding Gerd and the camper cab with light.

"Turn that off, Jesse," the man said. "Sorry . . ." he started to say, but the driver was whispering something to him, and suddenly he was out of the car, a rifle in his hand, the glint of a badge on his shirt.

"Put your hands in the air, mister," he told Gerd. "And you, too, ma'am."

The one called Jesse and the driver were both out of the car now, and they both had rifles too. "Cover them, Jake," the man with the badge said, reaching into the cab and unslinging the tommy gun from its place on the back of the driver's seat.

"Duane, the woman's bleeding," Jake said, excitement in his voice.

"Make sure you don't get any on you," the sheriff said, moving around to the camper's rear. They heard him open the doors. "There's a dead man in here. No, he's breathing. Sonovabitch."

Amy and Gerd exchanged glances. Where was the other man?

The sheriff came back. "Jesse, bring that guy in the back down to the jail. Be careful with him." Jesse giggled, and went to do it. "Okay, you two," the sheriff said, "walk."

They walked, a hundreds yards or so, down to where they'd first seen the glow of light. "Blount County Sheriff's Office, Locust Forks" it said above the door. The man called Jake opened the door, took off the "Gone Fishing" sign, and preceded them in. The sheriff brought up the rear and, still holding his gun on them, took two pairs of handcuffs from his desk drawer. He threw them to Jake.

"Behind the back," he said, watching while the cuffs were snapped on. He lit a cigarette and sat down behind his desk. "So what have we got here?" he asked dryly. "Bonnie and Clyde?"

Amy examined the two men; it was the first chance she'd had to see their faces. The sheriff was a man in his forties, thickset with a round head and cropped blond hair. Jake was his opposite, wiry and dark with a lugubrious face.

"What's your name, lady?" the sheriff asked her.

"Bonnie," she said.

He didn't smile. "Bonnie," he repeated softly. "Yeah."

The one called Jesse dragged Kuznetsky across the threshold and let him down, with surprising gentleness, on the wooden floor. "Duane, there's two more machine guns in the back and some big crates with weird markings on them."

"Is there now? Take him through to the cells and then go get the guns."

Jesse turned to obey like an obedient dog. His face, Amy noticed, was too young for his body, much too young. There was something wrong with him.

"Maybe I'd better look at those crates," the sheriff mused. "Watch 'em, Jake."

"I wouldn't open them," Amy said as he headed for the door.

He turned. "And why's that, lady?"

"It's dangerous stuff."

"What is?"

"It's . . . a new type of explosive."

He walked back to his desk. "From where?"

"Paradise," Gerd said.

"Shut up, Clyde." He looked at them both, then ground out his cigarette in the brass ashtray and picked up the telephone. "C'mon, c'mon," he muttered. "Mary Beth," he said at last, "yeah I know what time it is. Business. Get me the state police in Huntsville."

He waited, staring at Amy. She stared back.

The operator was talking. "It's dead? Then try Birmingham," he said. Cradling the receiver in his shoulder, he lit another cigarette. "It's ringing," he told Jake. "What the . . . there's no lines out? Hey, Mary Beth, what's going on?"

He put the phone down, walked across to Amy. "There's someone out there messin' with us, Bonnie. Ain't there?"

She looked at the floor.

He grabbed the front of her blouse and yanked her to her feet in one violent jerk. She felt a moment of nerve-tearing pain, then the warm wetness of blood flowing out of the reopened wound.

"How many?" he was asking.

Gerd leaped to his feet, but Jake prodded him hard in the stomach with a rifle barrel and sent him sprawling back across the bench.

"Two," she said.

"You lying bitch," he said, shoving her back onto the bench. "Jake, take him into the cells and stay with him. Jesse, take her upstairs."

"She's bleeding, Jake."

"So what?"

"Shall I clean her up?"

"You behave yourself. Just make sure she doesn't go anywhere."

"Where'll you be, Duane?" Jake asked.

"Right here, with a rifle pointed at the door. It'll be light in a couple of hours, and then we'll go out and get whoever it is."

☐

Paul dropped from the telephone pole the last few feet to the grass, then sat on his haunches for a few moments, a shadow among shadows, trying to ignore the splitting pain in the back of his head. On the other side of the road the breeze rustled the pines, but the night was empty of any other sound.

He'd had two pieces of luck: return to consciousness and the wirecutters still being in his pocket. And perhaps the location too. Locust Forks—population 896, according to the town sign—was only about half a mile from end to end and considerably less wide than it was long. He'd found no road entering the town from the east, and the hill he was now skirting seemed to rule out access from the west. But he had to make sure.

He clambered down a bank, waded across a stagnant ditch and up the other side, walking into a barbed-wire fence at the top. He cut himself a hole to get through as well as removing a four-foot length just in case.

The moon had almost set now, turning orange and bathing the buildings to his right in a ghostly luminescence. He trotted across the field, slipped, and fell headlong, catching the barbed wire against his thigh and burying his face in something that smelled like rotting cabbage. He lay there for a moment, silently laughing at himself. "Two eagles" Schellenberg had called them, and here was one of them tripping over vegetables in the dark.

He moved on, crossing two more fields and cutting his way through two more fences before he reached his starting point at the town's northern end. Just the one road, then. And they'd be doing no talking on the telephone. But there wasn't that much of the night left, there were at least three of them, and they had the guns.

He squatted down and cut the barbs off the last foot of each end of the wire, then twisted those ends into loops. It wasn't very flexible, but it would have to do. He began edging his way down the street, keeping to the darker shadows of the western sidewalk.

☐

Jesse laid Amy out on the sheriff's bed and disappeared. She heard running water through the adjoining door; presumably it was the sheriff's kitchen. It was extremely hot, or had the wound made her feverish? She could feel the sweat pouring down her face.

He came back with a bowl of hot water and what looked like a piece of bed sheeting, gently opened up her blouse, and carefully wiped away the blood from around the bullet gash. Then he just sat there, the bloodied sheet in his hand, staring at the space of bare flesh between her belt and her brassiere.

"Thank you," she said, trying to lift herself up, trying not to let fear creep into her voice.

He helped her forward, and for a second she thought she'd misjudged him, but his hands wrestled with the hook on her brassiere. Successful, he pushed her back down, and like a little boy peeking under a stone, he eased the cups off her breasts with the palms of his hands. Looking into his eyes, she found an innocent evil that terrified her far more than any sign of lust.

He didn't touch her for a long time, just stared as if transfixed by her naked breasts, the droplets of sweat rolling down between them. Then he reached out a hand and stroked a nipple with the edge of a thumb. Not once did he look at her face. Leaning forward, he put his mouth around the other nipple, sucking gently, his eyes closed.

She squirmed violently, felt the blood flow again.

He let go, looking horrified, and held the sheeting to staunch the renewed flow and made a clucking sound in his throat.

☐

Paul stood on the side of the street opposite the jail, examining the lighted sheriff's office. The lights seemed to be on in every room, up and down, but in ten minutes he'd seen only one hint of movement, someone upstairs carrying a bowl. It didn't look very inviting. Someone must have picked up the phone and put two and two together. They were waiting for him.

He crossed the street in a wide semicircle, avoiding the patch of light thrown from the windows and open door, and worked his way around to the back of the building. The lights were on there, too, throwing the shadows of the window bars across the remains of an old tractor. The back door was locked.

He made his way back down the side, but stopped when he heard Gerd whistling the first notes of "Lili Marlene," which seemed to come from a point only feet away through the clapboard wall. The whistling was swiftly followed by a grunted "Shut up" and the sound of footsteps.

"Keep the bastard quiet, Jake," another voice said, this time from the right, toward the street.

Which meant the third guy was probably upstairs, and

probably with Amy. Stupid, Paul thought. They shouldn't have separated themselves. He looked up, then remembered the rain barrel and pipe at the rear.

☐

Amy had never felt so much like screaming. If he'd said anything, just one word, it might have been bearable, but the silence, the look of schoolboy curiosity on the middle-aged face, even his concern over her wound . . .

He unbuckled her belt, breathing with little gasps, a small trace of spittle forming at the corner of his mouth.

"If you take off the handcuffs, I could help," she said, fighting to keep her voice steady.

He didn't even seem to hear. She felt him tugging at her skirt, pulling it below her knees, felt a drop of moisture fall on her bare thigh. He was dribbling uncontrollably, a glistening of tears in his eyes.

She closed hers, heard an inhuman gurgle, and almost fainted. But suddenly the hands disappeared, his head jerked back violently, blood spurting as Paul wrenched the barbed wire tight across his throat. It seemed to go on silently forever, then he let the body down onto the bed and lifted her up, and she sobbed into his shoulder. "Paul, Paul . . ."

"Ssshhh," he murmured in her ear, and they sat for a moment in silence, her body quivering as the tension dissolved. Then he stood her up, pulled up her skirt and fastened the belt, replaced her brassiere and buttoned her blouse with a doctor's detachment. He went through the dead man's pockets, but there were no keys for her handcuffs.

He gestured for her to stay where she was and went through into the sheriff's kitchen. There was a sharp hunting knife hanging on the wall, but it wasn't a weapon for throwing.

He went back past her to the top of the stairs, crawling forward to extend his view of the office below, but all he could see was the corner of a desk, the bottom of the open street door, and floorboards. He lay there thinking. He could go down with the dead man's rifle, probably get the sheriff, and if Gerd was still conscious they'd manage the other man between them. But the whole town would be awake, the camper's tire still wasn't fixed, and the crates were still in the camper. He couldn't fire the gun.

The sheriff didn't know that, though.

He felt a tug at his ankle, turned, and found Amy sitting behind him. She indicated with her head for him to follow her back into the room, then whispered in his ear. "The sheriff told this one to behave himself. If I make noises as if he isn't, maybe he'll come up."

"Maybe he'll call his man down," Paul whispered back.

She shrugged. "And when he doesn't come?"

"Okay."

She got back on the bed. "Please, no," she said in a trembling voice. "Please don't"—this time louder.

"Jesse, whatever you're doing, don't," the man downstairs shouted up.

Amy groaned, a long shuddering groan that seemed to go on and on.

"Jesse!"

"Aw, let him have some fun," Jake shouted.

"Yeah, and you'll explain it all to the Feds, I suppose. Jesse, answer me!"

"Come and get the pig off me," she sobbed.

"Jake," they heard the sheriff say, "go up and bring 'em down here."

Paul took up position behind the door, the hunting knife held in his hand like a brush, as if he were about to cut a line on a wall. They could hear Jake tramping up the stairs, and Amy began to groan again as he opened the door. "Jesse . . ." he began, then the knife slit his throat from ear to ear, splashing blood down his bare chest.

Paul lowered him silently to the floor, picked up his rifle, and signaled Amy to walk in front of him. As they began their descent the sheriff glanced up at her, still handcuffed, then resumed his watch on the door.

"Put the rifle down, Sheriff," Paul said softly, and the man's head jerked around, his mouth dropping in disbelief. He laid the rifle down on the desk in front of him.

"Throw the keys for the handcuffs onto the floor over there."

"You . . ."

"Shut up. I don't want to use this gun—it'll wake up the whole town—but if you're going to do that anyway, then it won't make much difference. . . . The keys."

He reached into his shirt pocket, threw them where he'd been told. Paul unlocked Amy's handcuffs with one hand, holding the rifle aimed at the sheriff with the other.

"Let's go and get our friend," he said, pointing the sheriff toward the door that led through to the cells.

Gerd was waiting for them. "You took your time," he said.

Paul unlocked the cell, and pushed the sheriff in. "I thought you'd have started a tunnel by this time."

"Where's my brothers?" the sheriff asked.

"They're dead."

The sheriff sat down on the bunk, his head between his hands.

"We have to talk," said Amy from the next cell. She'd been examining Kuznetsky, who was still unconscious but seemed to be breathing regularly. "But not in front of him," she said, reappearing and nodding in the sheriff's direction. "And we'd better get the lights out."

Without waiting for an answer, she walked through to the office and up the stairs. Her feet faltered at the top, but she went on in, ignoring the two corpses. When she came back down Gerd was fixing the "Gone Fishing" sign back in the door window. Paul came through from the cells, switching off the office lights.

"There's something you don't know, Paul," Amy said, grateful that she couldn't see his face in the dark. She told him what she'd told Gerd back on the road.

"And this was Berlin's plan from the beginning?" he asked bitterly.

"Yes."

"And the sixty men on the U-boat?"

She said nothing.

"The bastards."

"We never thought they were saints," Gerd said. "Or even normal people, come to think of it. Anyway, we're stuck with the plan. And no matter what we think of the bastards, we've still got to get out of this country."

"How long to change the tire?" Amy asked Gerd.

"Ten more minutes. I'll get on with it." He opened the door, looked right and left, then came back in. "We've forgotten their car."

"When we leave I'll drive it," Paul said. "We can dump it a few miles down the road. . . . No, why don't we take it, use it as a recon vehicle? I can keep half a mile ahead and look out for trouble."

"Right." Gerd disappeared.

Amy and Paul sat in silence, each absorbed with the other. He wondered where the woman who'd sobbed on his shoulder not ten minutes before had gone; she remembered the look on his face as he'd tightened the barbed wire around Jesse's neck. It was for the best, she thought; at least she knew now that neither of them were the same people who'd fallen in love all those years before. Or did she just want them to be different? Stop it, she told herself. Gerd was right: all that mattered for now was getting out of America, or all four of them would be dangling from nooses, or whatever it was that happened to murderers in this state.

And then she remembered the sheriff, opened her mouth to say something, but closed it again. It was up to her this time. She didn't know why, but it was.

The camper pulled up outside the door. "You and Gerd bring out Smith," she told Paul, and went out to find her bag in the front seat. After screwing together the revolver and a silencer, she waited for them to come out, and as they were maneuvering Kuznetsky into the back, she walked again through the office, trying to conjure up anger against this man who'd let his idiot brother slobber all over her. It didn't work. The moment she saw his petrified expression the anger dissolved, leaving her with nothing but logic. Quickly, Amy told herself. She aimed and fired before he had time to speak or shout, one bullet through the chest, then another through the head.

The dull pops seemed to echo through the cells, and she turned to find Paul staring at her as if he'd never seen her before.

"We can't leave any witnesses," she said, almost succeeding in keeping the tremor out of her voice.

"Makes sense," he said automatically.

She walked straight past him and out to the camper. Gerd was already behind the wheel. She got in beside him, heard Paul gun the motor of the convertible, and they were on their way again. As they left the shelter of the buildings she could see the first hint of dawn in the eastern sky.

eleven

LIEUTENANT JEREMIAH ALLMAN examined his watch by the light of his car's headlamps. It was 4 A.M., another two hours till dawn, perhaps an hour and a half. Not that he particularly wanted to see the scene in the cold light of day. Seven corpses, one of them just a kid. And they still hadn't found the fireman. Of course he might have been one of the gang. If it *was* a gang.

It didn't look like an ordinary holdup: two of the victims bore the signs of execution rather than simple murder. It would help if he knew what the train had been carrying; maybe Walsh would enlighten him when he arrived from Bridgeport.

"There's nothing in the car," one of his subordinates called out.

"Just get the plate number down—we'll check it when we get back. No, you might as well go back now." When was he going to get radios in his cars? "No, wait," he said. Christ, he hated being called out in the middle of the night. His brain refused to function. "Let me think. Check the plate, that's the first thing. Then check the area for strangers—the hotels, realtors, everything. Huntsville and Scottsboro first, then spread out."

Was there anything else? No. Whoever they were, they'd done a first-class job of covering their tracks. No witnesses left alive, telephone wires out, just like a military operation. But why had they left the car? Tried to turn it and overshot, he supposed. And they hadn't stripped off the license plates. Clumsy. It didn't fit in with the rest.

He realized the sergeant was still waiting. "Okay, that's it. . . . Oh, hold on." Another car was coming up the valley. "The cavalry," he murmured to himself. How in the hell was the sergeant going to get his car out? What a goddamn mess. He rubbed his eyes and waited.

It was George Walsh, who was quite human for a Fed. They'd worked together against the moonshiners, with a little hindrance from the Treasury men, a few years back.

The two exchanged greetings and Allman showed Walsh around the exhibits. The FBI man whistled under his breath, chomped his gum, and scratched his ear. "Well," Allman said at last, "what was in the goddamn train?"

Walsh looked, if possible, even less willing to talk. "Crates," he finally said, making the most of the word's consonants.

"Crates containing what?"

"Army people wouldn't tell me. I pointed out that it sometimes helps to know what you're looking for, and they gave me this." He showed Allman a diagram. "That's the marking on them. It must be some military secret—probably supplies of krypton. They're flying two men down from Washington now. I'm just here to keep you company until they get here."

"Thanks. How many crates? How big?"

"Ten. Three foot by two foot by two."

"A truck for certain, then."

"Has to be. No tracks I suppose?"

"Ground's too dry. We might find something when it's light, but I wouldn't bet my pension on it. This was a real peach of a professional job."

□

The streets of Birmingham were bathed in the light of half-dawn and virtually empty. A few trucks making deliveries, the occasional paperboy on his bicycle, and one police car parked near City Hall. Its occupants, as Gerd drove the camper past, were deeply involved in a conversation with Paul, all three men being bent over a map spread out on the vehicle's hood. Ten minutes later Paul overtook them again and resumed his position a quarter of a mile ahead.

They drove southwestward now, through the heart of an industrial area that seemed to Gerd more like a stretch of the Ruhr than Alabama. There were more people on the streets, most of them in blue overalls. The road passed under a series of railway bridges, then rose sharply to display a line of huge blast furnaces silhouetted against the rising sun.

"I never realized it was a place," Gerd said to himself.

"Where?" Amy asked through a yawn.

"Bessemer. We just passed the sign. It's a steelmaking process, but I never knew it was a place where they made steel."

"Oh."

He laughed. "I was a teacher once."

"Teaching what?"

"Science."

She pulled herself upright in the seat and gazed out at more factories, their tall brick chimneys standing out against the blue line of distant hills. "Did you like teaching?" she asked.

"Some of the time." He lit another cigarette. "But in the end there's only one thing science teaches you—that all truths are relative."

She glanced sideways at him. "And isn't that a useful thing to learn?"

"Not in a world run by true believers."

☐

In Huntsville, Jeremiah Allman put the phone down when Walsh got back from the airport with the two men from Washington.

"Sam Benton," the taller one introduced himself. "And this is Don Mitchell. Any developments?"

"Would you like to fill me in first?" Allman asked.

It was Mitchell who answered. "There's a distinct possibility that foreign nationals are involved. In other words, enemy action, Japs or Germans."

"Japs would be rather noticeable around here."

"Yeah, probably Germans."

"And are we going to be told what's in the crates?" Allman asked.

"I'm sorry, but no. Not without Roosevelt's say-so, anyhow. But it would be hard to exaggerate how important it is we get them back."

"Fair enough," Allman said. "Here's where we're up to. The hunting lodge on McCoy Mountain—that's about ten miles from where the train was stopped—was hired out last Saturday to a guy named Joe Markham. The realtor in Scottsboro said he had a woman with him when he picked up the key, and she was also there earlier when they first looked it over. Some business associates were going to join them later. Markham had a Tennessee accent, about five foot nine, a hundred and fifty pounds, dark hair, brown eyes—do you want all this now?"

"No, just get it out," Benton said. "The woman?"

"He didn't see her clearly either time; she stayed in the car. Black Buick, by the way. She had dark hair, sunglasses— that's all he saw. Could have been just a hooker for Markham's friends."

"They're checking the lodge now?"

"Yeah, and we're still waiting for Washington to come through on the car plates."

A sergeant arrived with coffee and a sheet of paper. "The lodge is empty," Allman read out. "Clean as a whistle."

The telephone rang. Walsh listened, made notes, and put the receiver down with a grim expression. "You'd better get a forensic team up to the lodge," he told Allman. "They've traced the car," he explained to the others. "It was hired by a man in Washington two weeks ago. He doesn't fit Markham's description—he was a big man with a Midwest accent. But he did give a German name—Doesburg. Address in New York."

"Give that here," Mitchell said. He was already asking the operator for the FBI's New York Central office.

Walsh and Allman looked at each other. "Now if you were a German commando team humping a truckload of crates containing krypton, where would you be heading?" Walsh asked.

"Germany."

"Right. The quickest way home would be through Georgia or South Carolina."

"How long would it take?" Benton asked, standing up to examine the map behind Allman's desk.

"Twelve hours minimum."

"So they haven't got there yet, and they're not going to risk a pickup in daylight—"

"They could be going south to the Gulf," Mitchell said, joining him.

"Why would they do that? It would add about a thousand miles to the sea journey."

"Yeah, but they'd know that we'd know—"

"Yeah, yeah, there's no end to that."

"I don't think we're dealing with people who are relying on luck to get away," Mitchell insisted.

"Jesus, German commandos in Jackson County," Allman muttered to himself.

"That's not for publication, Lieutenant," Benton told him. "Okay, Don, they could have gone south. Walsh, work out how far they could have gotten by midday in any seaward direction and then start phoning around. Get Birmingham, Atlanta, and Columbia to put blocks on all the major roads. Tell them what we're looking for, not what's in the crates."

"I don't know what's in the crates."

"Right, right." He looked up at the map again, then at his watch. "We've got about twelve hours to catch these bastards."

☐

Wim Doesburg was in the bath when they hammered on his front door. He heard Elke shout that that she was coming, stepped out, and wrapped his bathrobe around him. It was impossible. Even if things had gone wrong, they couldn't be here this soon.

He stepped into the hall and was almost knocked over by a tall young man in plainclothes. At the door there were two uniformed police with drawn guns. "What is . . . ?"

"Wim Doesburg?" the man said, flashing a card at him.

"Yes, but . . ."

"FBI. We have a warrant to search this house."

Doesburg controlled himself. Let them search! It would take them forever to find anything incriminating.

The FBI man looked into each room. "Come in here," he said, entering the kitchen. "We have some questions."

Doesburg followed him. "There must be some mistake," he said, conscious that he was parodying a thousand Hollywood villains. "What's your name?" he asked belligerently.

"Kowalski. It says on the card. Okay, you can start," he told the other plainclothesmen who had just appeared in the hall. Doesburg heard one of them ascending the stairs. Oh God, he thought suddenly. The money.

"Mr. Doesburg, have you rented a car in the last month?"

"No."

"In Washington. A black Buick."

"I said no. I don't drive. I've never driven a car in my life." What was happening? Was this something else entirely? "Ask anyone around here if they've ever seen me drive a car," he added hopefully.

"Do you know"—Kowalski consulted his notebook—"an Aaron Matson of 221 Mountain Boulevard, Knoxville?"

Knoxville. Could it be Sigmund? "No," he said calmly. "Who is he?"

"Was. He was shot dead in Knoxville this morning."

"That can hardly concern me. Or are you suggesting I can be in two places at once?"

"Do you know a Joe Markham?"

"No."

Someone was coming down the stairs. "Found this, Charlie," he said, putting the pile of notes on the table. "About four thousand dollars, I'd say."

Kowalski looked at Doesburg, raised his eyebrows.

"My savings," he said indignantly.

"Get dressed," Kowalski said, "we're going downtown."

"But . . ."

"Now."

In the back of the car Doesburg held his wife's hand, trying to communicate the need for silence. There were tears in her eyes and he realized, with something of a shock, that he had no idea how she'd react under pressure. She didn't know everything, but she knew enough.

They were separated the moment they arrived, and Doesburg was led to a small windowless interview room. He was left on his own for several minutes, then Kowalski came in with an older, gray-haired man who didn't bother to introduce himself.

"I'd like to see my lawyer," Doesburg said immediately.

"Bullshit," the man said, in a quiet voice that somehow seemed full of menace. "I'm not going to play games with you, Herr Doesburg. You know what this is about and I know what this is about. You're thinking that we have no proof, and you're quite right. But we'll find some, starting with a trace on that money and finishing by taking your house apart brick by brick. We may find it too late, but not as far as you're concerned. For you, there's a straightforward choice. You talk now and you get fifteen years. You don't talk now and you go to the chair. Which is it to be?"

Could they trace the money? Perhaps. He wouldn't want to stake his life on it. And if they had Markham, he was done anyway. But that, he realized with a flash of insight, was all irrelevant. The only one who knew his address was Kroeger, and if Kroeger had talked, then he must too. He sighed, looked across into the man's blue eyes.

"What do you want to know?" he asked.

□

For a few seconds Amy was conscious of bumping up and down, but it was the cessation of motion that finally woke her. They seemed to be in the middle of a forest, and the sun shining down through the yellow-green foliage invested everything with amber light.

"We've been driving through this for about ten miles," Gerd said, "so I thought it was time to get off the road." He yawned, stretching out his arms above his head. "And I was having trouble keeping my eyes open," he added.

"Where's Paul?" she asked, noticing the empty convertible in her side-view mirror.

"Call of nature, I expect," he murmured, his eyes already closed. "Wake me when the war's over."

She was extremely hungry. In the back of the camper Kuznetsky seemed much the same, though perhaps there was more color in his face. She took a can opener and a tin of peaches from the supply box and opened it on the camper's hood.

Paul reappeared, his face and hair glistening with water. "Stream over there," he explained, leaning across her and digging a hand into the tin.

The consciousness of his body forced her to move away. "You can get some sleep too," she said.

"Someone'll have to stay awake."

"I'm not driving," she said levelly.

But there must have been something else in her voice.

"Are you okay?" he asked, touching her lightly on the shoulder.

"Fine," she said. "I'm just fine." She walked off toward the stream.

☐

Benton and Mitchell arrived in Savannah early in the afternoon. There was no fresh news from Huntsville or New York. Benton called New York and was told that they were bringing Doesburg in now. "Half an hour," the voice promised.

It was an hour before the call came through. Benton listened, moved his finger down the coastline on the map in front of him. "Got it," he said into the phone. "Anything more precise?"

"Where the road hits the sea," New York told him. "There's only one, according to our German friend here."

"We're on our way." He put down the phone, showed Mitchell Ossabaw Island on the map. "Everything set?" he asked.

"The troops are lined up for inspection outside."

The phone rang again, Washington this time. "Benton? Charleston just called us. They've had a reported sighting of a U-boat. Someone called in from Folly Beach—place just outside the city—said it was heading south about a half mile out."

"Anything else?"

"No, the caller got hysterical after that, started screaming about a German invasion, and then hung up."

"I take it the Navy's on the way."

"And how."

"Right." He hung up, clapped Mitchell on the shoulder. "Let's go get 'em."

Ten minutes later they were sitting in the cab of an army troop transport, the first in a column of ten rumbling south along the Jacksonville road.

☐

Kuznetsky emerged into consciousness, seemed to be looking through a large glassless window at angular beams of sunlight shining down through strange tall trees. Was it the forest, a dream of the forest . . . heaven perhaps, old Father McIl-roy's paradise situated somewhere high in the sky above St. Cloud. . . ?

A figure blocked the window. Could it be hanging in midair?

"Jack . . . Yakov," it whispered. Yes, they were him. How could he have two names? "Don't be greedy, Jack." "But . . ." The trees were so beautiful—why was this person blocking them out, coming closer, feeling his forehead, a cool hand, the smell of clean hair. Nadezhda? No, it was someone else, he knew that. Nadezhda was far away. Who was it then? It was important he know, but his head hurt, felt like cold fire.

"Try to sleep. Everything's fine." He obediently closed his eyes. The story must be finished, he thought. Good night, Mama.

Amy pulled the blanket up to his chin and walked back to the others, feeling the wound in her side. Paul was sitting against a tree, trying to flick a cigarette into his mouth. Like a little boy again, she thought. A little boy who cut throats.

"How do you think Smith is?" she asked Gerd. "Will he come through?"

"There's no way of knowing. He's a strong man, but head wounds. . . ." He shrugged. "I'd better look at you," he said, getting to his feet. She held the blouse up across her breasts as he carefully inspected the wound. The blood had clotted in the gash, a brown groove in a patch of blue flesh. "How's it feel?" he asked.

"Stiff. And it itches."

"Good signs." He went to the camper, got a roll of bandage, and replaced the dressing she'd lost in Locust Forks. "You'll be okay in a few days." He smiled at her.

"Thanks," she said. His kindness was almost unbearable. "I'm going to wash my face."

She walked off toward the stream, feeling close to despair. If Kuznetsky died, what could she do? Even with him they'd never have gotten this far without the two Germans. And what would she do with them? With Paul? They might reach the coast, they might reach Cuba, they might even reach Sweden. And then? At some point Paul and Gerd had to be silenced, had to be, or it was all for nothing. And she didn't know if she could kill them.

"Where exactly are we headed?" Paul asked when she returned, his gaze fixed on the map that he'd spread out on the convertible's hood. "Mon Louis," she said, pointing it out and moving away. "It's a small fishing port. French-speaking. There's a shrimp boat waiting to take us to Cuba."

"Hired?"

"Yes. No questions asked, a nice big fee."

"When?"

"We're supposed to sail at midnight." She looked at her watch. "We should be leaving soon."

"The U-boat's been sighted by now, hasn't it?" Paul asked.

"Yes," she said coldly. "I expect it has."

□

Sam Benton stood at the top of the path that led down to the rocky beach. It was a damn shame in some ways, a damn shame. They'd come for a battle and found nothing but one empty and broken crate and a dead man in a car. The Navy had gotten all the glory. Well, almost all of it—the Bureau had nabbed the big wheel in New York.

"It's Markham all right," Mitchell said, joining him. "Found a book under the front seat—Civil War battlefields, something like that—got his name inside the front."

"That's that then."

"Well . . ."

Benton looked at his partner. "Well what?" he asked irritably.

"I don't get it," Mitchell said. "It doesn't add up."

"It doesn't add up," Benton repeated sarcastically. "We've got this empty crate, we've got Markham's body, we've matched the car left by the train with the one those kids saw here on Wednesday night. Markham hired the lodge. The German in New York, the guy who arranged the whole goddamn spree— he told us this was the pickup point. . . ."

"He said the pickup was supposed to be at ten P.M."

"So they got here early."

"Why was it traveling on the surface? That doesn't make sense. They'd be dead ducks."

"How d'you know it was?"

"The sighting."

"Hell, I don't know."

"And why was it moving south when they got it?" Mitchell went on doggedly.

"Oh Christ, that doesn't mean anything. It had seen our boats, and was making a run for it."

Mitchell sighed. "Yeah, you're probably right. But why did they shoot Markham?"

The "probably" irritated Benton still further. "How should I know? They must have fallen out among themselves. . . ."

"The moment they arrived?"

"Orders from Berlin, then. He knew too much. Christ, what does it matter now?"

"Yeah. Okay." There must have been a reason. "We'd better unblock the highways," he said. "And I'm hungry."

□

Paul had seen the roadblock when he was still half a mile away, but there'd been no way to avoid it. In the mirror he could see the camper pulling up two cars behind him.

The state troopers finished with the truck in front and

one of them waved him forward, a bored expression on his face. As the truck picked up speed Paul accelerated the convertible through the space between it and the troopers' car. A burst of gunfire would have been nice, but he had only two hands and he wanted to stay on the road.

Looking back, he could see that gunfire hadn't been necessary; the troopers were already pulling their car around and giving chase, the siren beginning to wail. He rammed his foot down, feeling an exhilaration as the wind swept past him.

The first thing was to get off the highway and clear it for the others, but at the moment he had a river on one side, railroad tracks and a forest on the other. And the troopers were slowly reducing the distance between them.

He was at the turnoff almost before he realized it, and the wheels screeched and squealed as he swung into the side road, bouncing across the inlaid tracks and climbing sharply upward through the trees. For a few seconds the pursuit vanished, then reappeared in his mirror about a hundred yards behind as the road straightened out. He could see the officer in the passenger seat talking into a radio. That was bad news.

For a mile ahead the road was straight and empty. Paul unfastened the door beside him so only the car's motion kept it closed, checked the position of the tommy gun on the seat, then skidded the car to a halt with his door broadside on to the pursuit. Kicking the door open with his foot as he picked up the gun, he raked the oncoming car before the dust thrown up by his skid had begun to settle. Through it he saw the windshield explode into fragments, two heads thrown back, the car careening sideways off the road to glance off one tree and into another.

He walked across to the wreck, tommy gun at the ready, and stood there listening to the voice shouting, "Hal, what the fuck's happening, come in. . . ." Both men were dead. "Hal died in the war," Paul murmured to himself and the trees.

He got back behind the wheel, leaned over and examined

the map Amy had given him. The road he was on wasn't marked, but with any luck it should join up with one that was.

After about ten minutes he reached an east–west highway and turned west. Almost immediately he passed a truck stop, a long one-story café with a dozen or so vehicles parked in the lot. He drove on until he was well out of sight, then pulled the convertible off the highway and drove it deep into the trees. There he examined the map again, measuring distances against the scale with the barrel of the Walther. He was about 120 miles from Mon Louis, which didn't seem far. But then they'd been only ten miles from the Kremlin.

It was almost seven o'clock, and the sun was sinking fast. It would be worth waiting for dark, he decided. Paul sat there for half an hour and let his mind rest.

When the last glint of orange had gone from the sky, he put the map inside his shirt, the Walther in his jacket pocket, and with the tommy gun slung over his shoulder walked back to the highway. It was lighter outside the trees and he waited another ten minutes before making his way to the truck stop.

There were about twenty people inside, and the smell of frying meat made his mouth water. All those years ago the one thing he'd loved about America was the hamburgers. He flattened himself against the side wall and, reaching up on tiptoe, cut through the telephone line where it entered the café, then walked stealthily around the back to the parking lot on the far side. The car closest to the highway was another convertible, so he decided on the one parked next to it, a black Pontiac. The door wasn't locked. He took off the brake and pushed it into motion with his shoulder, finding it easier as the slope took over. He jumped in, letting in the clutch a hundred yards or so down the highway.

He traveled east, toward Selma, and a few miles farther on he saw a police car coming toward him, its siren wailing. The tommy gun was ready, but the cruiser just sailed past, ignoring him. So far so good. But in fifteen minutes they'd be at the truck stop, and the car's disappearance might have been noticed. The troopers would radio Selma and . . . at this rate he'd have to change cars every ten miles to Mon Louis, and leave a trail that any fool could follow in the process. He needed a car whose theft wouldn't be noticed for several hours.

He put his foot down harder on the gas, and within ten minutes he entered a town alongside a railroad track. He was running parallel with a train. Now if it was going south. . . . He stopped to look at the map, and found that it must have *come* from the south. A pity, but the station would be a good place to dump the car he was in. The police didn't know in what direction he was headed.

He followed the train into town, keeping the orange glare of the locomotive in sight between the buildings, and reached the station only a minute or so behind it. After parking the car away from the single streetlight, he sat there wondering what to do. He'd have to leave the tommy gun, that seemed certain. He pushed it under the front seat and was opening the door to get out when another car almost hurtled into the yard. A man leaped out and raced to the train platform just as it was pulling out.

Paul smiled beatifically. A third piece of luck in twenty-four hours; someone somewhere liked them. He watched the train clank out of the station, waited to check that there were no arriving passengers, then recovered the tommy gun from its hiding place and strolled calmly across to the man's car. The key was still in the ignition.

☐

They drove south through the cotton fields, through ramshackle settlements full of black children and small towns that all looked the same, through Megargel, Uriah, Bay Minette, strange names for a strange land of bright colors and fading endeavor. As the sun went down it seemed to Amy as if the golden light transformed each vista into a sepia photograph, pushing time backward a century and more. And then, with darkness having fallen, the movie screens, set high in the fields, their flickering images reflecting from the roofs of their wheeled congregations, seemed only to emphasize the point, to offer a present that was too unreal to hold back the past.

It was past ten when they crossed the bay bridges and drove into Mobile, a larger version of the same picket and neon mélange. Amy bought a newspaper while they were stopped at a city intersection. There was no mention of train holdups, no mention of U-boats. "Nothing," she told Gerd. "But I wouldn't expect anything, not with our cargo."

"Perhaps we imagined it all," he said, swerving to avoid a cab that had cut across him. "Christ, don't they teach Americans to drive?"

"You're in the wrong lane," she told him sweetly.

"And what happens when we get there?"

"The boat should be waiting. The *Lafayette*. Captain's name is Warren. He lives on the boat."

"I thought you said it was French-speaking."

"Not completely."

"What's he know?"

"Nothing. As far as he's concerned, we just want a ride to Cuba—one that doesn't involve customs inspection. But he's expecting only two people."

"Hmm. People who haven't been shot up, presumably."

"I thought we'd imagined all that."

☐

Mon Louis looked French. It was a small fishing community built on a narrow peninsula between the bay and an inlet, with wooden houses and a long, sheltered anchorage crammed with shrimp boats. The first two people they stopped spoke a French that neither could understand, the third, on hearing the name *Lafayette*, spat a long stream of tobacco juice between his feet and gestured them toward the end of the dock.

There they found the boat, one of the least prepossessing in sight, faded paint from the deck down, rust from the deck up. But it was floating.

There was no one aboard. "I'll start loading," Gerd said. "The invalid first." He glanced up and down the waterfront, but there was no one in sight; all the noise seemed to be coming from a bar about two hundred yards away.

Gerd had lifted Kuznetsky down onto the dock when the car arrived. It was Paul. His eyes had lost the bitter expression she'd seen in the forest, but he avoided looking at Amy. "A frog among princes," he murmured, looking at the *Lafayette*. "Nothing's too good for us eagles, eh?"

He and Gerd carried Kuznetsky along to the boat, then lifted him across and onto the deck. Gerd noticed that the tide was in—either good planning or luck. Probably the former, he thought. But for the kid everything would have gone like clockwork.

"You'd better sit down," he told Amy, noticing how unsteady she looked. "I said you'd be better in a couple of days, not hours."

She watched as they hauled the ten crates out of the camper, onto the dock, and across to the boat. "You were always complaining about the lack of exercise on the U-boat," Paul said as Gerd, the job finished, sat down and wiped his brow.

"You can unload them all at the other end," Gerd said. "We'd better find the owner of this pleasure cruiser before the tide turns. No, you stay where you are," he told the other two. "I need to practice my French."

"I'll take a look at Smith," she said, not wanting to be left alone with Paul.

Gerd found Warren, a short, wiry man with a shock of black hair above a crowded face, playing dominoes in the bar. He was about fifty, and judging from the skin on his face, he'd spent a lifetime in the sun. Gerd introduced himself as Jack Smith.

"You're early," Warren said curtly, concentrating on the game.

"What about the tide?"

"An authority on the sea, eh? What about the tide?"

"It's turning."

"Plenty of time. Have a drink." He passed over the bottle of bourbon, called over his shoulder for another glass.

It was delicious, but not, Gerd decided reluctantly, the ideal lining for an empty stomach. The game went on, and he fought to restrain his impatience. At last Warren got up, called over a young man who turned out to be his son and crew, and accompanied Gerd back to the boat. Both fishermen were mildly drunk.

Paul came out of the cabin, and leaned against its side. "Okay?" he asked Gerd.

"What happened to him?" Warren asked, looking past Paul at the inert Kuznetsky. "Hey, I was told two, not three passengers. . . ."

"Be more company for you," Paul said lightly.

"And it's four," Amy said, emerging from the shadows in the bow, her hands behind her back. "You were paid for the journey, not by numbers."

"Who the hell are you people?" Warren's son exclaimed, backing toward the side.

"Tourists," Paul said succinctly, bracing himself for a lunge. Why the hell hadn't he thought to have a gun on him?

"Hold on," Warren said calmly. "I'm sure we can agree on something here."

"We'll throw the camper in as extra payment," Amy said coolly.

"Okay, I'll have to move it off the dock."

"No." Her voice was harsher than Paul had ever heard before.

"Look, lady . . ."

She stepped into the light, bringing the Walther out from

behind her back as she did so. "Cast off," she said to Gerd.

Warren laughed nervously, pushed his son. "Take the wheel. Madame here wants to leave."

They were under way in a few minutes, chugging down the bay toward the open sea. "We didn't stay long," Paul muttered as he and Gerd watched the last lights of the shoreline slipping past.

"Long enough. We'll have to watch them day and night now," he added, indicating the cabin where the two Warrens were talking softly to each other.

"How long's this trip going to take?"

"Two days," Amy said, joining them. "It's over six hundred miles. I don't think they'll give us any trouble, but it might be a good idea to throw the tommy guns overboard rather than have to carry them around."

"Good idea," Gerd said. "Let's do it now." He disappeared into the crew quarters, took a quick look at Kuznetsky, and returned with the three guns. The men in the wheelhouse had stopped talking, were watching with open mouths as he and Paul sent them arcing over the side.

"I'll take first watch," Paul said. "I'll wake someone if I feel like collapsing."

The others laid out blankets on either side of the foredeck, and Paul sat down with his back against the bow railing, his service revolver in his lap. Amy heard him and Gerd talking about someone called Burdenski, fell asleep wondering when they'd first met each other.

twelve

PAUL rearranged his legs to make himself more comfortable, tried to remember which of the stars was which. The sky must be very different this far south, he thought, because he couldn't make head nor tail of it. Warren stood in the wheelhouse a few yards away, both hands on the wheel, a pipe in his mouth. His son had bedded down somewhere in the stern.

He looked at Amy's upturned, sleeping face, watched her hand brush something from her cheek, felt a lump form in his throat.

He forced his gaze back to the sky, made out the veil of the Milky Way draped across the heavens. What the hell had happened by the train? Gerd still hadn't told him the full story. The image of Smith shooting the injured man in the back of the head kept flashing into his mind, and the feeling of revulsion that had accompanied it. Why? he wondered. Why was it worse to kill people in cold blood than to kill like an animal? The man had known nothing; it had been almost merciful. Because we are animals, he answered himself, and we fear machines.

He found himself staring at Amy again, remembering kissing those gray eyes, feeling those legs that now shifted under the blanket shifting then against his own. . . . *Damnit*, that had been someone else, not this woman with a gun and a voice that could turn you to stone. But sleeping she seemed . . .

He'd read the paper while Gerd had been looking for Warren back in Mon Louis. Russians outside Warsaw, Americans all over Normandy. It wouldn't be long now. He might yet outlive the war. And then what? The farm? It would be like Russia again, a life dictated by the seasons. He never wanted to see snow again; he still had the snow dream, as Gerd did, and probably thousands of others: the beautiful white blanket, white velvet sewn with silver sequins, so lovely . . . suddenly thawing into mud and flesh, as if a face had been pulled away to reveal the pulsing muscles and pumping blood. . . .

Stop it, he told himself, you're not asleep now. He wouldn't go back to the farm, the country. A city then, full of new buildings, living people, endless activity.

"Life in the country is just like life in the city—a hundred years earlier." He could still hear Uncle Berndt say it, the droll inflection, the malicious twinkle in his eye. Well, his uncle had died in his beloved Bremen, had stubbornly sat in his fourth-floor office, probably with cigar in hand, as everyone else crouched in the shelters and the RAF opened their bomb-bay doors.

He wouldn't mind losing the last hundred years. What had been happening in 1844? They'd been building railways, exploring Africa, looking at steel mills as if they were magic creations. People had been optimistic then, one way or another. Hadn't Marx written the Communist Manifesto that year? Now *there* was optimism for you. And Germany hadn't even existed then, not as a unified state. Perhaps it would be that way after the war: a hundred small states within a civilization, just getting on with existence, making watches and toys like the Swiss.

It was one in the morning, time for something to eat. He raised himself gingerly to his feet and walked back to the cabin.

□

The first thing Kuznetsky noticed was the movement of the floor, the easy rocking motion of a buoy on water. Either he was being rowed across the Hesperus or they'd made it to the Gulf. The latter, he guessed, wincing as the muscle movement of a smile shot up the side of his face. He carefully felt for the wound, found his head swathed in bandages.

Someone came in, a man to judge from the footfall. He closed his eyes and played unconscious as the visitor rummaged around at the far end of the cabin, then observed the man's back through slitted eyes. It was the younger German, Paul. He closed his eyes again as the man walked back past him.

Alone again, he tried to remember what had happened. The train, the rush of feet in the darkness, the blow on the side of the head. How long ago had it been? At least twenty-four hours if they were now at sea, which they were—he could smell the salt.

So what was the German doing here? She must have brought them—no one else knew. But why? It couldn't be betrayal or he wouldn't still be alive. And if it wasn't betrayal, then what had she told them? Christ, his head hurt. She'd have to do the thinking for a bit longer yet. He drifted back into sleep, the throbbing in his skull keeping time with the throbbing of the engines.

□

When Amy woke it was light, the first flash of the sun glinting on the eastern horizon. The boat was chugging through an empty sea, deep blue and calm, beneath an empty sky that seemed to lighten as she watched. She stood up and stretched, forgetting for a moment the wound in her side. The sharp pain pulled her up short, but fortunately she didn't open up the scab tissue.

Gerd was huddled in the wheelhouse with Warren, who appeared to be explaining the controls. She joined them. Warren seemed almost asleep on his feet, but at least daylight gave his face a basic friendliness that she hadn't suspected the night before. Perhaps she'd overreacted by pulling a gun on him, perhaps he really had only wanted to move the camper. He looked at her now with something approaching awe. He finished with Gerd and went to lie down in the stern next to his snoring son.

Gerd didn't look much livelier. She made herself some coffee and asked him to go through what Warren had shown him. There was nothing to it.

"Go to sleep," she said, "I'll be fine."

"Smith's better," he told her, "he's sleeping now."

"Good," she said automatically, and watched him slump wearily down onto the foredeck beside the sleeping Paul. She supposed she was glad, but she'd never really doubted that he'd pull through. His sort always did.

She knew what they had to do with Paul and Gerd. It was obvious—they'd leave them in Cuba. There was no reason for them to go back to Europe, and after what she'd made up about their being Berlin's sacrificial lambs, surely they wouldn't feel duty-bound to carry on fighting the Führer's war. It was simple. No need for Kuznetsky to kill them. No need for her to worry. Paul would soon be gone again, pushed safely back into the past.

She gripped the wheel, checked the compass heading, pushed her hair back from her eyes. Another thirty-six hours. She didn't want to think about anything else, just to get it over, come through to the other side. There must be other things she could occupy her mind with. . . . But there weren't—everything in her life seemed to return to the same place, the same feelings, the same knot of experiences she couldn't untie. . . .

The rasp of a match being struck on the wheelhouse door spun her head round. It was Paul.

"Sorry," he said, lighting the cigarette. "I didn't mean to startle you."

She turned her face back to the sea. "It's just weariness," she said. There was no hostility in his face, which somehow made it worse. *Go away*, the voice in her head screamed.

"Amy," he said quietly, almost gently, "I've something to tell you. It doesn't make any difference now, but I want to tell you anyway."

"Yes?" she said in a small voice, but her eyes still would not meet his.

"I never got your letters. I would have answered them, the way I felt then."

"Then how—"

"They came to my family's farm. My mother read them and destroyed them. She was afraid I'd leave, go back to America. I would have. But . . . my father had just died, and I don't think she'd yet come out of shock. Anyway, I never saw them. She told me about your letters years later, in 1939. Thought she was dying, wanted to confess her sins. She didn't die, of course. She's still alive now as far as I know." He stopped, and she could feel his gaze on her face. "I just wanted you to know," he said.

"As you said, it doesn't make any difference now." Her voice felt like it belonged to someone else. "But thank you for telling me."

"Well, life is full of might-have-beens." His cheerfulness sounded forced. She turned to face him and saw, for the first time, the strain behind his eyes, the toll the last eleven years had taken. She wondered if he saw the same in her.

"You've hardly changed at all," he replied to the unspoken question.

"Perhaps not on the outside." She wanted this conversation to end, to have never been. "Smith's better," she said desperately.

"Wonderful," he said with all the old irony. "He'll be up and executing people before we know it."

"It was necessary," she said fiercely, "you know it was."

"It always is," he replied coldly.

"Anyway, you'll have his company for only another thirty-six hours."

"Why?"

"There's no need for you and Gerd to go home, back to the war. Especially after the way Berlin's treated you. And they're expecting only two passengers on the freighter."

He digested this information for a minute or more, lighting another cigarette. "Are you and Smith . . . more than partners?" he asked.

"No." The question hurt. She wondered if it was meant to.

"And what are we supposed to do in Cuba—beg?"

She felt like screaming. "There's more than fifteen hundred dollars left from the expenses," she said with a calmness that seemed to tax every nerve in her body. "The war will be over in six months."

Silence.

"Amy . . ."

"What?" she asked sharply.

He sighed, ground out the cigarette. "Nothing. I'll talk it over with Gerd. Give me a turn at the wheel." He almost pushed her aside, took the wheel, and stared straight ahead.

"South southeast," she said, moving away toward the stern.

"Yes, Paul," he muttered to himself after she'd gone, "it pays to know which way you're going."

☐

She leaned against the stern rail for several minutes, the two snoring Warrens behind her, then ducked inside the cabin. Kuznetsky was awake, half out of the bunk. She pushed him back and sat down beside him. "Everything's under control," she told him in a whisper. "The Germans still think we're all on the same side, and we're leaving them in Cuba."

"Well done," he murmured. "Now tell me how."

She explained what had happened, what she'd told them, then got him something to drink. "They're good soldiers," he said, apparently to himself. But before she could ask him what he meant, he'd drifted back into sleep.

The rest of the day dragged by, each of them taking turns at the wheel as the *Lafayette* carved its passage through the blue-green sea. By noon the heat was becoming unbearable, and with Warren's help Paul and Gerd rigged up a makeshift awning on the foredeck. Amy spent the hours either sitting with the sleeping Kuznetsky or talking with Warren in the wheelhouse; even his inexhaustible stream of tall stories was preferable to another conversation with Paul.

He and Gerd had found a pack of cards and were playing under the awning, though neither of them looked as if he had his heart in the game. She studied Paul's profile, remembering the very first time she'd seen him, playing chess in the lounge on the *Bremen*. She loved him—there was no harm in admitting it to herself. It didn't make any difference now. There were more important things than love.

The sun went down in a golden burst, the twilight seemed over as soon as it came, the stars grew sharp in the sky. Amy went back to see Kuznetsky, found him sitting in the stern, the Walther beside him, staring into space. He smiled at her, a distant smile, said nothing. She had the fleeting impression that he was absorbing energy from the sea, like some mythical monster, somehow both benign and terrible, and in that moment felt almost resentful at how easy it seemed for him, how hard it was for mere mortals like herself.

☐

The next day seemed to pass more quickly. The *Lafayette*, growing lighter as its engines consumed the drums of fuel, seemed to pick up speed, to almost skim across the water. Amy seemed more relaxed after their announcement, and Paul wondered if their reunion had caused as much turmoil in her heart as it had in his. He would soon know.

By noon the Cuban shore was visible on the horizon, and two hours later they were passing beneath the sullen remains of Morro Castle and threading their way into Havana harbor. The *MV Balboa*, flying the Swedish flag, was anchored in the reach, a squat freighter with three masts and an incongruously small funnel. Gerd hailed the lookout, who disappeared to find the captain. They tied up against the ship's side.

"Well, this is good-bye," Amy said to Gerd.

He looked over his shoulder at Paul, who was standing with his hands in his pockets in the stern, and received a nod. Kuznetsky was sitting on the wheelhouse steps staring into space.

"We're coming with you," Gerd said, loud enough for everyone to hear.

He saw what looked like panic flash across her face. "Why?" she asked, a hint of supplication in her voice. He looked at her, failed to catch her eyes. Was she that desperate to leave Paul behind? It seemed ridiculous.

"We're going home," he said gruffly, watching Kuznetsky, who was now fully alert, glancing first at him and then at Paul. "There's plenty of room," he continued, nodding at the bulk of the freighter towering above them.

Kuznetsky relaxed, leaned back on his elbows. "It's up to you," he said offhandedly. Life or death, he thought to himself. He felt sorry for Amy.

"Ahoy there," a voice shouted from above. "I'll throw down a ladder."

"I'll go," Kuznetsky said as the rope ladder snaked down out of the sky. "Get the crates untied," he said over his shoulder as he began to climb.

☐

Amy watched the sling descend, watched Gerd maneuver the first crate into it and wave it back up. *Why, why, why?* The word kept echoing in her brain.

"You might as well give Warren the fifteen hundred dollars," Paul said, suddenly appearing at her side.

"Yes, I might as well," she said, and went to do so, feeling utterly numb.

☐

The *Balboa* sailed on the evening tide, and it was hardly out of the harbor before Kuznetsky, sitting alone in the bow, was approached by one of the Swedish crew.

"Bjorn Sjoberg, Comrade," the man said in a low voice. "Do you have any instructions for me?"

"None for now."

"Who are the other two men?"

Kuznetsky grinned. "Two serving German officers."

Sjoberg showed his astonishment. "How—"

"Don't worry, I'll deal with them when the time comes." He looked out across the sea. "How will your captain react if they are suddenly missing, do you think?"

"Difficult to say." Sjoberg had recovered his poise quickly, which encouraged Kuznetsky. "He won't turn the ship around and search the Atlantic for them, but he might ask awkward questions. And he might arrange a police welcome in Gothenburg."

"That won't matter. You contacted Rodrigues?"

"Yes, he'll have watched the loading."

"Good. Moscow will take all the necessary steps."

thirteen

"YOU HAVEN'T TOLD Zhdanov, I suppose," Fyedorova said with a malicious grin. "I seem to remember you told him there was no chance of a German atomic bomb."

"There still isn't," Sheslakov snapped. "And no, I haven't told him," he added more thoughtfully.

"Intriguing though, isn't it?" she said in a similar tone. "It's hard to find any reasonable explanation for the presence of the two Germans."

"There must be one. The question is, what will we do about it?"

"Nothing."

"We do have a U-boat, you know. It was grounded in the Gulf of Finland in 1942. It's been repaired and it's ready for service."

"What service?" she asked.

"Well . . . I'm considering sending the Swedish boat an escort, even perhaps transferring the uranium to the U-boat at sea."

She swung her legs to the floor in the familiar move. "No," she said earnestly. He waited for the explanation as she went through the usual process of putting her thoughts in order. "For one thing," she said, "it's too elaborate. You're seducing yourself with your own trickery again. For another, and much more important, imagine Kuznetsky's reaction to the sudden appearance of a U-boat. He'll throw the stuff over the side."

Sheslakov looked at her appreciatively. "Why didn't I think of that?"

"Because you're itching to interfere. Look, the Germans must still think it's a German operation, so there's no reason for them to do anything before the ship reaches Gothenburg. And even if they do discover something before that, what can they do? They can't hijack a Swedish ship with the crew and our people against them. It's much more likely that Kuznetsky will dispose of them before the ship reaches Sweden."

"Nothing then," he muttered.

"Just make sure Gothenburg is swarming with our people when the ship comes in, including a few German-speakers in case the need arises."

"Right. And if necessary we can dispose of them when we dispose of the other two."

"What?"

"I forgot to tell you." He passed across a sheet of paper bearing the General Secretary's signature.

"For reasons of state security," she said impassively. "And us?" she asked him.

He shrugged. "A good question. I doubt whether we'll be sent advance notification."

☐

The days passed, blue seas giving way to green, calm waters to the rolling ocean swell. On clear days the thin line of the American coast was visible on the western horizon, emphasizing the distance still to be traveled.

Of the four of them, only Paul showed any inclination to mix with the Swedish crew, and this, it seemed to Gerd, had more to do with avoiding the three of them than with any genuine desire to play nonstop poker in the galley. He understood his friend's need, but felt unable to share his means of assuaging it.

For many days he was haunted by the expression on Amy's

face that afternoon in Havana harbor. It had seemed out of all proportion when measured against what he knew of her and Paul. He sensed that she was hiding something, but he had no idea what it might be.

As the *Balboa* plowed northward this absorption faded, giving way to another. Sitting in Schellenberg's office all those weeks before the whole business—America, atomic bombs, trains, and U-boats—it had all seemed quite fantastic, a crazy game that the mad masters of his country had decided to play.

Now, with the crates sitting out there on the deck, a few weeks at most from Germany, he was experiencing a growing feeling of revulsion at the thought of delivering them. Did he want to see himself as one of the men who'd brought Hitler a weapon like that? "Defeat will have its compensations," he'd told the U-boat captain, and that had been an understatement. Leaving the U-boat that night had been like stepping out of the war, giving him his first chance in years to look at the whole ghastly mess from the outside. And he knew now, as clearly as he'd ever known anything, that a German defeat would be the best possible outcome for everyone, the German people included. A swift defeat moreover, while the country was still in one piece.

And here he was helping to prolong the war, perhaps even to change its outcome. He didn't want that. Aboard the U-boat they'd heard Hitler's account of the bomb plot against him, the chilling voice announcing the revenge to come. And though a part of him still, almost reflexively, condemned the conspirators for breaking their soldier's oath, the rest of him, most of him, had never felt prouder to be a Wehrmacht officer.

God knows, they should have acted sooner. They'd been blind, completely blind, and once the war had begun their eyes had been looking outward, their minds full of that shameful intoxication with victory, with sheer motion really, right up to that dreadful month outside Moscow.

But that was the East, not the middle of the Atlantic Ocean. Was it too late for treason? If he and Paul heaved the crates overboard, it wouldn't make him very popular with Smith or Amy or the reception party that would be waiting in Sweden—in fact it might well prove to be their last meaningful act on earth. But as the days passed the vision of those crates sinking through the Atlantic swell seemed more and more like the only appropriate swan song for his war.

□

Kuznetsky spent his days sitting in the bow, hardly moving for hours save to light his cigarettes, staring ahead at the ocean still to be crossed. He had decided to kill the Germans on the penultimate night of the voyage. By then, he reasoned, he would be fully fit again, and there would only be around thirty-six hours for Torstensson to discover that two of his passengers had gone over the side. Twelve hours would have been better, but he didn't completely trust Amy, and had told her it would be the final night. If by some chance her feelings got the better of her it would be too late.

Not that she'd shown any such inclinations when he'd told her. "You know they have to die," he'd said on the occasion of their only conversation since leaving Havana.

"There's no other way, is there?" she'd said simply, not even avoiding his eyes.

"There never has been. From the moment Sheslakov drew up the plan those two were dead, one way or another."

She'd picked up on the name quick enough. "I'm slipping," Kuznetsky had said, "no one should have known that name."

"Do I have to die too now?" she'd asked with the same, almost unreal detachment.

"There's a good chance that both of us will be considered unnecessary risks. You knew that, didn't you?" And she had—he could tell by the expression in her eyes.

"It's insane," she'd said quietly, "but it makes perfect sense."

□

Back in her cabin, its walls seeming to mock the dreadful openness of her mind, Amy sat on the floor, her back against the bunk, her legs splayed and straight like a little girl's.

It did make sense: that was what seemed so terrifying. It made sense that Paul should die, should be killed, if not by her then at least with her active connivance. It made perfect sense. Richard had died for the same reason, and Joe, and the guards, and the boy who had appeared from nowhere. And Paul would die. To make it all work. If he didn't, it wouldn't work. Her feelings had no power to change the logic of it.

She wanted Paul, but only for herself. She wanted it all to work, for herself perhaps, but for others, too, and that was the difference. At times during the days at sea the distinction had escaped her, her motivation had been impossible to pin down in words, and she'd wondered whether she'd spent ten years trapped in an illusion. But she hadn't.

The distinction *was* real, the struggle *was* real, existing outside as well as inside herself. She couldn't release herself from it even if she wanted to. If Paul's death was the price demanded, then she would pay. It wasn't what you felt that counted, it was what you did.

She could remember the very day Aunt Rosa had said that to her mother. The two women had been arguing, as they often did, but this time with more anger than usual, and at the end of the argument they'd hugged each other. She had watched from the stairs, had rushed to join the hugging, not knowing what it was for but knowing that it was important.

Aunt Rosa. She had a picture of herself and Effi sitting in that same kitchen listening to one of Aunt Rosa's "history lessons" as they prepared the evening meal. The man in the factory working all day and getting next to no money, the owner in his big house sitting around doing nothing, getting richer and richer. And how they should even feel sorry for the rich man, because all his riches were things, cold and empty things.

It must have been in the month following Aunt Rosa's release from prison; she'd been weak, thinner than before, but her face at that time had seemed almost luminescent, like the pictures of the Virgin Mary in stained-glass windows. And she and Effi had sat there, sometimes not understanding what this wonderful woman was saying, but captivated by the face and the kindness and the simple intensity of belief. The world could be better, fairer, more human.

Fables for children perhaps. But they'd carried a truth she'd never been able to deny, because all the people she'd ever loved—all except Paul—had lived it, had worked and struggled and died for something beyond themselves. And their deaths had not been an illusion.

The Soviet Union might be; she didn't know. But the alternative was not: an American world in which no one cared for anything but themselves and Aunt Rosa's cold and empty things. If the material in the crates could prevent that, they were worth any cost.

Only a few more days. Kuznetsky would kill Paul and then he and she would die. It was fair and just.

There was no other way.

☐

Kuznetsky looked at his watch as he inhaled the cigarette. It was almost two in the morning. He checked the Walther once more and sat for another ten minutes adjusting his eyes to the darkness.

"Thy kingdom come, the Party's will be done," he murmured to himself as he stood up. "On earth as it is at sea."

The two Germans had taken separate cabins. Perhaps Paul

had hoped to resume his affair with Amy, perhaps they were fed up with each other's snoring. Either way, it simplified matters.

He stepped out onto the deck, found the light brighter than he'd anticipated. The sky was overcast, but every now and then the moon would find a thinner layer of cloud to shine through, bathing the freighter and the sea in a silvery glow. A few miles to the south, the dark bumpy line of the Shetland Islands divided the ocean from the sky.

The sea was choppy rather than rough, and not as noisy as he'd hoped. Still, Sjoberg had arranged for the helmsman that night to be a Party sympathizer, and he himself took the stern watch. No one would hear anything. He took the strangling cord from his pocket, stood outside Gerd's door, and listened. Nothing. He eased the door open and slipped noiselessly inside, closing it behind him. There was no one in the bunk.

He went to the cabin next door, but it was empty too. A white square shone in the gloom, a note pinned to the mirror. He struck a match and read it: "Amy, Bremerhaven Bahnhof, 14 July." For an instant Kuznetsky saw the expression of surprise on his own face in the mirror, an expression he'd forgotten he had.

He went back on deck, walked purposefully back toward the stern. Above the sound of the ship's passage he heard a scraping noise, recognized it from the loading in Havana. They were moving the crates. He peered out around the corner of the ship's superstructure, saw the silhouettes of the two Germans pushing a crate toward the starboard rail, and as the sky momentarily lightened, he caught a glimpse of a body, Sjoberg's, lying motionless on the stern deck.

Somehow they'd found him out, and had decided to take the uranium to Germany on their own. He felt almost proud of them.

He worked his way nearer, dodging silently through the crates of general merchandise stacked amidships until he was no more than ten yards away. Raising the Walther with both arms extended, his feet splayed to compensate for the ship's motion, he took aim at the back of Gerd's head.

He couldn't do it. Didn't want to do it. They deserved to see his face as he pulled the trigger. Private executions were bad enough, and even then the victim could see his executioner.

As he stepped forward the moonlight suddenly brightened, giving his entrance an almost theatrical quality. The two Germans stiffened, then relaxed as they saw the gun, relaxed in the way he had once seen a Siberian tiger relax, with a casualness that obscured the alertness of their poise. They didn't expect a chance, but were ready for one if it came.

"Where are you planning to go, gentlemen?" he asked softly.

"We're sleepwalking," Paul said, edging away from Gerd. Kuznetsky stopped him with a flick of his wrist.

"We decided the Führer's genius didn't require any assistance," Gerd said sarcastically.

Kuznetsky smiled at his own misjudgment and admired them even more. "They're not intended for your Führer," he said. "Or Nazi Germany."

A tiny voice inside him said, "Let them go," but was instantly silenced by the familiar voice of duty.

"Somehow," Gerd said, "that doesn't seem as surprising as it should."

☐

Amy lay awake on the bunk watching the play of light on her cabin walls. Another twenty-four hours. What could be wrong in spending the last night with Paul? It would change nothing. In the dark there would be no deception, in the dark their love would be real. And the thought of it, of one more meeting, one last immersion in that other world, had held her together through the weeks at sea.

221

She climbed out of the bunk, wrapped a blanket around her shoulders, and left her cabin. The iron plate felt cold beneath her feet. She went to tap on Paul's door but it was ajar, the cabin empty, the note shining on the mirror.

□

"Why?" Gerd asked, almost disinterestedly. His gun lay on the crate, hidden from Kuznetsky by a bag of food they'd brought for the journey. If only it wasn't lying with the butt farthest away from him.

"Why?" Kuznetsky seemed to find the question ridiculous. "I serve a cause I believe in. Could you say the same?"

"No."

"You're not an American," Paul said flatly.

"I was. I chose another country." He still couldn't pull the trigger. It wasn't finished. "I, too, was at Khimki, Povorovo, Lyalovo," he said.

They looked at him. Did they understand? Did he?

"My comrades, and my sense of duty, they died together in the snow," Gerd recited slowly. "But they didn't, did they? They should have, but they didn't. Only the comrades died. And," he said, looking straight at Kuznetsky, "the duty remains."

"I'm sorry," he heard himself say.

"Does Amy know?" Paul asked abruptly.

"No," Kuznetsky lied.

Gerd lunged for the gun, but succeeded only in knocking it across the crate and onto the deck. The Walther coughed, pumping a bullet through the side of his head, and whirled in search of its other target. Paul scrambled for the fallen gun, realized he wouldn't reach it, and looked up in time to see Kuznetsky topple forward as Amy's bullet smashed through the back of his right knee.

Paul started forward, was stopped in his tracks by the gun aimed at his heart. "No," she said, "no."

He looked up at her, a woman with bare feet in a nightdress, a blanket hanging from one shoulder, a gun held rock-steady in both hands, tears pouring down her cheeks.

"What now?" Paul asked.

She tore herself away from his face, from the question, picked up Kuznetsky's gun, then Gerd's, and threw them over the side. Below her she saw the lifeboat bobbing on the waves.

She turned back to Paul, wiping the tears from her eyes. She had to know. "Do you love me?" she asked with a terrible simplicity.

He studied her face, thought for a moment she'd gone mad, but her eyes were shining with some other fire. Joy it looked like, and maybe that was madness. He smiled up at her, the old self-mocking smile. "Do you always point guns at men when you ask them that?"

"I've never asked another man that, Paul."

He leaned over and closed his dead friend's eyes, looked down at the deck. "Yes," he said.

"Get in the lifeboat," she said softly, lowering the gun.

"Am I going alone?"

"You know you're not." She turned to Kuznetsky, who was smiling, a smile she couldn't begin to understand. "You don't need me anymore," she said.

"They will hunt you to the ends of the earth," he said without malice. "But you know that."

Amy had a momentary impulse to hug him, to wish him well, but she turned her back and followed Paul over the side.

epilogue

Washington, D.C., 1945

AGENT DON MITCHELL sat in the director's anteroom, leaning forward, his elbows on his knees, twisting his hat in his hands. He'd been there for more than an hour, and even the secretaries on the other side of the room were beginning to treat him as part of the furniture.

He knew why he'd been summoned, though he hadn't expected it to be Hoover in person, and he hadn't expected it to be so soon. His report had gone in only the day before.

He thought back to his moment of inspiration and laughed. He'd been at the movies with Fay, he couldn't even remember the main feature. The "B" had been a crummy two-reeler about the romantic moonshiners and the boring G-men. And right in the middle the boys had sat in a diner discussing the tactical niceties of shifting roadblocks—"Frank'll go through and make the gap" one had said. And he had remembered the guy who'd killed those two cops near Selma that night. He'd wanted to know.

He had sent down to Selma for the police report, to Birmingham for the Locust Forks report, taken the hijack file out of its cabinet, and put them all together. It was all there, had been all the time. The car that had broken through the roadblock was the one stolen in Locust Forks; the prints

225

found on the bars in the Locust Forks jail matched those found on the train.

He had sent down to Selma for the bullets that had killed the two policemen. They'd been fired from the same gun that had killed the guard on the train. That had convinced even Sam Benton.

But he'd still wanted something more. It was almost a year now, so there was no hurry. He took a long weekend and the train down to Birmingham, where he hired a car and drove south through the Talladega Forest to Selma. If they'd gone through the roadblock at around 7 P.M. they must have holed up someplace during the day, and this looked like an ideal spot. For one ridiculous moment he thought of stopping to look for clues.

In Selma he got the names of the witnesses to the incident, and from one of them, a middle-aged woman with the sort of Southern accent you could spread on bread, he found what he wanted. Their car had been in the line, and behind them there'd been a camper. She remembered because she'd been struck by the face of the woman sitting in the passenger seat.

Mitchell had showed her the photograph of Amy Brandon.

"Yes, sir, that's her."

That had been enough. He'd driven back to Birmingham and taken his train home, wondering what had happened to them, almost admiring them in spite of himself. What ruthlessness, to deliberately sacrifice one U-boat and leave the way clear for another. And it had worked.

He'd written the report the moment he'd gotten back, but Benton had dissuaded him from turning it in for a week. "What's the percentage?" his partner had asked, and sitting there in Hoover's anteroom, he was beginning to wonder. But duty was duty, and he didn't find that as old-fashioned as Benton did.

He had only a few minutes more to wait. Director Hoover

greeted him warmly and seated him in a plush armchair before taking one himself.

"Mitchell," he said, "I've got two things to say to you, and I wanted to say them both myself, man to man."

"Yes, sir."

"One, you've done a very fine piece of detective work, and that will go on your file."

"Thank you, sir."

"But the substance of it will not, because of the second thing I have to tell you. The case is closed, Mitchell. And I mean closed."

"Sir . . ."

"Let me finish. Mitchell, I'm sure you can see that nothing can be gained from publicizing this matter. The war with Germany is over, and whether or not those commandos or agents or whatever they were got back to Germany with the stolen material . . . well, obviously nothing came of it."

"Yes, sir, but—"

"What may not be so obvious to you is the danger any publicizing of this story might do to the United States of America." Hoover stood up and walked to the window, his hands in his vest pockets. "Japan will be beaten before Christmas, and the soldiers will come home. But the FBI, Mitchell, fights an endless war. We are America's first line of defense. The enemy changes but we do not, and the American people have the right, the *right*, to have a Bureau they can respect and trust."

"I understand, sir." And he did. They'd made fools of the FBI, and no one was going to know.

Hoover smiled for the first time, a baring of the teeth that had nothing to do with amusement. "I'm sure you do, Mitchell. Use your talents on today's enemies, not yesterday's."

PAUL loaded the last fertilizer sack onto the back of the pickup, fastened the tailgate, and whistled for his dog. She came tumbling out of the freight office and leaped up obediently onto the front seat. Paul raised a hand in farewell to the clerk and pulled the pickup out of the station yard. He was driving down the town's main street when one of the two local policemen, the new one he hadn't met, flagged him down.

"Paul Brent, isn't it?" the officer asked, leaning into the cab and fondling Rosie behind the ears.

"That's right. You're Pete Ackerman, right?" He extended his hand.

"Thought I'd tell you. Your brother-in-law has arrived from America—I just saw him over at the hotel asking for your address."

"Thanks," Paul said automatically, gazing into space.

"Sure."

Paul pulled out of his trance. "Thanks again," he said, "I'll be seeing you."

He parked the pickup outside the hotel, found Betty at the desk. He and Amy had stayed there while they were rebuilding the farmhouse; their daughter, Elisabeth, had been born there. Betty and her husband, Jim, had been the first real friends they'd made in New Zealand.

"Hello, Paul—"

"Is Amy's brother here?"

"No . . . what's the matter?"

"Where did he go?"

"He drove out to your place, about fifteen minutes ago—"

He was gone, accelerating up the street, praying he wouldn't be too late.

☐

Kuznetsky drove slowly up the valley, savoring the countryside. He liked New Zealand's South Island, there was a touch of Siberia's wild emptiness about it, a place for beginnings, not endings. And at this time of the day, as the falling sun lit the tops of the trees, the valleys seemed like darkened paths in a never-ending forest.

He turned off onto a side road that wound upward alongside a narrow rushing stream. After half a mile the valley suddenly widened, and at its farthest end he could see the house, surrounded by tall trees and sheltered by a steep hillside. He'd told her the ends of the earth, and here they were.

He stopped the car, lit a cigarette, and watched. The lights were on in the house, smoke curling from the chimney into the twilight sky. It was not *the kind of house in which the landlord settles down.* He felt pleased for them, absurdly pleased.

He'd spent almost a year searching for Nadezhda, pestering every committee he could think of, cashing in every favor he'd ever earned. She'd vanished off the face of the earth. And then one day he'd been buying a ticket at Belorussia Station and recognized Yakovenko in a group of men drinking tea in the office next door. Yakovenko told him she had been killed, had been dead even before he left for America, cut down by a group of retreating Germans who'd blundered into their forest hideaway.

The news had stunned him; he knew that now. The body still worked, even his knee after a fashion, the brain still worked, but everything else in him was dead. There was a generation of Nadezhdas, and for that he was grateful—his life had not been wasted. But they were not for him; the new world had a right to be free of the terror that had made it possible.

He got out of the car, gun in hand, remembering the sad look on Sheslakov's face at their last meeting. The old proverb—you can bring a horse to water but you can't make it drink—crossed his mind. He smiled grimly and began walking toward the house.

□

Amy saw the car pull up under the trees, the sudden spark as the driver lit a cigarette, and she knew who it was. She'd known he would come one day, known it in her bones.

She took Elisabeth out of the cot, praying that she wouldn't wake up, and carried her into their bedroom. "Ssssh," she said to the sleeping baby, as her mother had said to her all those years before.

Back in the front room, she turned off the lights and peered out through the crack between curtain and frame. He was walking, limping, up the dirt road toward the house. She sat back in the chair and waited, listening to his feet crossing the yard and climbing the steps up onto the porch. There he stopped, and in the silence she could hear Paul's pickup hurtling up the valley.

He heard it too. He knew she was behind the door in the corner—that's where *he* would be. He smiled to himself and walked across the threshold, slowly, deliberately, his gun pointing down at the floor. He never saw Amy sitting in the shadows, or the shotgun that scattered his life away, only a flashing vision of a forest split by sunbeams rushing into night.